THIS NETTLE DANGER

Center Point
Large Print

Also by William MacLeod Raine
and available from Center Point Large Print:

Courage Stout
Clattering Hoofs
The Black Tolts
Long Texan
The Trail of Danger
Square-Shooter

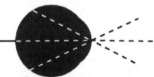

**This Large Print Book carries the
Seal of Approval of N.A.V.H.**

THIS NETTLE DANGER

William MacLeod Raine

CENTER POINT LARGE PRINT
THORNDIKE, MAINE

This Center Point Large Print edition
is published in the year 2017 by arrangement with
Golden West Literary Agency.

First US edition: Houghton Mifflin
First UK edition: Hodder & Stoughton

The text of this Large Print edition is unabridged.
In other aspects, this book may vary
from the original edition.
Printed in the United States of America
on permanent paper.
Set in 16-point Times New Roman type.

ISBN: 978-1-68324-556-8 (hardcover)
ISBN: 978-1-68324-560-5 (paperback)

Library of Congress Cataloging-in-Publication Data

Names: Raine, William MacLeod, 1871-1954, author.
Title: This nettle danger / William MacLeod Raine.
Description: Large print edition. | Thorndike, Maine :
    Center Point Large Print, 2017.
Identifiers: LCCN 2017031084| ISBN 9781683245568
    (hardcover : alk. paper) | ISBN 9781683245605 (pbk. : alk. paper)
Subjects: LCSH: Large type books. | GSAFD: Western stories.
Classification: LCC PS3535.A385 T48 2017 | DDC 813/.52—dc23
LC record available at https://lccn.loc.gov/2017031084

CONTENTS

Chapter		Page

The Wire Cutters

I

It was a night of scudding clouds from back of which a pale moon emerged occasionally for a few moments. Out of the darkness the mountain range came vague and shadowy. A trail of sorts, steep and rocky, ran up the hogback, one good enough for a horse but impossible for a wagon. Looking up at it, the cap rock seemed a sheer precipice, but Bruce Sherrill knew there was a break in the wall through which the cowpony could pick a way. The animal took the last stretch with a rush, scrambling up like a cat, the hard muscles of the flanks standing out like ropes.

From the far end of the cleft Bruce looked down into a black gulf of space at the bottom of which Squaw Creek followed its winding course. A pinpoint of light stood out of the emptiness like a beacon. It was from the Gilcrest ranch. The roan picked a footing through the obscurity with the sureness of a trained Western mount.

The lower slope was dotted with small pines, but the grove ended before Bruce reached the creek, giving place to thick brush that slashed his legs and snatched at the stirrups. A trace paralleled the stream, and he took it out of the gulch into a small park where the light he had seen from the summit of the hogback reappeared. He opened a poor-man's gate and closed it behind him.

When he rode into the yard he found three other horsemen waiting there. One of them, Pete Engle, was holding Dave Gilcrest's white mule Jenny.

' 'Lo, Bruce,' Pete said. 'All here but Flack.'

Pete was a small man, his face lined with wrinkles of anxiety. He wore dusty boots run down at the heels, soiled jeans, and a patched shirt that had once been blue before many washings had faded it. Care rode heavily on Pete's narrow shoulders. Five reasons made the struggle to earn a livelihood harassing. He had a wife and four children, and it was impossible to forget that the wolf was never more than two jumps from the door of his cabin.

Gilcrest came out of the house followed by his wife, a tall gaunt woman in a loose gingham dress. She had apparently been good-looking once, but years of toil and worry had etched lines in her face and dried the sap from her body. She might be twenty-nine or thirty.

The newcomer swung from the saddle to meet her. Unlike most of these nesters, Bruce was instinctively courteous to women. This was something they could not get from their own men, and they liked it in him. But tonight Sarah Gilcrest was preoccupied with her fears. She brushed aside his greeting.

'This is a crazy business,' she broke out sharply. 'They'll lay for you-all. One of these nights there will be a rookus—and then what?'

Sherrill's smile was friendly and disarming. 'Don't worry, Mrs. Gilcrest. We expect to use wire cutters for weapons.'

'I s'pose that's why you're all packing guns,' she retorted tartly. 'If you want to know, I worry every minute Dave is night riding.'

'There are a hundred miles of wire around the Pitchfork spread,' Bruce reminded her. 'What chance would they have of picking us up at any one point?'

'Now, old woman,' Gilcrest interrupted mildly. 'If you would just quit frettin'.' He was a big hulk of a man, bow-legged and barrel-chested, with a long drooping mustache too large for the homely, puckered face.

The sound of hoofs came down the wind. Out of the darkness a big bony horse took shape. Riding it was a man with a sly hatchet face and small searching eyes set too closely. He carried a long muzzle-loading rifle.

'Just in time, Flack,' Engle said.

Bruce glanced around. 'If you're all ready, we'll start,' he suggested. The youngest man present,

9

he had been tacitly chosen as leader. Soft-spoken and gentle of manner, he had, however, a driving force.

With the exception of Pete Engle, who was an old-timer and knew this country from the grass roots, all the others but Bruce had within the past few years come a thousand miles in covered wagons to try a hazard of new fortune in this raw frontier land. Bruce was of another genus. He was from a good family, well-educated, and had brought with him the means to buy several hundred head of cattle to stock the ranch on Bear Creek that he had homesteaded. But this fight was his as well as theirs, for he had filed on land upon which the cows of a big outfit had run for a dozen years and had fenced a stretch of the creek to keep out Bar B B stuff.

They rode down Squaw till it emerged into the open foothills leading to the undulating plain. The stream took a sharp turn to the east, but they still pointed south to avoid climbing the spurs that, rooted in the range, ran down to the flats below. For the most part they traveled in a silence broken only by the creaking of saddle leather and the sound of moving horses. These men were going on a grim and perhaps dangerous errand. They were not gay and casual young cowboys who joked about everything.

Flack drew alongside Bruce and moved knee to knee with him. 'Looks like rain,' he said. 'This country sure needs it. I don't ever recollect seeing Squaw so empty of water before.'

Sherrill agreed briefly that this was true. He did not like Flack. The fellow had a mean spirit, and there was something ratlike about the quick beady eyes in the longjawed face.

'I'm certainly a chump,' Flack continued, with a furtive look at his companion. 'I done forgot my clippers.'

'Thought you were going to a dance, I reckon,' Bruce replied, a touch of contempt in his voice.

'I sure must of been wool-gathering, doggone it,' Flack admitted humbly.

Bruce did not accept this explanation. His guess was that the man had left the cutter at home deliberately, to mitigate his offense if they should be caught.

'Anyhow, someone has to hold the horses while the others work,' Flack mentioned more cheerfully. 'I can be the wrangler.'

'So you can,' Bruce answered dryly. 'And if Daly's riders jump us you'll be all set for a getaway.'

'Now that ain't nice,' reproved Flack virtuously.

Bruce made no comment. A spur touched the flank of his mount lightly. The roan began to dance. 'Steady, Blaze!' its rider ordered. By the time Bruce had the cowpony quieted, he was riding beside Cal Malloy, a tubby little man with a round moon face.

'Flack forgot his clippers,' Bruce told the fat man.

'The damned yellow-belly is full of tricks,' Malloy snapped, disgust in his voice. 'He'd be a fine partner to side a fellow if he got in a jam.'

Engle pulled up his mount and the others joined him. They had come to a barb-wire fence. Bruce turned his horse over to Flack, but he carried his saddle gun with him. The sound of the clippers punctuated the silence of the dark night. All three strands of wire were cut between each post for a hundred yards, after which the men remounted and rode along the fence for a quarter of a mile and repeated the demolition for another stretch. This was not the first time they had slashed the 'bob-wire' of the enclosures of the big ranches, and they went at the job with ruthless efficiency.

While the others were at work Flack took charge of the mounts, but apparently there were too many of them to manage easily. They bumped into one another as they swung to and fro restlessly.

Cal Malloy called to the wrangler irritably. 'Bring those horses nearer and keep them close to us. If you can't handle them I'll swap places with you.'

'They're millin' around,' Flack explained. 'Keep your shirt on, Cal. I'm bringing them up.'

The nippers were getting dull. After the third attack on the barb-wire Bruce called to Pete, who was at the head of the line, 'We'll call it a day.' He straightened, nerves suddenly tense. On the light night breeze there had come to him the drum of hoofs. 'Fork your broncs, boys,' he cried. 'They're on us.'

The nesters raced for their mounts, grouped half a stone's-throw distant. Pete stumbled on a grass bump and went down. Saddle gun in hand, Bruce waited for him to pick himself up.

Out of the darkness a rider galloped, far ahead of his party. He dragged his horse to a halt and fired at Pete, who was just getting to his feet. The bullet plowed into the ground. His second shot was a hit. Pete ran, limping. Before the rider could pull the trigger again Bruce had his saddle gun in action. The weapon dropped from the hand of the rider. He clung to the horn in front of him for a moment, then slid from his seat.

With one sweep of his eyes Bruce took in the situation. Flack had not waited for his companions but had turned loose the horses and was galloping away to save his own hide. Three of the wire cutters had reached mounts. One of them, Dave Gilcrest, was holding a pony for Pete, now only a few yards from him. Blaze was vanishing in the distance, running at the heels of Flack's big bay. The attackers were coming out of the murk not a dozen yards from him.

Bruce caught the rein of the riderless horse beside him and vaulted into the saddle. He swung the animal round, pulled it to a gallop, and sent it over grounded wire into the big pasture.

On the Dodge

II

There was a moment before the clatter of the guns sounded, the time it took for the cowboys to realize that Ben Randall was lying on the ground and one of the wire cutters escaping on his horse. Bruce lay low in the saddle, driving the buckskin to its fastest speed. Bullets whipped past him. One thudded against his calf just above the boot top. In a dozen seconds he was out of range of accurate shooting.

But he held the horse to a gallop, for he knew that already the pursuers must be pounding across the pasture. First, he must see they lost him in the darkness. After that he must make plans for the future. This would be no safe country for him if he had killed Ben Randall. Old Jeff Randall would see to that. The Diamond Tail was lord of justice in this part of the territory, and the rough old-timer who ruled it would be no impartial judge.

He had been lucky in the horse he had commandeered. The buckskin had a broad deep chest and a big-barreled body. It was not overtired. Bruce guessed that its legs would stand up for the grueling test they might both have to face.

15

The rider swung sharply to the left, still traveling rapidly. The black night surrounded him like a wall. He had no time to let the horse pick its way. All he could do was hope that a leg would not be broken in a gopher hole.

Presently he pulled up to listen. A coyote yelped in the distance, but no rumor of horses breaking through the brush reached him. For the time he had evaded the enemy. This did not greatly elate him. He knew that before morning every mountain pass would be blocked and every ranch on the plains be on the lookout for him. He must have been recognized. Bill Cairns had been staring at him when he jerked the horse around to start his flight.

He kept going, but at a more reasonable gait. He was not quite sure why he had cut into the pasture, unless it had been to divert the hunt from his companions, particularly poor Pete. It would have been safer to make directly for the mountains and try to get over one of the passes before it was closed. The chase would concentrate on him. He was the only one of the raiders yet identified and the one who had shot young Randall.

Not counting the peril into which the shooting had brought him, Bruce was unhappy at what he had done. He was no killer any more than he was a horse thief, but now the word would go out that he was both. What else could he have

16

done? Before Pete reached the horse Gilcrest was holding for him Randall would have finished him if he had been let alone. Bruce had been given a fraction of a second to decide. It had to be Pete or Ben. A man in a fight had to stand by his own side.

The boot of the fugitive was already soggy from the blood dripping into it. When he had time he would have to give it attention. But he could not do that now. He was cut off from his own ranch, even if he had dared go there. Before daybreak he must be out of the valley and in the hills. There were draws and pockets where he might find a temporary hiding place among the aspens or the scrub oak. Down here in the rolling plains he would not have a chance. He decided to make for the Sleepy Cat Range.

Bruce did not deceive himself about what would befall him if he was captured. He had been too long a thorn in the side of the big ranches. His cool light insolence, the lash of his quick tongue, the encouragement his aid gave the hoe men, had marked him for punishment even before the jaws of this trap had closed on him. Unless he had miraculous luck he was due to be rubbed out before the sun of the coming day set.

He pointed northeast, holding the buckskin to a road gait. It would not do to be in too much of a hurry. The strength of the horse must be conserved. It would have to travel far over a wild rough country, and it must have enough stamina left for a hard race if he were seen by one of the posses combing the hills for him.

Light was already breaking in the eastern sky when he cut the wires of the Pitchfork pasture and rode out of it into a draw leading to the foothills. A small stream ran down it, and he plodded beside this for miles, working steadily deeper into the approaches to the range. He found what he wanted at last, a gulch running into the cañon, its floor sown with young pines behind which he could conceal the buckskin. Without unsaddling, he tied. There was no feed here. The animal would have to wait till he found a grassy pocket higher up.

Bruce limped back to the brook, the saddle gun in one hand. The wound in his leg was paining a good deal. That was something he had to endure. Before it was better it would be a good deal worse. Beside the stream he sat down and pulled off the boot. His blood-stained stocking clung to the calf. It took more resolution than he had to tear the cloth free. Instead, he put the leg into the running water and let the current wash the stocking loose. This hurt, but he stuck it out. His hope was that the clear, cold runoff from the snow would cleanse the wound and prevent poisonous infection. The handkerchief that had been around his neck he washed, and after it had dried in the warm sun he tied it around the wound. The sock he threw away. Slowly he inched the boot on again, setting his teeth to keep from grunting. He drank deeply, and washed his face in the cool water. After the buckskin had drunk he headed again upstream.

He had not gone a dozen yards when he heard voices. A party of his hunters were coming up the cañon. Swiftly he wheeled the horse, rode back to the gulch, and moved into the pines behind a great boulder. Bruce watched the party draw up to water. His stomach muscles tied into a cold hard knot. He could see the discarded sock lying beside a rock not a dozen yards from them.

'Might have gone up this gulch,' a cowboy said.

'Not unless he could climb out by his eyebrows,' another differed. 'There's a twenty-foot rock fall straight up and down at the top. Could be hiding in the pines.'

The man who spoke next was Bill Cairns, wagon boss of the Pitchfork. He was a wall-eyed man with a leathery brown face. Hard muscles packed the frame of his big body. 'Could be, but isn't. Not that bird. He's way up in the range, ridin' like the heel flies are after him. He'd be a chump to fool around down here.'

'Mebbe so.' The cowboy who had spoken first pulled out a revolver and sent a bullet crashing through the pines. 'That's for you, Mr. Sherrill, if you're roosting there.'

Cairns turned on the young fellow angrily. 'What you trying to do—warn him we're around?'

'You said he wasn't there,' the young rider retorted sulkily.

'He isn't. But don't pull any of that funny stuff when we get higher, Wally. Save your bullets till you see the son of a gun.'

The foreman pulled his horse, splashing as it went, out of the water. He rode upstream. The others followed in single file.

Bruce reclaimed the sock and buried it in the creek beneath a rock.

A mile below this point he had passed a rocky gorge down which in the rainy season a torrent poured. He rode back and turned into it. Looking up that boulder-filled steep, Bruce doubted if a horse could make it. But he had not any other choice. He could not turn back into the valley. Nor could he follow the creek, knowing that Cairn's posse was ahead of him. He set the buckskin at its job.

He had to get out of the saddle long before they reached the top. Every step on foot up the gorge tortured him, but he set his teeth and took the pain. All his thought had to be given to the task of maneuvering the reluctant horse up the narrow rock-strewn bed. They made it, after a hard pull.

Bruce found himself on a plateau, one side of which dropped down to a small mountain park and the other fell almost sheer to the foothills below. There was on it no sign of human life. He rode to the end of the prong and looked down at the sea of grass stretching to the far horizon. In the pleasant sunlight it was a fair sight to see. No doubt a gentle breeze was rippling through it, though he was too far away to verify his guess.

He made out the windmills of the Pitchfork, and nearer a sparkle of light that must have come from the sun glinting on a line fence. Bruce frowned. That fence was a symbol of war, the spoils of which were the water and the grass on that wide undulating plain.

It was unfortunate, Bruce thought wryly, that he was of a temper that saw both sides of a question. Better be a thorough partisan and know that you are a hundred per cent right and your enemy entirely wrong. The tired nesters and their gaunt parched women could vision only one angle to this quarrel. They had come a long weary trek to homestead this land and these insolent cow barons flouted the law and made it impossible for them to live in their homes.

All of Sherrill's sympathies were with these poor underprivileged nesters, but there was some justice too in the claim of the cattlemen. For a score of years they had been the Men on Horseback, lords of all they surveyed. They had fought the Sioux and the Cheyenne, had endured droughts and blizzards while building up their herds. Their cattle had roamed over a hundred miles of free grass. By use they had a claim to it, if not by law. Then the hoe men came in to fence the creeks and plow the meadows, cutting off the cattle of the big ranches from feed and water. In retaliation, to protect their herds, the old-time cattlemen began to fence all the land in sight.

Though the sympathies of Bruce were with the newcomers, he had an uneasy feeling that nature was on the side of the range men. This was pasture land, too dry for farming. The plow would destroy the native grasses, and the land would be lost forever.

None of which reasoning justified the big outfits in fencing thousands of acres of government land to prevent the small fry from running their poor herds on it. The arrogance of the Randalls and the Dalys and the Applegates would not in the end avail them. They could frighten away this or that homesteader. They could rub out another accused of rustling calves belonging to the Pitchfork or the Bar B B, but they could not stop the tide of hoe men looking toward the cow country any more than Canute could sweep back the sea. The empire of the cattleman was doomed.

Bruce dropped from the plateau to the mountain park that bounded it. At the far end of this was a thick clump of aspens running up into the entrance of a small gulch. He rode across the park, skirted the aspens, and descended into a pocket where the grass was good. After he had picketed the horse he pushed up into the gulch to a cluster of great boulders tossed together fifty feet from the floor of the trough. He lay down to rest, and in spite of his throbbing calf fell into troubled sleep.

Hours later he was awakened by rain beating in his face. The sun had vanished, and the whole sky was a heavy gray. It had set in for a long rain.

He limped down into the pocket and saddled the buckskin. If any of his hunters came this way they would notice the circle of cropped grass where the pony had been picketed. But that was a contingency against which he could not guard. The weakness of his situation was that no planning could extricate him. It was not possible to know in what direction he might run into enemies.

Linda Applegate Shows Anger

III

Within the hour he caught sight of riders moving along a ridge above him, their figures vague in the misty rain. He drew back into the pines and waited until they had passed from sight. Already night was beginning to fall, earlier than usual on account of the heavy weather. He decided to stay in this timbered park until daybreak.

That he would have a bad night he knew. The cold rain had chilled him to the bone. He was very weary and in a good deal of pain. For twenty-four hours he had been without food, and he guessed he was running a fever.

After several attempts he got a fire started close to a projecting sandstone bluff. The wood was wet and several times the struggling fire threatened to give up the ghost. It ran to smoke rather than heat.

There was little hope in him. The mountain passes must both be guarded. He dared not shoot game. Twice he had crossed streams in which he had seen trout. They might as well have been in Africa for all the good they did him. Eventually he would be forced to work back to the ranch country from which he had escaped. He was cut off from his allies as completely as if a prison wall had surrounded him, and in any case they were too weak to help him.

He slept fitfully, waking now and again from the pain of his wound and from the penetrating cold. Dawn broke clear. He was saddling when he saw riders once more on the lip of the park, this time traveling in the opposite direction from those he had sighted yesterday. One of them pulled up and pointed a finger down at him. Somebody let out a yell of triumph. The hunters scurried about, trying to find the quickest way down from the rimrock.

Bruce pulled himself into the hull and made for the opposite ridge. When he reached the top he looked back to see riders strung along the flat he had just left. He had no choice now. With the hunters so close on his heels he had to let himself be driven back into the ranch country and hope for a miracle. Recklessly he raced down the steep slope, rubble slithering from the hoofs of the buckskin. He galloped down precipitous gullies and came to a long ledge overlooking the plains. Perhaps he was trapped. All he could do was to keep going, watching for any break in the rock that might lead to the foothills below.

His pursuers were out of sight for the moment, and they had not yet appeared when he found a rain gutter made by flood storms and turned the horse into it. This was a beggar's choice, but the buckskin reached safer ground below, during half of the descent sliding on its haunches.

A hill crease tempted him, and he took it instantly. Far back he heard the shout of one of the posse, but at least they had lost him for the moment. The draw led to open ground. There was a fence before him and beyond that the buildings of the Bar B B ranch house. He grinned wryly. His long flight had brought him to the very door of his chief enemy. Most of the cattle shut off from water by his homestead fences belonged to Cliff Applegate.

Linda was making a rice pudding when she heard a horse moving toward the house. She glanced through the window. The buckskin was the favorite mount of her cousin Ben Randall, but the man in the saddle was not Ben. She was startled. Ben lay at home, near to death. That villain Bruce Sherrill had jumped his horse and escaped on it. Except at a distance she had never seen the fellow, but this must be the man. Her stomach muscles tightened, not from fear. While he lowered himself from the saddle, heavily, as one does who has been hurt, her gaze did not lift from him. He came to the porch, limping.

The girl was surprised at the appearance of the man she saw in the doorway. He was haggard, his eyes sunken from pain and fatigue. One shoulder leaned against the jamb, as if for support. She guessed he was completely exhausted, though his twisted smile was one of mocking self-derision. What very much astonished her was that she found no evil in the face of this man whom she had for years heard denounced as a scoundrel.

'Couldn't make it,' he said, lifting the Stetson from a head of crisp reddish hair. 'Your friends were too smart for me. They cut me off from the passes.'

The planes in the fresh young face set like those of a hanging judge. She was thinking of Ben Randall, the boy with whom she had gone to school and ridden the range and hunted deer. Her heart hardened, to reject any appeal this young fellow might make.

'So you come to me for help—after killing my cousin,' she flung at him bitterly.

The news that Randall was dead disturbed him, but he had no time for dwelling on that now. 'Thought you might like to be in at the kill,' he corrected, still with the thin brittle smile. 'They are beating the hills back of your place. In ten or fifteen minutes they ought to be here.' His body sagged a little. He leaned more heavily against the jamb.

'If they find you here—'

'There won't be any time for last words, will there?' he cut in flippantly.

'Get on that horse and ride away,' she ordered, stormy lights in her dark eyes. 'I can't save you—and I wouldn't if I could. You'd better hurry.' Her gaze swept out of the window to the hill folds back of the house. No horsemen were yet in sight.

He came into the room and put a hand on the back of a kitchen chair to steady him, still with that fixed ironic grin turned on her. There was something a little wild in his look, as if he might be out of his head.

'Don't you hear me?' she snapped. 'If they are really there, as you say, they'll take you out and hang you.'

'Sounds reasonable,' he agreed.

'You fool!' the girl cried. 'Haven't you a lick of sense? Fork that horse and light out, if you don't want to get what you deserve.'

'You're a true Applegate,' he said. 'No fooling you. Give the dog a bad name and hang him.'

Anger boiled in her, and back of it an increasing dread. She hated this insolent scamp, but there was a growing panic rising in her. She did not want him taken to be killed—not here, before her eyes, after she had seen him in such dire need.

'What is it you want—food?' she demanded. 'If it's that, I'll get you some. But I won't have you here.'

'Quite right,' he agreed. 'Evil communications

corrupt good manners. I learned that in my copybook.'

Her exasperation was about to burst over him, but he did not give it time. His knees collapsed, and he pitched down at her feet in a faint.

A Good Samaritan

IV

Linda stared down in great surprise at the prone lax body of the fugitive. From it her gaze went through the window again to search the hill creases. She caught sight of a horseman for a moment and then he disappeared in a draw. Sherrill had told the truth, they were hard on his trail.

Already she had decided to save him if she could. Her thoughts came in stabbing flashes. First, she must get the horse out of sight before they emerged from the foothills. That done, she must hide the hunted man. Not upstairs in her bedroom. She could not carry him up. In the storeroom off the kitchen. Neither her father nor her brothers went in there more than once a week.

She ran out and pulled herself to the saddle on the buckskin. There was a brush-filled gulley at one side of the house where old tin cans and garbage were flung. It angled in the direction of a hayfield for a hundred yards or more. Near the lower end she led the animal down the steep bank and tied it to a young willow.

As she hurried back to the house Linda saw that the hunters were out of the foothills and moving toward the ranch. In another five minutes they would be tramping up the porch steps.

She caught the unconscious man under the armpits and dragged him across the kitchen floor into the storeroom. A flour barrel and one containing molasses stood at the far wall and behind these she left Sherrill. His hat and the saddle gun she brought in and concealed under some empty gunny sacks. There was no time to make sandwiches, for she could see a group of men coming through the gate, but she took in and left her unwelcome guest a jug of milk and a plate of bread and cold beef. The door of the storeroom she closed.

When a rap came on the door she was stirring the pudding, a song on her lips. She stopped singing, 'Don't you remember sweet Alice, Ben Bolt,' to let in Bill Cairns and four Pitchfork cowboys.

'Morning, Miss Lindy.' On the ugly mouth of the foreman was an ingratiating smile. Ever since the girl had been fifteen Cairns had looked at her with a covetous eye. 'Haven't seen anything of that young fellow Sherrill, I reckon?'

Linda's eyes were wide with surprise. 'Is he around here, Mr. Cairns?'

'You bet he is. Not far away. We drove him down from the hills and lost him at the rimrock. But he had to come this way. If you'd been lookin' you must of seen him pass.'

She stared at him. 'You mean—right by the house?'

'Mighty close, headin' for the river.'

'Unless he's around one of the ranch buildings,' Wally Jelks amended. 'Hoping after we've passed to cut back into the hills.'

Cairns showed his tobacco-stained teeth in a grin. 'Smart boy, Wally. Maybe you're right. Have a look-see in the stable and the bunkhouse.'

'How about that coffee you promised us, Bill?' a youngster asked.

'I'll make some right away,' Linda said. 'Won't take me but a few minutes. If one of you will grind some in the mill.'

Three boys headed for the coffee grinder, but in spite of his bulk the foreman was there first. 'Take the others with you, Wally, and search the buildings. Make sure he ain't squattin' behind the roothouse or anywheres. I'll stay with Miss Lindy, seeing as she's got a license to be scared of this murderin' scoundrel.'

'I'm not afraid of him,' the girl said promptly, an angry flush on her face. She had noticed Wally Jelks's satiric grin as he started to follow the others from the room. His thoughts were as clear to read as the open page of a book. Cairns wanted to be alone with her. Probably the range rider had observed the sly greedy looks with which the foreman had watched her furtively at dances.

'You're a young lady and don't understand,' the Pitchfork major-domo told her with smug righteousness. 'Some of these fence-cuttin' hoe men are bad characters—this fellow Sherrill, f'rinstance. A girl like you, pretty as a painted wagon, ought to have a good man to protect her.'

'I have three—my father and two brothers,' she said stiffly. 'Nobody with any sense would dare to insult me.'

Her dark hard eyes drilled into his. His reputation with women was bad. If he had any ideas about her he had better forget them now.

'Right,' he agreed. 'Still and all, Cliff hadn't ought to have left you alone while that villain is still prowlin' around.'

'Perhaps you had better tell him so,' she suggested, with a thin contemptuous smile. Cliff Applegate was not one to take advice on so personal a matter, certainly not from a man with Cairns's record.

An angry red poured into the back of the foreman's leathery neck. He was thought to be a tough hard fighting man, and he was full of vanity. To have this young woman tell him off so neatly was annoying. He was a man of no subtlety and blurted out his resentment.

'You got no call to ride me because I'm trying to protect you from this skunk we're aimin' to rub out. You've always been so high and mighty. What's the matter with me, anyhow?'

33

'If you'll finish grinding the coffee I can start making it,' she suggested.

'You've always acted like you hated me,' he complained.

She corrected that impression. 'You're quite wrong. I'm afraid I've never thought of you one way or another.'

He strode up to her, his face purple with rage beneath the tan. His strong fingers closed on her shoulders and bit into them. 'By God, you will,' he swore. 'No woman can talk thataway to me.'

Her small fist smashed into his face.

A man had opened the door and was standing there. He said, in burlesque of the current melodrama, 'Unhand that villain, maiden.' Rod Randall, an older half-brother of her cousin Ben, was smiling at them in frank enjoyment. He was a lean-loined, broad-shouldered fellow, dark and good-looking, with black eyes and a strong jaw. Linda called him cousin, but he was no kin except by the courtesy of marriage. She had seen a good deal of him, but she did not understand him very well. She was a little afraid of him. He had the unconscious arrogance of one who means to take from life what he wants. It sometimes made the girl uncomfortable to suspect that one of his unnamed wants was Linda Applegate. She thought about him a good deal, as a young woman does concerning a man who may some day be important in her life. Her instinct warned her to avoid him. She suspected he was ruthless, that no woman would mean enough to him to find happiness beside him. And yet somehow he fascinated her.

It was like him not to rush forward to her assistance, to act as if this were a pleasant comedy for his entertainment.

'He's making an annoying fool of himself,' Linda told the newcomer. 'But I don't need any help. I know how to handle his kind.'

Randall laughed. 'Pick on someone of yore size, Lindy,' he drawled. 'Bill doesn't weigh much more than two hundred pounds.' He offered mock sympathy to the Pitchfork man. 'Maybe I could hold her long enough for you to make a brcak for yorc horsc and a gctaway.'

'I wasn't hurtin' her any,' Cairns growled.

A change came over young Randall's face, amusement banished from it as the flame is from a blown candle. His eyes had grown hard and cold, the warning of half-scabbarded steel in them.

'You'd better not,' he said, his voice and bearing arrogantly contemptuous. 'Keep yore dirty looks on your own kind. If you ever annoy Miss Applegate again I'll cut your hide off with a quirt.'

'I was jest funnin' a little, Rod,' the foreman mumbled. 'No need to get so bossy about it.

Why, I stayed here to protect her from that fellow Sherrill.'

'Her own family will do any protecting that's needed,' Rod answered. 'Don't forget that.'

They heard the cowboys coming back. Their spurred boots dragged across the porch.

'Nothin' doing,' Jelks announced. 'He isn't here.'

'Who isn't?' Randall asked, and the situation was explained.

'We'll take off,' Cairns announced, his voice a snarl.

'Not without our coffee,' a towheaded cowboy objected in surprise.

'Of course not,' Linda said. 'I'll hurry it up.'

'Sherrill has probably ridden across the pasture to the river and will try to hide in the bushes,' Jelks guessed.

'I could of told you that all the time,' Cairns flung out spitefully. 'He's not jugheaded chump enough to stick around here to be caught.'

They drank their coffee and left. From the window Randall watched them ride down into the pasture.

'I'll drift along after them presently,' Randall told his hostess as he sauntered back. 'Like to be there when they get the fellow.'

She thought he moved with the undulating grace of a panther. Sometimes it seemed to her there was menace in his motions, a suggestion of a banked power to pounce if the occasion came. He flicked at the table with the end of his quirt.

'So Mr. Cairns has ideas,' he mentioned, his smiling eyes on her.

'I'd rather you didn't say anything about this,' she said. 'I'll handle it.'

His grin remained. 'You already have, I'd say. Competently.'

Linda did not like that. As a younger girl she had been known to have a gusty temper not under very good control. For the past year or two she had been trying to live this down.

'What could I do when the fool laid hands on me?'

'No criticism here,' he said.

'How is Ben?' she asked.

'I've been riding all night,' Rod answered. 'But a Diamond Tail hand reached our camp this morning with the news Doc says Ben might make it if he has luck. Why in time did he have to race in before the others and get a slug put in him?' He moved to the door. 'So long, little wildcat. Be seeing you.'

She watched him ride away, a flat-backed graceful figure, and as soon as he reached the pasture she opened the door of the storeroom. The wounded man was conscious.

His gaze took in the slender graciousness of her young body, the face with a beautifully modeled bone structure. There was a hint of temper, perhaps of willfulness too, in the hostile eyes. No doubt she had been spoiled. He thought her capable of violent emotions.

'You have visitors,' he said.

'They have gone.'

'Didn't they want to meet Mr. Sherrill?'

His insouciance set a spark to the resentment in her. 'I'll make this clear,' she declared coldly. 'I'm not going to joke with you. There's no friendship between us. To me you are just a killer I hate. But you're here—wounded. There's nothing I can do but take care of you.'

'A good Samaritan.'

'As soon as my father comes you'll be his responsibility.' She said it with angry bitterness. 'Now I'll look at your wound.'

He shook his head. 'No. Why take trouble to patch me up for so short a time?'

She glared down at him. If she had been a little girl she would have stamped her foot. 'Haven't you any sense?' she cried, withdrawing her threat illogically. 'I want to fix you up so you can travel, so that you won't be killed here by my people.'

'Fair enough,' he agreed. 'Inconsiderate of me to drop in, but your friends were crowding me. Any port in a storm, you know. Too bad I had to annoy you. The patient is ready, doctor.'

She brought water and clean rags, knelt beside him, and dressed the wound. It was a neat job.

'Doc Bradley couldn't have done better,' he said approvingly.

She noticed that he had drunk the milk and eaten some of the bread and meat. 'I'll get you a snack to take with you,' she said.

He got to his feet slowly, still light-headed. 'Why?' he wanted to know. 'I'm just a killer you hate. Your conscience is clear now. I can make it off the Bar B B without any more food. Thanks for your charming hospitality.'

'I'm not thinking about you.' She wanted him to be sure of that. Her voice was sharp with censure. 'I want you to get far enough away so that it won't be Applegates who meet you.'

He hobbled into the kitchen and his glance went out of the window. 'Sorry to disappoint you. We're a bit late. Enter Cliff Applegate all loaded for bear.'

Her glance shuttled to the window and back again to him. The color had drained from her cheeks. 'I'll help you upstairs,' she told him instantly. 'Quick.'

He hesitated. 'What's the use? You can't keep me hidden here, even if you wanted to.'

'Do as I say.' She caught at his arm and drew him toward the stairway. 'Hurry—hurry!'

He limped up the stairs, leaning on her, and was pushed into a bedroom. 'Don't make a sound,' she warned.

'Lindy!' her father's voice called.

'Be right down,' she answered, and shut the door behind her.

The first glance told the uninvited guest that it was the girl's own bedroom. The furniture was plain and simple, but everything in the room had the woman's touch that made it homelike and attractive. Dotted muslin curtains hung at the window. A neat rug was on the floor. On the bed a patchwork counterpane made perhaps by Linda's mother was as fresh as if it had been finished yesterday. His eyes picked out the titles of half a dozen books on a shelf—the poems of Tennyson and Longfellow, *David Copperfield*, *Guy Mannering*, *Jane Eyre*, and a three-volume edition of Shakespeare. The exquisite neatness showed that the young mistress gave her belongings scrupulous care.

He tiptoed to the bed and sat down on it. He knew this would be only a short reprieve, but she had wanted it that way and he had not found physical strength to resist.

Breakfast at the Bar B B

V

Cliff Applegate said, 'We're hungry as wolves.'

He was a big man, with a broad reach of shoulders, a thick chest, and the heavy muscular spread that comes to an active outdoor man in the fifties. The eyes in his bony determined face had been bleached from squinting into ten thousand summer suns. They held a touch of arrogance, due to the power that success and possessions had brought him. His sons, Cliff and Brand, were tall, long-legged young fellows, strong and spare of flesh, but it was an easy guess that in time they would look very much as their father did now.

'I suppose you haven't had any breakfast,' Linda said.

'We've forgotten what little we had,' Brand laughed.

'Have you heard this morning how Ben is?' young Cliff asked.

'Still hanging on,' his sister answered. 'Doc Bradley says he has a slim chance. Rod told me. He was here for a minute.'

Linda looked at the pudding in the oven, found it done, and put it on a side table. She began preparing breakfast for her men. It occurred to

41

her that it might be wise to show an interest in the chase from which they had just returned.

'Did you get Sherrill?'

'No. He seems to have found him a hole and pulled it in after him,' Brand replied. 'But he can't get away. The passes are plugged up. He'll be driven down into the valley.'

'Bill Cairns and four Pitchfork boys dropped in and stopped for coffee. They said they jumped him up in the hills but lost him afterwards.'

'Then he is still in the hills,' Cliff, Senior, said.

'Not if they are right,' Linda explained. 'They think they drove him down to the river right close past the house here.' She put roasted coffee beans into the mill and ground them.

The men went out to wash up while she made biscuits and cooked the steaks. But before she started she flew upstairs to her patient. She had intended to tell him to lie on the bed, but she found him already there, his dusty boots on a newspaper.

'You'd better have them off,' she said, and caught hold of a heel and toe.

'Don't bother,' he advised her, 'unless you don't want me to die with my boots on.'

She paid no attention to his sardonic remark. The boot on the wounded leg she eased off as gently as possible. Beads of perspiration stood out on his forehead. His teeth were clenched.

42

'I'll get you water soon as I have time,' she promised curtly.

'I say thanks. You haven't told them yet.'

'That's my business,' Linda replied brusquely. 'You stay here and keep quiet.'

'Why not?' An ironic smile twitched at his mouth. 'This isn't my day for whooping it up. I can get along without visitors nicely—except you.'

An angry flush swept into her cheeks. 'I'm not doing this for you, but to keep my folks from being the ones who kill you.'

She left the room and hurried downstairs. Swiftly she put three large steaks on the stove to cook and measured coffee from the drawer under the grinder into the pot. Her motions as she mixed the biscuits, rolled them out, and put them in the pan were sure and fast. When the men came stamping into the house she was nearly ready for them.

'It's time Bud Wong came back from town,' she told her father. 'He's had time to gamble away all his money and get on several sprees. If I were bossing that Chinaman he wouldn't get off so easily. He's been away nearly a week.'

'Do you good to cook for a spell, honey. We can take it.'

'You'd better. First one complains I resign.'

They ate like men who had been starving on a desert island. Linda brought plate after plate of hot biscuits to the table. She watched them vanish almost as if a magician had waved them away.

The girl gathered information while they fed themselves. 'How did this man Sherrill come to shoot Ben?' she asked. 'I know Ben and some of the Diamond Tail boys caught him cutting wires.'

'That's the answer,' Brand said. 'Guns started smoking.'

'Who began firing?' Linda persisted.

'I reckon Ben did, but that doesn't matter. He was on his fast buckskin ridin' hell for leather like he always does. Soon as he got close enough he cut loose. Bill Cairns says Ben hit one fellow. He could see him limpin' as he ran. Then Sherrill shot Ben outa the saddle, grabbed the buckskin, and lit outa there before they could get him.'

'Ben was shot in a fight then. He wasn't ambushed.'

'That's right,' her father confirmed. 'But there wouldn't have been any fight if these fellows hadn't been cutting Pitchfork fences.' After a moment the ranchman added: 'There's nobody in the world I have less use for than this man Sherrill, but I will say for him that I don't think he would kill from ambush. He's a hardy devil and doesn't fear God or man.'

'How did the Pitchfork riders know they would be cutting wire at that place just then?' Linda inquired.

There was a long moment of silence, broken by her father.

'Don't ask so many questions, honey,' he told her.

His answer surprised her. She could see no reason for secrecy, unless perhaps the cattlemen had brought in a range detective to check on the nesters, one whose identity must be kept under cover.

Brought up in a world of men, her impudence encouraged since she could first toddle, Linda was not easily suppressed.

'What's the matter with that question?' she demanded.

Brand grinned at her. 'Little girls should be seen and not heard.'

'Maybe they oughtn't to be seen either,' she said, a little heat in her voice. 'I've decided to accept Aunt Mary's invitation to visit her. I won't be gone more than two or three months.'

'Now—now, honey,' her father interposed. 'Don't get sore. Brand is just foolin'.'

'I'm not sore,' she flung back. 'I just want to go away and play with my dolls for a while— to some place where a lot of men won't always be dragging mud into the house for me to clean up—and dropping their clothes any place they take them off—and coming home at all hours for meals—and giving me such a nice time generally. I'm damned tired of it.'

The ranchman was shocked. 'I haven't heard you use that word since you were a little trick about four years old. It's not nice for a young lady.'

'Oh, I'm a young lady now, am I, too old to be spanked?'

'I paddled the boys too for letting you hear them use the word,' he reminded her. A bit fearfully he took up her complaint. 'I didn't know you were so tired of us, honey.'

The gentleness of his voice reproached her. She knew that of all the world he loved her most. Her warm fond eyes smiled at him. She did not know why she had flared up anyhow.

'Forget it, Dad. Once in a while I get tired of staying at home and running the house, especially when you come home with secrets I'm not to know because I'm only a girl and of no importance.'

'Who said you were of no importance?' he asked. 'You know better than that, Lindy. It's only that we're kinda pledged not to tell anyone that particular thing.'

'That's all right, then.' She turned on him her mocking impudent grin. 'I won't have to accept Bill Cairns's offer to become his missus, will I?'

Her father's hand stopped, with a buttered biscuit halfway to his mouth. 'Did that scalawag dare—?'

She interrupted his resentment. 'Not quite. What he said was that I needed a good man to protect me. I told him I had three. I gathered that the good man he was thinking of wouldn't leave me alone to the mercy of this desperado Sherrill the way my men do.'

'Maybe he is right. I ought to have left one of the boys here.'

'Do you think Sherrill would hurt me?'

'He's in a bad jam. You can't be sure what he would do.'

'Don't worry about him,' Cliff, Junior, said. 'He's not going to be with us long.'

'About Bill Cairns,' Brand commented. 'If he bothers you any, sis, let me know.'

'Are you the head of this house, Brand?' his father inquired with displeasure. 'I'll look after my daughter when it is necessary.'

'It won't be necessary,' Linda told them decisively. 'I can take care of Mr. Cairns without any help. I've already put a flea in the ear of the big lug.'

'If he crooks a finger at you I want to know it.' The ranchman looked at Linda sternly. 'And don't let me hear of you flirting with this scoundrel the way you do with half the boys you meet. He's no good.'

'I'm certainly dumb,' she told herself out loud. 'I ought to know by this time you can't take a joke. I wouldn't look at Bill Cairns if he was the only man in the world. And I don't flirt with anybody. I have to be polite, don't I?'

Her father ignored the question. 'We'd better make the calf cut this afternoon. Some of our boys ought to be getting back soon.'

He caught up his hat and left the house.

Linda Changes
Her Father's Mind

VI

Linda gave her patient a drink and washed his face with cold water. She looked down at him, frowning.

His twisted grin was apologetic. 'I'm a white elephant on your hands, Miss Applegate. Sorry.'

She was worried. The buckskin in the gully would be discovered soon, and then the place would be searched. She could not keep the wounded man here without somebody finding out he was in the house. Yet it was plain he was in no condition to travel. He needed a doctor, but he would have to do without one. Before nightfall he might be beyond medical aid, unless he was still concealed.

'I don't know what to do with you,' she answered. 'If you stay here my father will find out, and even if you could travel I couldn't get you away without being seen.'

'Better tell him I'm here,' he advised. 'You won't be to blame for what happens to me.'

'I don't see why you had to come blundering in here of all places,' she broke out in exasperation. 'You know how we have despised and hated you for your contemptible conduct. On top of that you have to shoot my cousin and come here to hide.'

'Annoying,' he admitted. 'There isn't any out for me, Miss Applegate. I'm throwing in my hand.' He started to rise from the bed, but her strong arm pushed him back.

'I'll decide what's to be done,' she told him sharply.

'I have a slight interest in this,' he reminded her dryly. 'Much obliged for your kindness, but I won't impose on it any longer.'

'You'll stay right there till I make up my mind.'

She spoke imperiously, but it was her anxiety rather than her anger that influenced him. He might as well let her have her way. It would make no difference in the end.

He gave a gesture of surrender. 'All right. Whatever you say. Fix it up so you won't get into trouble.'

She left him, to go down and wash the dishes, her mind greatly disturbed. Her father was not a cruel man, not ruthless like her uncle Jeff Randall, but he could be stern and stubborn. There was no man he felt so bitterly toward as the one upstairs, and now the fellow had added surplusage by shooting down his favorite nephew. It was not likely he would show any mercy for him now. Probably he would not himself execute what he considered justice but would turn the offender over to the Randalls for punishment. At the Diamond Tail Sherrill would meet his jury, judge, and sheriff.

A jubilant shout outside startled Linda. She heard her brother Cliff's voice, excitement racing in it. 'Look what I found in the gully, Father.'

The girl's heart went down like a plummet. She knew what he had found. With the dish towel still in her hand she walked out to the porch. Cliff was leading the buckskin across the yard to the blacksmith shop where his father and Brand were standing with their saddled mounts.

'Ben's horse,' the ranchman said, and a moment later added: 'The Pitchfork boys were right. They drove him out of the hills.'

'Where to?' Brand asked. 'Where is he now? Did he hide the horse, figuring he had a better chance to slip down to the river on foot without being seen?'

'Or is he on this place right now?' his father asked. 'We'll find out about that first.' He turned to his daughter. 'You didn't notice any lone rider around here, Lindy?'

She cried, to gain time, 'Why, that is Ben's buckskin.'

'Yes. Sherrill must have been on it. He's either here or headed for the river on foot.'

She nodded quickly. 'Like Brand said, getting rid of the horse so as not to be noticed.'

'Stay here with yore sister, Brand,' the cattleman ordered. 'Cliff and I will search the outbuildings. If he's not there we'll go through the house. He might have slipped in while Lindy was busy.'

'Just what I did,' a voice said. 'But it was no go. I'm bucked out.'

Their eyes converged to the doorway. Bruce Sherrill was standing there, his hands in his trousers' pockets. The other men stared at him, for the moment dumb with surprise.

'That's a lie,' Linda said angrily. 'I hid him in my room.'

The guns of both her brothers covered the fugitive.

'What crazy nonsense is that, girl?' her father demanded.

'Can't you hear?' she retorted. 'I hid him— from Bill Cairns and his men—because he is wounded and I didn't want him murdered here, no matter what he has done. And when you came I hadn't made up my mind what to do. So I didn't tell you. I thought he might have a chance to slip away. Then somebody else could deal with him, not on our place.'

'Have you lost your mind?' the ranchman bellowed. 'Trying to stand between me and this killer. My own daughter. Goddlemighty! You ought to be whipped. Butting into other folks' business.'

She faced Applegate, her eyes hot with anger. 'He's been wounded, I tell you. He fell fainting

52

at my feet. I had just time to hide the horse and drag him into the storeroom before the Pitchfork men came. Would you want me to turn over to Cairns to be hanged a man who might be dying? Or to you either?'

Her father struggled to control his temper. Her defiance was outrageous. 'Why can't you act like a lady—instead of a—'

Words failed him. He could not find a simile. His face had dyed to a rich purple. As yet his rage was turned against the girl. He would deal with his enemy later.

'I don't claim to be a lady, whatever that is,' Linda flung back furiously. 'How could I be, brought up in a house filled with savages? If you were civilized you would understand that a woman can't turn a wounded man over to be slaughtered even if she does hate him.'

Applegate threw up his hand in a gesture that flung the girl aside for the moment. He glared at the man in the doorway—haggard, sunken-eyed, unshaven, but with the look of one unbroken and indomitable in the grim reckless face.

'You've gone too far at last,' Applegate cried harshly. 'When you shot Ben Randall you tied a noose around yore neck.'

'I shot him because he was trying to kill a man he had already wounded,' Sherrill answered. 'A friend of mine.'

'That doesn't go with us. Yore friend was

cutting a Pitchfork fence. No doubt he is a rustler.'

'No,' the wounded man denied. 'Just a plain homesteader fighting for his rights, a poor scrub nester no better than a worm in the eyes of you exalted bullies.'

'Even if Ben lives it won't do you any good. You've come to the end of yore trail, Sherrill. You've been warned times enough, but you were hell-bent on forcing a showdown. Well, you've got it.'

Bruce Sherrill flashed a quick look at Linda. She had not told him young Randall was still alive. He was glad to know it, even if it would not profit him.

'What are we going to do with him?' Cliff, Junior, asked. 'Take him over to the Diamond Tail?'

'I reckon that would be best,' his father said.

'Can't you see he is sick?' Linda broke out. 'He can't ride.'

'He's been riding for most two days,' Brand said callously. 'He can make out to do twenty miles more.'

'What kind of men are you?' the girl cried desperately. 'Apaches torture their prisoners. I thought you were decent white folks.'

'Keep outa this,' the cattleman ordered her. 'I won't stand for any more interference from you. Go into the house.'

She steadied her voice before she answered, to convince him that this was no hysterical outburst. 'I want to talk with you, Father—alone,' she said in a low voice.

'I've got more important business on hand,' he told her roughly. 'Later I'll tell you plenty.'

Her eyes held fast to his. 'We'll talk now—or never. I'm of age. I'd rather work in a railroad hash house than live here with men who have turned a wounded prisoner over to be murdered by his enemies. I'll leave—and never come back.'

Cliff Applegate stared at his daughter in astonishment. She had been pert and impudent often enough and had let her gusty temper fling her into occasional tantrums, but she had never before set her will to stand against him on a matter of importance. There flashed to his mind a vivid picture of how bleak and desolate life would be without her. But he brushed it aside. He was not going to let a slip of a girl, his own daughter at that, give orders as to what he could and could not do.

'I'll lock you in yore room, missy. I'll show you who is boss here. You've been spoiled. That's what is the matter with you.' He took a step or two toward her threateningly.

Her gaze did not falter. 'I mean what I say,' she answered, still very quietly. 'If you take this man over to the Diamond Tail or if you send for Uncle

Jeff to get him, I'll not stay here another day.'

Cliff reined in his anger, checked by a warning voice inside that was close to fear. He might be on the verge of a bad mistake. Linda was both proud and obstinate. Any one of a dozen young fellows in the district would marry her if she snapped her fingers at him. If he drove her too far, she might do just that, and regret it later.

'What is it you want me to do?' he asked harshly.

'I want you to keep this man hidden here till he is able to travel, then turn him over to the law.'

'The law!' snorted her father. 'And have a rustlers' jury turn him loose to start his deviltry all over again.'

'Of course it isn't fair,' she admitted. 'I know that. But there's nothing else we can do.'

'When we started to comb the hills for this fellow it was to rub him out for shooting Ben— and that's what he deserves,' the cattleman retorted. 'This is man business. You've got no place meddling in it.'

Linda ignored that. 'If you'd met him in the hills and he had died fighting, that would be different,' she persisted. 'But he dragged himself to our house sick and wounded. Let him stay here till he is well, anyhow, and then make up your mind.'

'And if our riders tell the Pitchfork and the Diamond Tail that he is here, what then?'

56

'They don't need to know he is on the ranch. Nobody need know except us four.'

'But Wong would know, after he comes back and starts cooking,' Cliff, Junior, suggested.

'Leave Bud to me,' his sister replied. 'He'll be close as a clam if I ask him.'

'She's got an answer for everything,' Brand said with a sarcastic grin. 'Soon as she is boss of the Bar B B we'll have to ask her may we wipe our noses.'

'You're blackmailing me,' the ranchman told Linda bitterly.

'I'm keeping you from doing something you would always hate yourself for having done. We've got to be fair even to an enemy. We can't revenge ourselves on him by being a party to his murder. I don't like him any better than you do, but I'm not going to lie awake nights ten years from now because I was afraid to tell you the truth.'

The ranchman turned his resentment on Sherrill. 'Get back into the house,' he ordered. 'Before some of our riders drift back and see you. I haven't made up my mind what the hell I'm going to do, but there's no sense standing out here yapping about it.' On Brand he swung round irritably. 'Better put this fellow in yore bed, boy, till I decide what's best.'

Linda knew she had won a victory, for the present at least. She was wise enough to make no comment and to become as unobtrusive as possible. Her father was furious at her, even though his judgment was already telling him she was right. A dominant man, his pride grudged being set straight by his own daughter.

The girl went into the house and stewed a chicken for their unwelcome guest.

VII

Before Bruce Sherrill had imposed himself upon them the Applegate family had been a friendly and closeknit one, but now their casual carefree life had been disrupted. None of them were happy. Linda was in the doghouse. Her father spoke to her only when necessary, and her brothers blamed her for the unfortunate predicament in which they found themselves. Though secretly glad they had not turned their prisoner over to the Randalls, they felt that they had betrayed their friends.

Brand came back from a visit to the Diamond Tail in a sullen temper. The family was at dinner when he walked into the room and joined the others.

'How is Ben?' Linda asked.

'Better. Doc thinks he has a good chance to make it.' Brand plumped out the grievance in his mind. 'I'm not going back there again. I felt like a skunk, sitting there and keeping my trap shut when the boys got to guessing where Sherrill could be. Whose side are we on anyhow?'

'I've wondered about that myself,' his father said bitterly.

'One thing is sure,' Cliff, Junior, contributed. 'When this gets out we won't have any friends among those we have always trailed with. They'll change the name of this ranch to the Double Cross.'

'We're doing the only thing we could do,' Linda submitted, rather humbly. 'You good as told me so yesterday, Brand.'

'You oughtn't ever to meet any of yore enemies, except with guns in yore hands,' Brand flared out. 'Take this guy upstairs. You look after him when he is sick and wounded, and you find out the cuss is human same as yoreself.'

Unexpectedly his father came out in support of the course they had taken. 'We'll live down any feeling there may be. I've been thinking that if Ben gets well even the Randalls may be glad after a while they didn't get a chance to hang Sherrill. But I'll be mighty pleased when he's well enough for me to take him to town and turn him over to the sheriff.' He added quickly, 'I don't like him any better than I did. He's one of these smart-aleck brash birds.'

'I never did meet a nester like him before,' Brand said. 'Most of them are sad-looking trash, meek but obstinate as a government mule. When one of them drops in at a round-up you feel like throwing a rope on him to drag the poor cuss up and fill his belly with steak and flapjacks. But this guy is different. He turns that you-be-damned grin of his on you and wants to know when the hanging is going to be.'

'Truth is, he isn't by rights a nester,' Cliff, Junior, cut in. 'He bought some of his land, and he is grading up his stuff same as we are. That whiteface bull of his is a jim-dandy. Trouble with him is he horned in too late and tried to grab off our range. Then when we wouldn't stand it he threw in with the covered-wagon riffraff.'

'Thanks for explaining him to us,' his father said sourly. 'He may be Jay Gould for all I care. He's a pain just the same. A born trouble-maker. Men like Sherrill have ruined this country. It was the finest place in the world when you were children. What will it be like in ten years?'

Since the first day of Sherrill's arrival Linda had seen almost nothing of him. Bud Wong prepared his meals for him and served them in the bedroom. From her brothers she learned that the wound was healing and that in a few days he would be able to travel. It would be a relief to get him safely out of the house.

One afternoon he hobbled downstairs and came into the sitting room where she was dress-making.

'What are you doing here?' she asked. 'Don't you know that one of the ranch boys might drop in any minute?'

'They are all down in the south pasture working stock,' he told her.

61

'A neighbor could come. They do almost every day.'

'I'm betting this is an off day,' he told her coolly.

'Of course it wouldn't matter to you if my father and brothers get in bad for protecting you,' she said, a small whiplash in her voice.

'You don't like me, do you?'

'No, I don't.'

'Yet you saved my life.'

'We all make mistakes.'

He smiled. 'I'm not going to get any change out of you, I see.'

She looked straight at him. 'You don't think I interfered on your account, I hope.'

'No, I'll acquit you of that. You were worried about the family conscience. But since it meant a good deal to me, you mustn't blame me for feeling grateful.'

'You don't need to. It might have been anybody.'

'But it happened to be Bruce Sherrill.'

'Unfortunately.'

He looked her over carefully, and what he saw he could not help liking. She had long well-fashioned legs, a lovely body slenderly full, a face a man could remember in his dreams. She moved with the fine animal vigor of one who loved the air and the sunshine, and in spite of her willfulness there was a certain gallant and defiant courage in her to which his heart responded.

'Some day you are going to change your mind about me,' he said, smiling at her.

'Am I?' Scornful words poured out to punish his audacity, but she felt a faint quickening of the blood. 'I see,' she replied with a curl of the lips. 'You're one of these barber-shop mashers who slay girls. You ought to have a nice little silky mustache.'

His smile persisted. 'Wrong guess. I'm not like that at all. But I don't need to tell you that. You know it.'

She felt herself flushing beneath the tan of her cheeks. He was quite right. She did know it. The look of scorn she had flung at him was not genuine. It was true that a flame of resentment against him burned in her, but it was also true that he interested her more than any other man she had met, unless perhaps it was Rod Randall. Her father and brothers were tough game Westerners, but their courage was fierce and defiant. Sherrill could meet danger with a mocking smile that denied its importance. His cool politeness could cover the sting of a whip. What was he like, back of this reckless front? He had given her a chance to find out, but she closed the door on it.

'It doesn't matter,' she said carelessly. 'In a day or two you'll be gone. I'll probably never see you again.' A heat beat into her voice. 'I hope not. Ever since you came there has been nothing but trouble in this house.'

He asked if he might smoke and when she gave permission rolled a cigarette. 'Trouble is good for people sometimes,' he suggested. 'It shakes them out of their complacency and forces them to face the truth.'

'What truth does it make us face?' she demanded, sparks of anger in her eyes.

'You're beginning to see that God didn't make this country millions of years ago just for the convenience of a few arrogant cattlemen. You'll never again hold the smug undisturbed belief that they are justified in trampling down poor settlers.'

She swept aside the waist she was making and rose, a tall slim figure stiff with rage. 'That's a fine thing to say, after my father and brothers hid you here and saved you, their worst enemy, protecting you from the just punishment you had earned. I knew you were a hateful person, from the first time I ever heard of you. I am surer of it than ever. Don't speak to me again, please.'

She walked out of the room into the kitchen, where Bud Wong was making apple pies.

'You want tell me something, Missie?' he asked.

'No.' The repressed violence in her exploded. 'That loathsome man! Is he going to stay forever?'

Bud Wong liked their guest, who made little

jokes showing friendliness. 'He plitty flesh,' the cook conceded.

'Fresh!' she repeated. 'He's the most impudent ungrateful scoundrel I ever met, as full of conceit as an egg is of meat. I wish I had let Father take him to the Diamond Tail.'

'He all light.' Bud turned his slant eyes on his mistress with a smile. 'He think Missie plitty nice.'

'He takes a strange way of showing it. Not that I care. He's a detestable person, and I hope he keeps out of my sight till he goes.'

They heard him limping across the sitting room to the stairway and slowly taking the treads. Presently Linda went back to her sewing, anger still churning within her.

She did not mention to the rest of the family the quarrel with Sherrill. It was her own private affair and she did not need any help from them. But she rehearsed what had been said after she went to bed, and the resentful memory of it was with her in the morning as she passed the door of his room on the way downstairs.

Her father was standing by the table reading something written on a page torn from a cheap tablet. He handed the paper to her.

She read:

I've stolen another horse to get to town. I'll leave it with Sheriff Humphreys.

Thought it better not to outstay my welcome. You do not want thanks from me for what you did, but you are getting it none the less.

Bruce Sherrill

'He's giving himself up, I reckon,' Cliff said.

She tossed the paper back on the table. 'We can do without his thanks. I never was so tired of a man in my life. He told me yesterday he had been doing us a favor by staying here because he had shaken our smug belief in our right to fight the nesters. His vanity is colossal. He needs a lesson.'

'He'll get one,' the cattleman answered grimly. 'I'm glad he has gone. I've made up my mind to come clean with your uncle about this whole business. He'll raise cane, and I'll have to take whatever he says.'

'Do you still blame me so much for what I did?' Linda asked gently.

'No. You were all right, honey. We couldn't turn him over to be hanged after he had come here wounded. I see that plain as you do now.'

He put an arm around her shoulders and gave her a little hug. She felt a warm glow in her heart.

'The fellow must of got up in the night and slipped out,' Cliff said. 'He was keepin' us fooled about not being able to travel. Only yesterday he told Brand that in three or four days he figured he would be able to make it to Redrock.'

'Yes, I expect he's chuckling now to think how he fooled us—after using us to save his life. He's one of these slick fellows smooth as butter.'

She turned away, hot anger in her dark eyes, to find out from Bud Wong whether breakfast was nearly ready. She hoped she would never see him again as long as she lived.

VIII

Linda sat beside her father in the buckboard when he drove down the valley to the Diamond Tail. She went for two reasons, because she wanted to see for herself how her cousin Ben was getting along and also because she wanted to be present when Cliff told her uncle what they had done in order to take her share of the blame.

The day was young, and the sun rising above the sandstone cliffs sent a sheen across the gray-green sage to the foothills across the valley. Hill-prongs jutted out from the mesa above into the plain, some of them eroded into shapes reminiscent of the fabled castles she had read about in Scott's novels. The pungent scent of sage mixed with dust rose to her nostrils. Once she caught sight of antelope in the distance slipping single file through the brush.

She had been born and brought up in this country, and all its scents and sounds, the hundred changing atmospheric appearances of desert and mountain, had been a part of her heritage. Life in the high plains, spent largely outdoors with sun and wind beating on her, had contributed to the radiant health that gave her eyes, her face, her hair, such an exciting vitality.

Her father pointed out men in the dip to the left of them stringing wire. He said grimly, 'Some the nesters cut ten nights ago in the dark of the moon.'

'You don't know who they were?' she asked.

'We don't *know*. They got away without being caught that time. I reckon yore friend Sherrill was one of them.'

'Is he my friend more than yours?' she inquired.

'No, he's no friend of any honest person who runs cattle here.'

'Will there be any more trouble? Or have they learned their lesson?'

'There will be more trouble—plenty of it. No way of ducking it. A slather of these poor fools who want free land are coming into the country to homestead. They don't use their heads. When they look over this open country, they never figure that it is all grazing land, too dry for the crops they are used to in Iowa or Tennessee. The only way to keep them out is to fence.'

'Isn't the government going to put a stop to that?'

He shook his head. 'I don't know. We've got a lot of wise lawyers back in Washington making laws for this cattle country without ever having seen it. They don't understand the conditions, and they don't take the trouble to find out. Our own congressmen and senators are all right, but they can't make those Easterners see how things are. Fact is, the general idea at Washington is that the West doesn't amount to a hill of beans anyhow, and it sounds good for them to make a hurrah about keeping the land open for the common people. Consequence is, a lot of no-account folk who can't make a go of it anywhere move out here and starve, after they have ruined the land for those of us who can use it.'

Linda had heard the cattlemen's side of this question for years, and she had always assumed it to be the right one, but now an unpleasant misgiving lurked in her mind. Maybe the homesteaders might have a just claim too. She brushed this out of her thoughts, resentfully, for she knew that Bruce Sherrill had planted it there.

The Diamond Tail ranch house was a long rangy log building, to which several additions had been made in the course of years. Looking down on it from the ridge above, one could see a huddle of other buildings—a bunkhouse, sheds, blacksmith shop, and small cabins. In contrast to the Bar B B, the place gave an impression of untidiness. In one corner of the big yard were worn out wagons, buggies, disconnected wheels, and rusty tools.

A boy of about seventeen shouted greeting to them as they drove into the yard. Linda waved a hand. 'Hello, Ned! How is Ben?' Ned was a younger cousin, a long-legged gawky lad who was just now wearing a friendly grin.

'Doing fine. Eats like he had been ridin' the range all day. He'll be tickled to death to see you, Lindy.'

Ben had gained ground surprisingly in the past two days. He was a dark lithe young man, very good-looking, with a gay and reckless charm that made for popularity. At sight of Linda his eyes lit.

'Time you came to see me,' he reproached, and drew the girl's face down to kiss her. 'Didn't you hear how close I was to Jordan's bank?'

'You had us all dreadfully worried,' she told him. 'I never saw such a boy for getting into trouble. We're so glad you're better.'

'Can't keep a good man down,' he answered cheerfully. 'Though I will say that Bruce Sherrill made a good try at it.'

'You think he meant to kill you?' she asked, to find out how he felt about it.

'You don't shoot at a man to do him any good,' he replied, with a laugh. 'Not that I blame him any. My gun was smokin' too.'

'Do you have to get into gun fights?' she chided.

His eyes twinkled. 'It's a bad habit—like flirting.'

'I don't flirt,' she said in swift defense. 'When

a man shows an interest in me I can't hurt his feelings, can I?'

'I reckon not. Anyhow, they all recover after a while. I haven't seen any die of love yet. What would you think about not hurtin' the feelings of a cousin who showed an interest in you?'

'I would talk over with him the other seventeen girls he is showing an interest in,' she told him, eyes dancing. 'Since I was told to stay only three or four minutes—I must go now.' After a moment, she added seriously: 'You're going to hear something about me you won't like.'

'You're not engaged?' he flung at her.

'Nothing like that. This is something altogether different. After we have gone your father will tell you, if you ask him.'

She left him filled with curiosity and joined her father and uncle on the porch. The first glance told her that Cliff had blurted out his confession. Applegate was glaring at his brother-in-law, a stubborn set to his jaw. Randall's mouth was a thin tight slit, but the eyes were the principal barometer of his rage. A bleak blaze of anger shone out of their flinty depths.

He was a bullnecked man, strong-jawed, with harsh features tied together to form a gross powerful face. There was a shapeless lumpy quality about his rounded shoulders and big body that sometimes reminded Linda of a swollen toad. But in spite of his weight there was no fat on him. A steel band of muscles crossed his thick stomach, and his great thighs were hard as steel. By reason of the drive in him he had become the leading man in the district, and he held his sway sometimes by bullying, again with suavity, but always to get what he wanted.

'So you had him in your hands and turned him loose,' Randall said, an ugly rasp to his voice.

'Put it that way if you like,' Applegate answered. 'He slipped away in the night.'

'He couldn't have slipped away if you had turned him over to me.'

'That's what Father wanted to do, Uncle Jeff,' Linda cried. 'At first. But I made such a fuss, on account of the man being wounded, that he gave way.'

'You made a fuss—and he let you have your way.' The biting scorn in Randall's voice stung like a lash. 'After this fellow had killed Ben, far as you knew.'

A dull flush burned into the face of the Bar B B man. 'Soon as I had time to think I knew she was right,' he said dourly. 'I hate this scalawag as much as you do, Jeff, but I couldn't turn a wounded man over to you to be killed after he had come to the ranch for shelter.'

'Very noble of you,' the other man jeered. 'Of course it wasn't your boy he shot down. Why should you care? What's a double-cross among friends anyhow?'

'You've no right to say that, Uncle Jeff,' Linda retorted. 'Father wouldn't throw down a friend any more than you would. He had to do what he thought right.'

Jeff turned his washed-out blue eyes on her. 'What you made a fuss to get him to do,' he corrected. 'Who runs the Bar B B—Cliff Applegate or a crazy girl he can't keep in her place?'

'That'll be enough, Jeff,' his brother-in-law warned. 'Linda is not in this. I played the hand.'

'You certainly played it fine. If there is one man I thought would do to ride the river with, I would have put my money on Cliff Applegate, and he cuts loose from his crowd to back the play of a murdering scoundrel who has done nothing but make trouble ever since he came to the territory.'

'We'd better go, Father,' Linda said in a low voice. 'There's no use talking to Uncle Jeff while he is in this mood. Pretty soon he'll say something we won't be able to forgive.'

'So you're the ones that have the forgiving to do,' sneered Randall. 'Well, you can't get out too quick to suit me. And tell your friend Sherrill when you see him that I aim to hang his hide up on a fence to dry one of these days.'

Cliff rose, reluctantly. If they left now it would

74

mean the break of a long friendship, but to stay longer would result in the exchange of more bitter words.

Two little girls rode into the yard and slid from their saddles. They turned their horses over to Ned and started for the house, each carrying schoolbooks in a strap. At sight of their cousin they broke into a run, pigtails flying.

'Lindy—Lindy!' they cried, and flung themselves into her arms. 'Mother's visitin' grandma. She'll be back in two-three days. She says she'll bring us over to see you awful soon. The pinto mare has a foal—the teeniest prettiest little thing. An' we have a holiday Friday.' They poured this information at Linda, interrupting each other eagerly.

Their father ordered them into the house gruffly. This scene of happy reunion did not fit in with his own feeling toward the Applegates.

The children were surprised and distressed. They had heard Jeff explode in anger, but he was seldom harsh with his little girls.

'Can't Lindy go with us and see the colt?' Molly asked.

'No, she can't.' He added brusquely: 'She doesn't want to see it or you either. Get along in.'

Lindy said, gently. 'We have to go now, Molly, but I hope you and Pearl can come and visit us very soon.'

Jeff set his stubborn jaw. 'They can't. If you're

lining up with the sodbreakers, we'll start from the chunk right damn now.'

The unhappy frightened children looked from one to another of the grown-ups and moved reluctantly into the house.

'As the Sparks Fly Upward'

IX

Sheriff Humphreys was not grateful to Bruce Sherrill for waking him at five-thirty in the morning to give himself up. What Humphreys wanted to ask him was why since he had got this far he did not keep going till he was out of danger. The truth was that this young man just now was dynamite to handle. From Randall the officer had received an indirect message to keep out of the hunt for Sherrill and let the cattlemen handle the matter. The sheriff had no desire to barge in, even though he was on the opposite side of the political fence from the big ranches. He had been elected by the votes of the little fellows opposed to the large outfits, by townsmen, nesters, rustlers, hoe men, and a few small stockmen. But he saw no use in raising an issue. His policy was to get along peaceably with as many citizens as he could. Now Sherrill had come along and dumped trouble in his lap.

For what stood out like a sore thumb was that he could not please both parties. The only hopeful feature of the case was the news that Ben Randall was getting better. If the boy had died old Jeff would have been quite capable of bringing armed men from the ranches some night and storming the jail to hang his enemy. Now he would not dare go quite that far. At least the sheriff hoped so.

'What you want me to do—have you tried for assault with attempt to kill?' Humphreys snapped.

'I thought maybe you would want to send posses out to arrest Bill Cairns and Ben Randall too,' Bruce suggested blandly. 'Three men were wounded that night. Ben shot Pete Engle and Bill Cairns sent me a pill. I don't suppose you share old Jeff's idea that it is all right to rub out us small fry but lese-majesty to hurt a Randall.'

'You know doggoned well I can't do that without starting a war,' the sheriff said irritably. 'Why couldn't you let sleeping dogs lie? If I put you in my jail they're liable to come hell-roaring in here to get you.'

Bruce laughed. 'I didn't think you would kill any fatted calf when you saw me.'

The officer relaxed. 'Well, come in and have a bite of breakfast. You can tie your horse to that young cottonwood.'

'I don't think I had better,' Bruce differed. 'It's not my horse, but one I stole.' He tied the reins to the saddle horn and gave the cowpony a cut with a quirt. The animal started down the street at a gallop. 'Hope he knows enough to go home.'

'Where is home for the horse?' Humphreys asked.

The face Bruce turned to him was as blank as a wall. 'Where he ranges,' the young man said.

'I notice you kept the pony so the brand was on the other side from me.'

'That might be because I thought you had better not know who owns it,' Sherrill answered, smiling by this time.

'Suits me,' grunted the sheriff. 'I don't want to know. I've got troubles enough.'

The mirth died out of Sherrill's eyes. He looked solemnly at his host, who was a pillar of the little church at the end of the street. '. . . Affliction cometh not forth of the dust, neither doth trouble spring out of the ground; yet man is born unto trouble, as the sparks fly upward,' he quoted.

The sheriff grinned at his irrepressible guest. 'No use quoting Job to me,' he said. 'I haven't his patience.'

Bruce pointed a reproachful finger at Humphreys. 'You don't know your Bible, deacon. Not Job, but Eliphaz, a gent who came to have breakfast with his friend Job and certainly rubbed his troubles in plenty.'

Mrs. Humphreys came downstairs to start the day and was surprised to see Bruce on the sofa rolling a cigarette. She had known him as a small boy before either of them had come West. He jumped to his feet. 'I've ridden forty miles to get my teeth into some of your beaten biscuits, Mrs. Humphreys,' he told her. 'Ever since you introduced me to them last time I ate here I've been dissatisfied with other food—so here I am.'

She was fat and forty, a wholesome good-looking motherly woman. 'My goodness,' she said, 'I thought—'

Her glance whipped to her husband for instructions. The situation was not clear to her. She did not know whether this cheerful young man was a guest or a prisoner.

'You thought I had forgotten those biscuits—and the fried chicken—and the raspberry jam. No, ma'am. When I am your husband's regular boarder do I get you for a cook?'

Mrs. Humphreys laughed. She had not put on her stays yet, not knowing they had company for breakfast, and her plump flesh shook like a jelly. She liked Bruce, as most people did. It was a relief to know his dead body was not lying crumpled in some fold of the hills, as her imagination had pictured. Instead, he seemed not to have a care in the world.

'I can't give you fried chicken for breakfast, but you're welcome to the beaten biscuits and the raspberry jam.' She asked her husband, from force of habit, 'Did you grind the coffee last night, Tim?'

'Don't I always?' he asked.

Bruce thought them a well-mated couple. The sheriff was a fat, friendly, easygoing man, and his wife had an unbounded admiration for him tempered by a maternal feeling that at times he was only a little boy acting big.

After the edge of their appetite had been dulled Humphreys raised the question in his mind. 'What in heck am I to do with you?'

Sherrill helped himself to more raspberry jam. 'Is that a rhetorical question, Sheriff? Or do you want advice?'

'I ought to put you in the calaboose,' Humphreys said, answering himself. 'But nobody wants you there. I sure don't. Your friends don't. I don't suppose you want to be shut up. The cattlemen would rather have you at your ranch or in the hills where there is no closed season on you.'

'Your reasoning points to one conclusion, doesn't it?'

Humphreys glowered at him. 'I'm sheriff of this county, young man, and sworn to do my duty.'

'Regardless of who it pleases.' Bruce nodded approval. 'But what is your duty? Let us look at the facts. The big ranches put themselves against the law by fencing government land. We cut the fences. Are we breaking any law? If so, point it out to me.'

The sheriff eased himself irritably in his chair. 'You know blamed well you were waving a red rag at the big outfits.'

'You're ducking the point. Of course it annoyed them. It annoys a burglar to be bitten by a bulldog while he is robbing a house. I claim we were inside the law. Any remarks?'

'Go on,' Mrs. Humphreys said. 'Tim is listening.'

'While we were peaceably cutting bob-wire—'

'With guns in your hands,' Humphreys barked.

'That country is filled with rattlesnakes and they are all out at night,' Bruce mentioned. 'Well, while we were at work along come a bunch of warriors and start shooting. Pete Engle is wounded, and young Ben Randall races after him to cut Pete down before he can reach a horse. I fired once. Far as I know that was the only shot from any one of our party. Isn't that a pretty good self-defense case? Pete and I are both hit. We are not really asking you to arrest young Ben Randall and Bill Cairns. Nobody is asking you to put me in jail.'

'What are you here for, then?'

'To put myself right with the law. Arrest me, then release me on bond. Everybody satisfied, including your conscience.'

'A lot you care about my conscience,' the sheriff grunted.

His wife said: 'Still, it's a good way out, Tim. Bruce has a right to claim self-defense, so without deciding on the merits of the case you release him on bond for the courts to settle the right of it later.'

Her guest nodded approval. 'A Daniel come to judgment! yea, a Danicl!'

'Hmp! Maybe Jessie is right at that. I'll see Judge Lanigan. You stay right here till I've talked with him.' Humphreys rose from the table and put on his dusty old black sombrero.

After the sheriff had gone Bruce suggested that he would like to saw wood for his breakfast if there were any chores about the place to do. His hostess told him there were none.

'How about me hoeing that corn in the garden?'

'Tim said you were to stay indoors,' Mrs. Humphreys told him. 'You look fagged out. No wonder, after riding all night. And you said you had been wounded. Where?'

'In the pasture. The night they jumped us.'

'You know that's not what I mean, Mr. Smarty. What about your wound? Is it serious? Hadn't I better have Doctor Bradley see it?'

'No need. A good fairy doctored me.'

She looked at him with shrewd inquiring eyes. 'You're keeping something quiet. All right. That's your business. But I'll bet a doughnut there's a woman in this somewhere.'

Bruce was quite willing to follow her advice about resting. He lay down on the bed in the room to which she took him and immediately fell asleep. When he awoke the sun was just sinking in the west.

Mrs. Humphreys heard him stirring and called

from the foot of the stairs that supper was just ready. Sherrill washed his face and combed his hair.

There was fried chicken for supper.

'Everything arranged,' the sheriff said. 'Light out when you like.'

Bruce said he thought he would get into another jam so that he could come back to this cooking and stay more permanently.

'If you are starting on your travels again what do you expect to do for a horse?' the sheriff inquired. 'By your way of it you have stolen two in a week. If you keep on helping yourself maybe some owner after a while will get narrow-minded and not like it.'

'Thought I'd have Sheriff Humphreys go down to the Elephant Corral and hire me one,' Bruce replied, a twinkle in his eye.

'Not on your life,' his host refused promptly. 'I'd look fine getting you a horse to skip out on.'

'If you feel that way about it I'll mosey down and get one for myself.' Sherrill took a large helping of whipped mashed potatoes and put it beside the chicken leg and wing on his plate. 'I'm going to hate leaving you, Mrs. Humphreys. If you ever think of taking a second husband I'd like to file an application.'

'I like the husband I have pretty well,' she said. 'But I'm some worried about you, Bruce. Where are you going from here? Are you sure you'll be safe?'

He did not tell her where he was going. The less the sheriff knew of his whereabouts the better. Whimsically he tilted an eyebrow at her. 'Now who would want to hurt *me?*' he asked.

Bruce Takes a Train

X

Bruce crossed the bridge and moved across a vacant lot to the corral. His eyes were vigilant and wary. Since he did not want to be recognized by anybody meeting him, his hat was pulled well down on his forehead. In a city a stranger aroused no comment, but in a small ranch town of the frontier he was observed and there was speculation as to the reason for his presence. Sherrill knew that one of the town loungers seeing him would not be quite satisfied until he was close enough for an identification. And if the man made out who he was everybody in town would know about it inside of half an hour. The cattlemen had spies in town of course. Before the sun set tomorrow Jeff Randall would get word that he had been here.

He got into the corral over the back fence and moved forward in the dark shadows of the wagon sheds. A man came out of the small office near the gate.

' 'Lo, Prop,' drawled Bruce. 'How you doing? Still got the idea that three kings beat a flush?'

The owner of the corral whirled on him. 'What

you doing here, you crazy galoot? Haven't you got any sense a-tall?'

He was a little man, excitable, with a high thin voice. His nickname was Prop because in an errant moment he had commissioned a wandering sign painter to hang from the box frame over the gateway a legend which read,

MATT ZANG, PROP,
ELEPHANT CORRAL, REDROCK

Another man came out of the office and gaped at Sherrill.

'Well, what d'you know?' he exclaimed. 'If it ain't Bruce!'

The man was Flack. He had been caught unaware. The lantern by the side of the office door lighted the sly mean face and caught the look of startled apprehension. More than once there had been an ugly thought in the back of Sherrill's mind. He had put it away, only to have it return. He could not believe that Bill Cairns and his riders had discovered them cutting wire by sheer chance. Somebody had given him a tip, and nobody knew in advance of the raid except those expecting to ride on it. Bruce remembered that Flack had come without his wire clippers, that he had volunteered to hold the horses and had kept them some distance from the men at work, and that at the first alarm he had turned the mounts loose instead of waiting for their riders. Had he expected the attack? It looked like it.

That Zang could be trusted, Bruce knew. He flung questions at Flack. How was Pete Engle? Had there been any trouble with the cattlemen since the night of the raid? Did anybody except themselves know who were the wire cutters that night?

Flack was suavely ingratiating. He was tickled to death to see Bruce. All his friends had been worried for fear he had been killed in the hills. Pete was doing all right, but somebody had burned his cabin down while he was staying at Gilcrest's recovering from his wound. Nobody had been at home when it was done. Flack was sorry to have to report that two of the haystacks in Bruce's meadow had been fired and his fences cut in forty places. There had been an attempt to destroy his house but his three cowboys had shown fight and the attackers had given up without success. The homesteaders felt pretty bitter at the high-handed outrages of the stockmen.

'Where are the Engles staying now?' Bruce asked.

'At the Gilcrest place. We're building them a new house right where the old one was. All the neighbors have turned in to help.' Flack went on to explain that he had come to town to get a new wheel for his wagon on account of a bust-up from a runaway.

'And while you were here you thought you might as well get a new hat and suit,' Bruce suggested.

Flack looked down at his new clothes uneasily. It was well known that he never had a dime to spend. 'My father died and left me some money—not much, just a little—and I figured I had looked like a tramp long enough and had better fix myself up decent like white folks.' His oily smile was not very sure of itself. 'Well, I'll tell the boys I saw you. They sure will be pleased.'

'Have you got your new wheel yet?'

'No. Yates didn't have one. He's sent an order to Cheyenne for it.'

'You're starting for home tonight?'

'Thought I would. I'll break the journey down the road a ways.'

'I might as well see you started,' Bruce said. 'You can tell me all the news as you think of it.'

'That's right. And of course the boys will want to know how you made out so long in the hills without any grub and just where you holed up so you couldn't be found.'

'Tell them I found manna in the wilderness,' Bruce answered lightly. 'With all the game and fish in the hills a man can't starve.'

Sherrill stayed with Flack until he saw him

disappearing down the road in the darkness. He had come to a sudden decision and he did not want the man to have an inkling of what it was.

Bruce returned to the corral.

'I want to borrow five hundred dollars, Prop,' he said. 'Do you know any guy can lend it to me?'

Zang rubbed his bristly chin in thought. 'I could get it at the bank tomorrow,' he suggested.

'I need it tonight,' Bruce explained. 'I'm taking a long trip on a train, but I don't want anything said about it.'

The keeper of the corral was a little surprised. Somehow he had not expected Bruce Sherrill to let himself be driven away.

'I reckon that's smart of you,' he replied, unable to keep a touch of disappointment out of his voice. 'They'll sure get you if you stay.'

'I'll be back—in about ten or twelve days, I should think. How about Kilburn? Think he could get it for me right away? I want to start for Casper soon as I can.'

'I'll ask him. Wait here till I come back.'

In a little more than an hour Zang returned. He handed Bruce a roll of bills, and the ranchman put them in his pocket without counting the amount. 'I'm much obliged to you, Prop. Mighty few men would dig up so much for a friend without asking a single question.'

'Hell,' Zang said, 'you're good as the wheat.

None of my business where you are going—or why.'

'I reckon you had quite a job getting Kilburn to open the bank and get the money.'

'He kicked some, but not too much. I didn't tell him I wanted it for you.'

'Good. Now I want a horse that will take me to Casper.'

Zang had only two. He recommended a flea-bitten gray. 'Not much for looks,' he said. 'But how that broomtail can travel!'

At Casper, Bruce took the train for Cheyenne. There he bought a ticket for Washington.

A Bullheaded and Cantankerous Man

XI

Cliff Applegate drew up in front of the Humphreys house and helped his daughter out of the buggy. The sheriff and his wife were old-time friends, and when Linda came to town she always spent the night with Jessie. There was a hotel in Redrock, but it was used only by poor derelicts who had no better place to go.

Jessie Humphreys ran out to meet Linda and kissed her warmly. 'Time you came to see us, after all your promises,' she cried.

'Father had to come for supplies, and as I wanted to match some dress goods I made him bring me,' Linda explained.

'I'll drive down to Prop's corral and leave the rig,' Cliff said.

'Be back in time for supper,' Jessie told him. 'Tim will sure be glad to see you.'

Linda cleaned up, put on a fresh dress, and went downstairs to join her friend in the kitchen. They chatted while Jessie worked. In the girl's mind there was something particular she meant to find out, but she wanted to have the older woman introduce the subject.

And presently Mrs. Humphreys did. 'You'd never guess who slept in your room last.' Since Linda gave it up, her hostess said, 'Bruce Sherrill.'

'Oh, that scamp.' Linda's voice and manner were hostile.

Jessie was a forthright person. What she thought, she was not afraid to say. 'I'm not so sure about that. Of course all of you at the Bar B B detest him. But the fact is I like him.'

'I think he is the most conceited, insufferable pup I ever met,' the girl answered with sharp emphasis on the adjectives.

Jessie's bright eyes fastened on her guest. 'When I was at the ranch you told me you did not know him.'

'I didn't then, but I do now.' Linda poured out the story.

'So you're the good fairy who doctored him.'

The young woman flushed angrily. 'He told you that, did he? That's like him—to boast about what I was forced to do. How could I help it when he was sick and wounded? Sometimes I wish I had let Father turn him over to Uncle Jeff.'

'He didn't say it was you. Only that a good fairy had looked after him.' Jessie added: 'It must have been hard on you all—especially on Cliff—to shelter the man he was hunting, one he hates so much.'

'Hard on us!' Linda exploded. 'When we

told Uncle Jeff he practically flung Father and me out of his house. Where do you think we stand with our friends? We're traitors—double-crossers—turncoats who have thrown in with the trash nesting in the hills. Oh, I know you feel differently about these settlers. They all voted for Tim. But when we see them plowing up good grass land—'

'It isn't because they voted for Tim that we feel sorry for them,' Jessie interrupted, quietly and firmly. 'You ought to try to be fair, Linda.'

The girl repented swiftly. 'I know it isn't, Jessie. You and Tim are the salt of the earth. Sometimes I get all mixed up about these homesteaders myself, especially lately. They are awfullly poor, some of them, and they have families. But we were here first, and if they had a lick of sense they would see this is grazing land, except some pockets along the creeks, maybe.'

'I think Bruce feels a sort of responsibility for them, even though he isn't a farmer himself,' Jessie said.

'What did he come here for—to give himself up?'

'He wanted it understood he wasn't an outlaw. If the law wanted him, here he was. But Tim felt there was no sense in putting him in jail. It was easy enough to get someone to go bail for him.'

'Where is he now?'

'We don't know. He didn't tell us where he was going. He rented a horse from Matt Zang and disappeared. That was three days ago.'

'I suppose he has gone back to his ranch to make more trouble.'

It was in Jessie's mind that some on the other side made a good deal of trouble too. News had reached town that poor Pete Engle's house had been burned down while he was still recovering from his wound. And Pete had a wife and four little children.

After supper Tim and Cliff sat on the porch and smoked. It was pleasantly cool there after a hot day, and when the dishes were done the women joined them. They were thinking about going back into the house when heavy footsteps clumped along the sidewalk and turned in at the gate. A squat ungainly figure shuffled up the path to the house.

The visitor was Jeff Randall. He peered at those sitting on the shadowed porch and let out a grunt of surprised exasperation.

'Quite a bunch of Mr. Sherrill's friends present,' he jeered.

The sheriff ignored that. He rose. 'I'll bring out another chair, Mr. Randall,' he said.

'Not for me.' The owner of the Diamond Tail waved the offer aside contemptuously. 'I don't belong here. I'm just one of those damned cowmen you were elected to fight, Humphreys.

I wouldn't expect any justice from a nesters' sheriff, and I'm not one of the kind of cattlemen who sit around and chin with fellows trying to ruin the country.'

The sheriff's voice was carefully amiable. 'Now you have that off your chest, Mr. Randall, I'll be glad to hear what I can do for you.'

'You can tell me where that skunk you turned loose is holed up.'

'Meaning Sherrill, I reckon.'

'Meaning Sherrill.' Randall added bitterly, 'The guest you had staying with you while you were fixing it with Lanigan to free him.'

'He left here Friday evening. I haven't seen him since.'

'When he left town he was riding Prop Zang's gray.'

'Was he?'

'You know damn well he was. Where did he go?'

'I don't know.' Humphreys repressed a desire to tell the arrogant ranchman that he would not give the information if he had it.

'I wouldn't be surprised if he had come back and was in this house right now.'

'He isn't here, Uncle Jeff,' Linda said.

Randall glared at her. 'Do I have to believe you—after you hid him from me for several days?'

'You don't have to believe any of us,' the

sheriff said firmly. 'I'm sorry you feel so hostile, but there's nothing I can do about that.'

Cliff had had about enough of his brother-in-law's domineering ways. 'What are you beefing about, Jeff? Tim hasn't got Sherrill tucked away in his pocket. You sent him word you could take care of the fellow without any official help.'

'So I could of, if you hadn't thrown down on me and hidden the scoundrel.' Randall slammed a heavy fist down on the porch railing, venom glaring out of the bleached blue eyes in the sun-and-wind-weathered face. 'If he ever gets where I can throw a gun on him, I'll blast the life out of the scalawag, even if he is yore friend.'

'That's wild talk,' Humphreys said. 'I hear Ben is getting along fine. Sherrill is under bond to appear here if the law wants him. After all, the Pitchfork boys wounded two of the other side. Doesn't that make it even steven? Once a feud gets started a dozen men might get killed.'

'The damned nesters were cutting a Pitchfork fence, weren't they?' Randall snarled. 'If they had all been shot into rag dolls they wouldn't have any just complaint. Don't think we're gonna lie down and let them ride over us.'

'Pete Engle's house was burned the other day. Haystacks have been fired. This can't go on. There is law in this country. In the end it will win out.' The sheriff spoke quietly, but with conviction in his voice. Back of his good-nature there was resolution in the man, and a stiff pride not easily aroused.

'If you're claiming I fired Engle's house you're a liar, Humphreys,' the Diamond Tail man flung out harshly, 'though I tell you straight that I'd back up whoever did it. Law! What kind of law do you call it that helps riffraff rob decent men of all they've been building up for twenty-five years? To hell with it.'

Randall turned and lumbered down the path, slamming the gate behind him. The clumsy tread of his feet died away in the distance.

A rueful smile creased the lips of Applegate. 'He always was bullheaded and cantankerous,' Cliff remarked. 'But I'm with him in most of what he claims.'

A shiver of prescient dread ran through Linda. 'It's such a lovely country,' she said with a sigh. 'And we are filling it with war and hate.'

The others made no comment. They were of the same opinion.

Ramrod Meets a Killer

XII

Ramrod Spindler, in charge of the Quartercircle D C during the absence of Bruce Sherrill, did not take his responsibilities lightly. He and the boys under him had repelled the attack on the ranch house made one dark night but they had not been able to prevent the firing of two haystacks and the cutting of the wire fence. Cattle had strayed, and Ramrod had not felt it safe to let Neal and Mark ride the range except together and armed with rifles. He was worried also about Bruce, but not so much so since he had received the letter from Denver telling him to have one of the boys meet him at Redrock when the stage arrived on the seventeenth.

What Bruce was doing at Denver Ramrod could not guess. The old cowhand had been afraid that his employer had been drygulched in the hills, though somehow he could not quite believe it. Sherrill was so vitally alive it was hard to think of all that energy stilled forever. Still, the coming of the letter had been a comfort. There was no other person in the world Ramrod could not spare rather than the man he served.

He decided to go to Redrock himself to meet

Sherrill. Neal and Mark were top-notch boys, but the weight of years had not quelled their carelessness. The wagon boss had been brought up on the frontier. He had been all through the Indian troubles, and when there was danger around he could be wary as a coyote. It was his job, one to which he had secretly pledged himself, to keep Bruce alive if possible, and he was not going to delegate the task. Since Redrock was the nearest town, both factions traded there. He would not have his friend step down from the stage into an ambush. That was one of Sherrill's weaknesses. He was too foolhardy—walked grinning into danger as if he thought God was carrying him in His pocket.

Ramrod started before daylight and reached town in the middle of the afternoon. Redrock was a cow town. It had been laid out by a Texan who had come up the Chisholm Trail and pushed his longhorns through Colorado to Wyoming. There was an old-fashioned courthouse square with business houses on the four sides facing it. Most of these had false fronts, on which were announced ownership and occupation. In some cases the signs were superfluous. On the sidewalk before the entrances to the Legal Tender and the Palace gambling houses old cards were littered. A cowboy sleeping off a drunk lay in the street close to the sidewalk where he had been deposited by a bartender just before Jake's

Place closed. Somebody had thoughtfully put a hat over his face to protect it from the sun.

The foreman of the Quartercircle D C tied at a rack in front of Doan & Devon's general store. He stepped to the sidewalk, rifle in hand. Since he had no other place to keep it, his idea was to ask permission to leave it back of the counter for an hour or two. This weapon was of no use to him in the town, where already he was facing enemies.

Bill Cairns and Wally Jelks were standing in the doorway talking with a Diamond Tail rider known as Quint Milroy. Cairns stopped, to watch Spindler as he came forward.

'I see you've turned into a two-gun man, Ramrod,' he jeered. 'Taking after yore boss, I reckon.' His gaze shuttled from the rifle to the revolver in the Quartercircle D C man's belt and back again.

'A three-gun man,' Jelks corrected. 'I'll be doggoned if he hasn't got a Winchester cased beside the saddle too.'

Ramrod shifted the rifle to his left hand casually, to wipe the perspiration from his face with a handkerchief. His guess was that the big bully was merely needling him.

'Hot as Billy-be-damn today,' he mentioned. He was not expecting trouble in this public spot, but it might jump up at him and it was well to have his right hand free.

'A regular walking arsenal,' Cairns prodded. 'A sure-enough wolf on the prowl. His night to howl, I expect, Quint.'

Milroy said nothing, but his glittering eyes did not lift from Spindler. Quint was a lithe slender man, poised and wary, with a reputation as a dangerous gun fighter. He was a recent importation at the Diamond Tail. The general impression was that he had been brought in by Jeff Randall on account of his prowess as a warrior.

Spindler was no 'bad man.' He belonged to the class of quiet resolute pioneers who had redeemed a hundred localities from the dominance of the swaggering killer and the furtive outlaw.

'You rate me wrong, Bill,' he said, with surface amiability. 'When a rifle needs fixing you have to bring it to town to a gunsmith.'

Cairns had a notoriously bad temper, which he let slip the leash when he did not think it too dangerous. 'Did it need fixing the other night when you were plugging away at some guys from the ranch house?' he demanded.

Ramrod smiled blandly. 'Oh, you've heard of that little rookus. Not much to it. Some boys had got hold of too much tanglefoot and were celebrating the Fourth of July a bit premature. You know how it is when whiskey, a gun, and a cowpuncher get stirred up together—they make considerable noise but usually don't do much harm.' He added, lightly, 'Be seeing you, Bill,' and pushed past him into the store.

The Pitchfork foreman glared after him, his ugly mouth set to a snarl. He did not like Spindler any more than he did the man's boss. Half of a mind to follow, he hung for a moment undecided.

'That will be all for now, Bill,' Milroy told him in a voice low but cold as a breath of wind over a glacier.

Sulkily Cairns nodded. It had not been his intention to call for an immediate showdown. What he wanted was to devil Spindler, roil his temper, and get away with it. Unfortunately the Quartercircle D C man had not been at all disturbed. It was Cairns himself who had boiled to impotent anger.

'Let's go get a drink,' he said abruptly, and clumped down the sidewalk.

Jelks followed him. Milroy stayed where he was, a thin smile on his saturnine face. He understood men like Cairns. They blew off to relieve their bilious tempers or to work up their rage to a fighting point. That was bad medicine. Much better not to insult a foe unless you were ready instantly to carry through. Even then words were generally surplusage. Quint Milroy did not waste his force in anger. He had schooled himself against emotion. Now close to forty, he had killed eight times. While still a boy, he had shot a rival in a quarrel over a woman, but since that day there had been no hatred in any of his shooting affairs. The instinct for self-preservation was well developed in him. He never boasted or swaggered, never traded before the public on his reputation. He kept to himself if possible, a man gentle of voice and manner, scrupulously polite. When he killed it was strictly in the way of business.

From a clerk he bought a cigar and lit it. Leaning easily against a counter, he was a picture of one at peace with the world. But he stood, as he always did, where nobody could get at him from behind. For him vigilance was the price he paid for life.

He watched Ramrod making purchases for the ranch, the alert brain back of the quick eyes studying the foreman. Some day he might be called on to deal with Spindler. Before that hour came, if it did, he wanted to know all he could about the reactions of his victim. Milroy did not depend only upon his deadly skill with a forty-five. He knew how to set the stage to minimize the chance of an opponent. It was his pride that he had no weakness, none of the handicaps of other professional gunmen. He did not drink or quarrel or embroil himself with women, had no Achilles' heel through which he might be destroyed.

Back from Luncheon at the White House

XIII

The arrival of the stage was the liveliest hour of the day at Redrock until the rattle of chips began after nightfall. For when Hank Sowers drew up in a cloud of dust opposite the courthouse, he brought with him news of the outside world. Ten minutes before the Concord showed on the hill summit at the end of the street, Ramrod tied two saddled horses at a rack in front of the hotel just below the stage office. In order not to call attention to them, he withdrew to the hotel porch and joined the chair sitters there.

Most of these were antiques, retired from the activities incident to making a living. Their main interest was gossip, and they turned on Ramrod with questions about the recent trouble between the cattlemen and the sodbreakers. The Quartercircle D C foreman showed a childlike innocence. He did not know what had become of Bruce Sherrill or how Pete Engle's house happened to catch fire. In a vague way he recalled that he had heard something about fence cutting, but the particulars had not reached him. There was a rumor he admitted, that Ben Randall had

105

been in bed from a gunshot wound. Maybe he had shot himself by accident while cleaning the pistol, if it was a pistol that had done the damage.

While Ramrod answered questions he kept an eye on the saddled horses. There was a rifle in the boot beside the saddle, and he did not want anybody to remove it while he was not looking. Spindler still was not expecting any trouble in town, but he had observed that Cairns and Jelks were crossing the courthouse grounds to the stage station.

They stopped in the road beside the hitch rack. Since they belonged to a cattle outfit they had of course read the D͡C brand on the shoulders of the horses Ramrod had just tied to the pole. They stood beside the animals discussing the meaning of this. Spindler had come to town alone and had brought two saddled mounts with him. One of them was Blaze, a roan never ridden by anybody but Bruce Sherrill. Did this mean that the foreman had come to town to meet his boss?

Cairns stepped to the side of the nearest horse and put a hand on the rifle in the case. For a big man Ramrod moved swiftly. Half a dozen reaching strides took him to the sidewalk.

'I wouldn't monkey with that gun, Bill,' he warned. 'It might go off.'

'Had it fixed, have you?' Cairns wanted to know, with a nasty laugh. 'Lear must of worked fast.'

Ramrod pushed between him and the roan, brushing his hand aside. 'Don't you know better than to fool with another man's gun, Bill?' he snapped.

The dull red of anger flushed into the leathery face of Cairns. 'Keep yore hands off me, fellow,' he snarled.

'Did I push against you? Sorry.' Ramrod's voice did not sound like an apology. It held a sharp note of command.

'This the gun Sherrill shot Ben with?' the Pitchfork man demanded.

'I wasn't present at any such shooting,' Ramrod answered stiffly.

'I was,' differed Cairns. 'A lot of scoundrels were cutting our fence. Too bad we didn't bump off some of them. We will onc of these days.'

'Y'betcha!' agreed Jelks.

'You talking about fences on government land?' Ramrod asked.

'Never mind what fences. When we put up bob-wire it's there to stay. You tell that to yore hoe-men friends.'

'I'll let you tell them,' Ramrod replied.

His gaze strayed to the end of the street. The stage had reached the hill summit, and the horses were pounding down the hill at a gallop. Hank dragged them to a halt in a cloud of yellow dust exactly in front of the stage office. The two Pitchfork men sauntered forward to watch the passengers pile out of the Concord. From it emerged a fat drummer, a lanky cowboy in chaps and big sweat-stained hat, and a young lady who had come to teach school at Redrock. The eyes of Cairns fastened greedily on the young woman, but deserted her at the sound of a cool mocking voice. Bruce Sherrill had stepped down from the seat beside Hank.

'Nice to meet you again when you are feeling peaceable, Bill,' it drawled. 'Last time we met you were pouring lead into me.'

The startled young woman heard the words and glanced in alarm from one to the other. The younger man was smiling derisively, but the big fellow to whom he spoke was bristling like a turkey cock. She hurried into the office. Wild stories about the West had reached her in Ohio, retailed by friends who were sure that a Wyoming cow town was no place for Mattie Adams, just graduated from Oberlin College.

'That's right,' boasted Cairns. 'You had just shot Ben Randall and stolen his horse. You were gettin' the hell outa there so fast I didn't get a good crack at you.'

'Maybe next time he won't be so lucky, Bill,' volunteered Jelks. 'A guy don't always have gilt-edged luck.'

'Another county heard from,' Bruce told the cowboy cheerfully. 'When you talk so ferocious, Wally, chills run all over me.'

Ramrod moved into the picture leading the two horses. 'Welcome home, Bruce,' he said.

'If he had been smart he would have stayed away after he lit out,' Jelks cut in sourly.

'The Pitchfork boys are a little on the prod today,' Bruce told his foreman. 'We'll have to try not to worry about that.'

Sherrill's glance picked up Quint Milroy across the road. He was leaning indolently against the fence, a cigar in his mouth. Though he was watching the group, he gave no indication of declaring himself in on any argument that might arise. The boss of the Quartercircle D C was glad of that. When Quint moved into a controversy the shadow of red tragedy was hovering close. But the killer's actions were unpredictable. He might be making up his mind at that very moment. It was time to go.

Bruce swung to the saddle. With Ramrod beside him he rode down the street and out of the square. Cairns watched angrily the two flatbacked riders disappear. Neither of them looked back to see if their enemies were drawing a bead on them.

'That bird Sherrill is the doggondest cool son of a gun I ever did meet up with,' Jelks said with reluctant admiration.

'He'll be dead inside of two weeks,' Cairns predicted. Almost in a murmur he added, 'Maybe in two hours.'

For a man with a time limit on his life Bruce

appeared unduly lighthearted. 'Good to get home again,' he said, and his glance swept the brown plain beyond the small town and the blue ridge of the mountain range on the horizon. 'This is where I belong.'

Ramrod looked at him doubtfully. 'I wonder if it is,' he questioned. 'There's trouble ahead, and you're in the middle of it.'

'I like elbow room,' Bruce continued. 'We've got it here. Back in the East you can't get away from crowds.'

'You been back East?'

'To Washington. I had a long talk with the Great White Father.'

The foreman stared at him. 'You mean the President?'

'Yes. You knew I was in his Rough-Rider regiment—got pretty well acquainted with him in Cuba. He's a man you can talk with easily. Had a ranch himself in Montana.'

'Hashed over old days, did you?'

'Some. We talked about bob-wire fences too.' He added, casually: 'While we were eating lunch at the White House.'

Ramrod guessed this for a merry flight of fancy. 'Hmp!' he snorted skeptically. 'Funny he didn't offer to make you ambassador to Great Britain since you are so chummy.'

'You don't try to get chummy with the Colonel if you have any sense,' Bruce explained, disregarding his friend's sarcasm. 'He's a man you could ride the river with, but he has plenty of dignity too. Nice and friendly, but you don't cross the line.'

'Did he have any ideas about bob-wire?' Ramrod asked.

'He did before I left. Of course, he didn't take my word about the situation. There's going to be an investigation.'

'I've heard of 'em,' Ramrod said dryly. 'When the committee reports, you'll have long white whiskers.'

Bruce differed. 'The Colonel is a hurry-up gent.'

From Doan & Devon's store a voice hailed them. Rod Randall sauntered down the steps. 'Want to see you, Sherrill,' he said. The words fell curt and crisp. Men on the street stopped to listen.

'It costs nothing, Mex,' Bruce answered coolly, and drew up.

Randall crossed the street with long light strides, gracefully as a cat, each step flinging up a spurt of dust from the road. The eyes of the men on horseback did not lift from him. They knew him to be reckless as well as arrogant and fearless.

'Thought you had lit out,' he said insolently.

'Wrong report,' Bruce replied. 'I own a ranch on Bear Creek.'

Ramrod shifted his position, so as not to be back of Bruce.

'Don't crowd me, Ramrod,' drawled Rod. 'No showdown today.'

'Good,' the foreman said. 'Gun fighting is bad medicine.'

'But necessary to get rid of pests.' Randall's voice was cool and scornful. 'I'm serving notice on you, Sherrill. If any more Diamond Tail fences are cut I'll come at you with a smoking gun.'

Bruce said quietly, 'I don't want any difficulty with you.'

'Then quit devilin' us, you fool, or I'll blast you sure as the sun sets tonight.' Rod turned contemptuously and walked back to the store.

The riders moved on. Ramrod said, 'Mr. Big serves notice, son.'

They dismounted in front of the sheriff's house. Bruce knocked on the open door. 'Important guests arriving,' he announced.

Mrs. Humphreys came to the door. She called over her shoulder to her husband, 'Here's your horse thief, Tim.'

Ramrod reproved her gravely. 'Don't call him names—not this Big Mogul. He's been eatin' at the White House with his side kick T. R.'

'Not really!' Jessie exclaimed.

'Honest Injun!' Bruce grinned at her. 'And the Colonel's cook isn't a patch on you.'

112

'He's fishin' for a supper bid,' Ramrod mentioned.

'I know he has kissed the Blarney Stone,' Jessie said. 'He is not fooling me a bit. Well, come in and wash up, as you had to do at the White House—if you ever were there.'

'That's a right big if,' Ramrod commented.

Bruce gave his hostess a hug. She had once been his next-door neighbor and Sunday-school teacher, before either of them had seen Wyoming or Tim.

'Just like his impudence,' Jessie declared, blushing, and vanished into the kitchen.

'Does a lawfully married husband have to stand for this?' Tim inquired.

Bruce clapped him on the back. 'Pistols for two, Tim,' he said, 'but not until I've had one more of Jessie's suppers.'

The eyes of the sheriff twinkled. He was not at all displeased. 'Wish I had had your cheek when I was a young rooster,' he said regretfully. 'You sure throw a long shadow with women.'

'They are sorry for me,' Bruce explained.

'Hmp! There was one here the other day isn't sorry for you. She's one you can't get to first base with, young fellow me lad.'

'Do I have to guess who she is?'

'Name is Linda Applegate. I don't know whose good fairy she is, but she sure makes it plain she is not yours.'

'Afraid she doesn't like me. Anyhow, she did her Christian duty. You ought to have seen her stand up to her father when Cliff wanted to turn me over to Jeff Randall for a Roman holiday. Nothing doing, she told him, and he had to take it.'

'Jeff dropped in while the Applegates were here. The old wolf is plenty sore at them. Feels they are traitors for shielding you.'

At supper Ramrod revived again the topic of Sherrill's visit at the White House. 'Did the President feed you beefsteak like this?' he inquired.

'I'll have to ask all of you not to say a word about that,' Bruce answered. 'He's sending a man out here to investigate conditions and I don't want the enemy to know about it until a report has been made. Our Washington representatives would start putting a lot of pressure on T. R.'

Ramrod said, 'I'm gettin' so I almost believe yore fairy tale.'

'I think you made a wise play, Bruce,' the sheriff approved. 'Nobody in Washington understands the West better than the President. 'Course we can't tell how he'll look at this thing. He used to be a cattleman himself. They say he approved of hanging rustlers when they controlled the law and couldn't be convicted. When our senators and congressmen get to him he'll hear the other side of the story. They will pour it on thick.'

Bruce knew that was true. But the President had already declared himself on the subject of fencing government land. Moreover, he had a strong instinctive feeling for the underdog. He did not like to see little people trampled upon by the powerful.

The whiplike crack of a rifle outside startled them. They stared at each other a moment before Bruce rose from the table.

'Stay here,' he ordered.

In the hall he picked up his saddle gun and cautiously opened the door part way. A bullet crashed through a panel. He closed the door. Ramrod and the sheriff were hurrying out of the parlor where they had been eating.

'Put out the lamps and get Jessie into the cellar, Tim,' he said. 'Someone has shot Blaze. I'm going out the back way to see if I can find out who did it.'

Ramrod went with him. They made a wide circuit, to strike the road fifty yards below the house. Darkness was falling fast, and at a distance they could not be seen. The shots had probably come from a grove of cottonwoods close to the bank of the river. They moved as fast as they could without making any noise. As soon as they struck the stream they followed the bank toward the shadowy bulk made by the trees. They heard the stir of horses, the creaking of saddle leather, and then the thump of hoofs pounding down the road at a gallop. Whoever had made the attack was getting away before the way of escape was closed.

There was nobody in the grove, and it was too dark to pick up any sign that might be there. The Quartercircle D C men walked back to the house. Blaze was lying in the dust before the hitch rack. The horse was dead.

'We ought never to have stopped here for supper with Bill Cairns in town,' Bruce said.

'Right,' agreed Ramrod. 'If we had come out before it got dark, one of us would have been lying there.'

The sheriff joined them. 'Better stay overnight,' he said.

'No,' Bruce decided. 'We've brought enough trouble to you. I'll get another horse and start for home.'

Half an hour later the two men were riding into the darkness.

Ben Faces a Showdown

XIV

Mary Randall, third wife of Jeff, came back from visiting her people at Redrock with a queer rumor she had heard, to the effect that the Applegates had picked up Bruce Sherrill, weary and wounded, had fed and nursed him, and sent him on his way. Of course there could not be any truth in it, since the Bar B B was tied up with the Diamond Tail and the Pitchfork in the fight against the hoemen. Nonetheless it disquieted her, for she had learned the story on pretty good authority. If there was anything in it, she knew her husband would be foaming at the mouth.

She found him irritable as a bear with a wounded paw. He was nursing not only a grievance but a hurt. The marriage of his sister to Cliff Applegate had cemented their friendship. He had liked all of the children. Now he felt an obligation to hate the whole tribe, and he had to stay angry at them to do it with vigor.

After two or three unhappy days she took her problem to Ben, whom she found sitting on the porch reading a magazine. Neither Ben nor Ned were her own sons. Ben had been six and Ned only a baby when at seventeen she had married

117

Jeff Randall, already close to fifty and with grown sons in homes of their own. Mary had been a good mother to her husband's little sons, and she had continued to love them even though she now had two girls of her own.

Ben put down his magazine and rolled a cigarette. He knew Mary was troubled and he could guess why. The situation did not please him either. The young Applegates had been his most intimate companions. His status with them was more that of a brother than a cousin.

'It's your father,' she said. 'He is unhappy, and all he can do about it is make life a burden for the rest of us.'

Ben nodded. He was very fond of this dark-eyed young woman who had given him love and care. More than once he had stood between her and his father's stiff intolerance.

'If there is anything I can do about it—' he said.

'I don't suppose there is. He sits there and broods, and if the children get in his way he barks at them.'

'Father has a memory like an elephant. Mighty little chance of his forgetting or forgiving. Matter of fact, I don't blame Uncle Cliff much—or the rest of them. What could Lindy do when Sherrill showed up wounded with Bill Cairns and his wolves hard on the fellow's heels?'

'Your father won't take that into consideration.

Bruce Sherrill had shot you down, so they ought to have turned him over to us.'

'I don't like these homesteaders any more than he does, but you have to look at things as they are. Sherrill wasn't gunning for me. He knocked me off to save that nester Engle. In a way I'm kinda glad he did. Engle has a mess of kids, and I'd feel like the devil if I had killed him.'

'Could you tell that to Jeff? Would it do any good?'

'I can tell him. Some day I'd have to get it off my chest anyhow. I'm not going to join him in a feud against the Applegates.'

'There are the children,' she sighed. 'They don't understand it. How could they? All their lives they have adored Lindy and liked the boys. Now they mustn't have anything to do with them or even mention their names. It's not reasonable. They'll come to hate their father.'

'The thing is poisonous,' Ben agreed. 'Hand me my stick, Mary. I'll have it out with the old man. He'll probably skin me alive.'

'I don't know what I would do without you, Ben,' she told him gratefully. 'You have more influence with Jeff than anybody else.'

'Yeah,' he scoffed. 'You sure owe me a lot. I started the whole mess. Serve me right if I got flung out on my ear.'

Mary gave him the walking stick and he hobbled to the small disorderly room his father used as an office. It was furnished with a plain table and two kitchen chairs. There was no carpet. A saddle with a broken stirrup and a bridle hanging from the horn had been flung into one corner. On the spare chair were a clutter of newspapers, a pair of run-down-at-the-heel boots, a dusty hat, a corncob pipe, and a sack of tobacco. Jeff Randall's huge shapeless body was huddled over the table. With a stub of a pencil he was working out the net returns from several carloads of beef he had driven to Casper and shipped from there. He squinted up at his son and said, 'In a minute.'

Ben put the hat, the pipe, and the tobacco on the table. The rest of the litter he swept from the chair and sat down. His father's school education had consisted of one term at a country school, and it made him sweat to get the correct answer to a simple problem in arithmetic. At every step of the process his mouth whispered figures sympathetically. Ben did not hurry him. He knew that what he was going to say would bring an explosion from the old man.

Jeff looked at the sheet of paper dubiously. 'You might check this, son,' he said. 'Save me from doing it over. I might of made a mistake.'

The young man added the columns, made the subtractions, and handed the paper back to his father. 'Right,' he said.

'I had eight of Cliff Applegate's stuff in one

120

car,' Jeff mentioned. 'I'll have to send him a check. He and I won't be doing business together any more.'

'Why not?' Ben asked.

Jeff glared at him. 'You know dadgummed well why not. Because he turned out to be a traitor.'

'Aren't you taking it too hard, Father?' Ben asked. 'Uncle Cliff had to do what he thought was right. He held Sherrill a prisoner till he found out whether I was going to make the grade. Knew our boys were so mad they were liable to act crazy.'

Jeff pounded the table so hard with a big fist that it jumped. 'Now my own son is throwin' in against me,' he shouted. 'By God, I won't stand it.'

'We want to be fair to Uncle Cliff, don't we?' Ben protested, voice and manner placatory. 'He had a wounded man who had flung himself on his hands for protection. He couldn't have done less for a stray dog.'

'This wasn't a stray dog,' his father roared. 'He was our enemy—and his. The fellow had killed you, far as Cliff knew.'

'Look at it this way,' argued the young man. 'I ram-stammed in with my gun smoking and likely would have killed Engle if Sherrill hadn't stopped me. If that raft of kids had been left fatherless because of me, I would have felt like a murderer.'

'You talk like a fool. I won't discuss this with you. Shut up yore mouth and do as I say.' Jeff was so explosively full that he reversed himself immediately. 'Engle had a gun in his hand, didn't he? You're too soft for this country. I ought to have whopped hell out of you when you were growing up and made you tough.'

Ben smiled, a bit grimly. He had not yet entirely forgiven his father for the numerous thrashings he had endured for boyish offenses.

'Get this,' Jeff stormed on. 'We've got to fight against this riffraff—or be licked. It's war. Either they lose or we do. It's not yore fault Engle has a passel of young uns. If he wanted a safe life he shouldn't come homesteading my water and plowin' up my land.'

'I understand that,' Ben agreed. 'What worries me is this business of Uncle Cliff. Say he did make a mistake. We can't cut loose from him.'

'I have cut loose from him,' Jeff corrected. 'It's done.'

'If we don't make up with the Applegates, Mary will be unhappy,' Ben continued. 'So will the children. They have been close to us long as I can remember. It's like cutting off an arm.'

'Don't tell me what I'm to do,' Jeff cried angrily. 'I'll decide who will be our friends and who won't. That girl Lindy may boss the Bar B B, but long as I'm alive I'll run the Diamond Tail and dictate its policies. Neither Mary nor you nor the children have a thing to say about it. I've been too easy with you all, but you'll walk the straight line now. Without making a chirp. Understand?'

For the first time in his life Ben had come into direct rebellion against his father. He was an easygoing young fellow who liked his fun, and he preferred the line of least resistance. But this involved a point he could not dodge. He had to stand his ground or admit himself a weakling. His eyes met those of the older man steadily.

'I'm not trying to run the ranch or decide its policies,' he said. 'This is a personal matter. I'm telling you that the Applegates are our kin. We can't forget that. It's not reasonable to like them one day and hate them the next because you say we must.'

'I don't give a damn whether you hate them,' the old man broke out. 'What I'm saying is that you are not going to have anything to do with them. That's an order.'

'I'm sorry.'

'Be sorry, but don't come sniveling to me about it. Just remember that I make the rules here.'

'I mean I'm sorry that I can't obey your order.'

Jeff's bulging eyes stared at his son. 'What?' he demanded.

'I'm a man.' Ben told him quietly. 'Free and twenty-one. I'll go with you far as I can, but I won't follow you when I know you are wrong. You ask too much.'

The ranchman jumped to his feet. For a moment Ben thought his father was going to attack him physically. Rage almost choked the huge cattleman.

'Then get out—and don't come back, damn you. Who the hell do you think you are? You eat my food and spend my money—and then tell me what you will and won't do. There's only one boss here—and I'm that boss. Get out, before I break every bone in your body.'

Ben walked out of the room. He realized that he had only made matters worse for Mary and the children. His father would be almost impossible now. But he did not see what else he could have done except knuckle down, and if he had done that he would have hated himself.

Jeff Randall was piling up trouble and misery for himself and for others, Ben knew, but the old man had fought his way to the top so ruthlessly that he had come to think his will was law. This corner of the world was his to rule. With the growth of power stubbornness had developed in him that had become tyranny. Of late the challenge to his dominance of the homesteaders had filled him with anger. What the Applegates had done was a more bitter and personal affront. Now his favorite son had sided with his enemies. Ben was afraid that the savage obstinacy of the man would drive him to excesses bound to recoil upon himself.

Linda Looks for a Way Out

XV

Ben Randall drew up at the Bar B B ranch house and shouted, 'Hello the house!' He was very tired from the long ride, and his side was aching. Both hands clung to the horn of the saddle.

Linda answered the call. Her sleeves were rolled up to the elbows and there were dabs of flour on the forearms. She had been making apple pies. That was one thing she did better than Bud Wong, and her father was particularly fond of the flaky crust. The sight of her cousin surprised her.

'Aren't you out of bounds?' she asked him coldly. The girl had nothing against Ben, but she did not mean to show any warmth until he had made known his own attitude.

He turned on her his winning smile. It had got him out of a lot of scrapes in their school days. 'I've come to take an interest in you, so you can't hurt my feelings,' he said, using her own words.

The eyes of the girl lit. She was much pleased that he had not joined in the animosity of his father.

'Does Uncle Jeff know about this interest you are taking?' she asked.

'I mentioned it to him.'

'And he said you were showing a nice neighborly spirit?'

'He told me to get the hell out of there and not come back.'

Mirth fled from the girl's face. 'Oh Ben, you mustn't quarrel with Uncle Jeff. Even though he is wrong, still he's your father.'

'The quarreling has all been done, and it was one-sided. I was meek as a lamb—tried to reason with him. He wouldn't have it.'

'I'm so sorry you had trouble on our account,' she cried.

'I didn't. It was on my own account. If a man is pushed to the wall he has to stand on his feet and say his piece. I said mine. I wasn't going to let him bully me into siding against you-all. Mary feels as I do, but her hands are tied and she can't do anything about it.'

He swung slowly and heavily from the saddle. She ran forward to help him, distressed at his condition. Of course he ought not to have ridden so far. Leaning on her, he got into the house. He lowered himself into an armchair and slumped down completely exhausted.

Her brothers were breaking horses in the corral. She ran to the door and called them. Brand was fastening a saddle cinch on a colt. He left the other men and moved to the fence.

'What you want?' he shouted. 'We're busy.'

'Come now, please,' she urged. 'Ben is here.'

Brand helped his cousin upstairs to a bedroom.

'I'd better get Doc Bradley,' he told his sister a few minutes later. 'Ben looks like a mighty sick man to me. He was crazy to ride so far.'

It was ten days before young Randall left the bed.

'We're turning this ranch into a hospital,' he said to Linda one day with a wry smile when she appeared with his dinner on a tray. 'I should think you'd hate to see a guy ride up to the house for fear he would fall off his horse and say, "Nurse me."'

'I hope you'll be the last,' she admitted.

'I reckon nobody has heard anything of Sherrill since he left Redrock on Prop's gray,' he said.

'Yes, he's back at his ranch. I didn't tell you while you were so sick. He came in on the stage one night and had supper with the Humphreys. While he was there somebody shot the horse he had tied in front of the house.'

Ben looked worried. 'Do they say Father had it done?'

'No-o. Bill Cairns was in town. He had words with Sherrill. Folks think he did it, but there was no proof.'

Ben was silent for a minute. 'Funny how one step leads to another. If I hadn't happened to be at the Pitchfork when word came that the nesters were going to cut the fence that night, I wouldn't be lying here, Sherrill wouldn't have been hunted, and you wouldn't have had to look after him. Father wouldn't have got mad at you and then at me. All the trouble since then flared up from that one night.'

She shook her head. 'No. It was coming anyhow. I see that now. You just set a match to an explosion ready to go off.'

'Maybe.' He put words to another thought troubling him. 'I wish I could have got along without leaving the Diamond Tail, but I don't see how I could. You know how bullheaded Father is. In his mind he'll pile the quarrel with me on top of everything else. I'm scared to think what he will do.'

'You don't mean against you or us?'

'Lord, no! He'll take it out on the homesteaders, or on one of them. On Sherrill probably. He'll blame him for everything that has gone wrong.'

'What will he do?'

'I don't know.'

Their eyes met. He did not want to tell Linda what he feared. He was thinking of Quint Milroy, the quiet deadly killer who had dropped in at the Diamond Tail and gone on its pay roll. Ben did not believe his father had hired the man to shoot down his foes. He had employed the fellow on account of his reputation, to frighten and scare away the homesteaders who were annoying him by interfering with the grass and water he needed for his herds. But given such a handy tool, in the

128

state of mind to which Jeff Randall had worked himself, what more likely than that the old man would use the gunman to rub out the leader of those interfering with what he considered his rights?

'Is there anything we can do about it?' Linda asked. There was a tight cold lump in her stomach. Two pictures flashed into her mind. One of Bruce Sherrill standing before her, gay and nonchalant, a whimsical smile on his face, making light of the danger crowding close to him. Another of him lying crumpled on the ground, a bullet in his heart.

'Not a thing.'

'We can warn him,' she protested.

'He doesn't need any warning—not after being hunted over the hills for days, not after having his horse shot down almost before his eyes. Of course the heat has cooled off a lot, since I took the right turn and made the grade. There isn't exactly an open season on him now. But he knows the old man isn't going to quit.'

'So we've got to sit here and let murder be done,' the girl cried unhappily.

'It may not come to that. If he is on his ranch he won't take any chances.'

'How can he help it, if somebody lies in the brush waiting to get him? There must be a way to stop it. What's the law for? Why doesn't Tim Humphreys do something?'

129

'What can he do? The law moves only after crime has been committed, not before.'

'So we had better just forget the whole thing and let your father kill Bruce Sherrill,' she said bitterly, in a surge of revolt.

He looked at his cousin, a new thought back of the watchful eyes. Was it possible she had any interest in Sherrill outside of that dictated by impersonal humanity? The man had been in her house a week, so close that she could not escape his presence. There were qualities in him that might touch a woman's fancy—his good looks, gay insolence, and that manner of ease contact with the outside world gives. Add to that the situation, a fugitive being hunted for his life, with her standing between him and death.

Linda must have guessed what he was thinking. A wave of color beat into her cheeks and up to the roots of her hair.

'I don't like him any better than you do,' she whipped out. 'I detest his impudence—and what he stands for—and everything about him. But that's no reason why I should stand aside and let him be killed by an assassin. We've got to do something, Ben.'

Ben loaded his fork with mashed potatoes and gravy before he answered. 'Nothing we can do,' he retorted, sharp irritation in his voice. 'It's got beyond us.'

His resentment was not at her but at the

situation that had trapped him. He understood her horror at waiting with folded hands to let tragedy develop, and to a degree he shared it. Yet what responsibility of his was it if Bruce Sherrill got himself killed because he had hell in the neck and would take no warning? Ben and the Quartercircle D C man were lined up on different sides of this feud. They had never exchanged a civil word. How could he prevent a bitter and vindictive old man from following his urge to destroy an enemy he hated?

Linda's reply touched this very point. 'If we could get Uncle Jeff to see he is in the wrong, that there is a better way to settle this trouble—'

'What better way?' he demanded. 'You can't compromise this fight. Either the cattlemen win or the homesteaders do.'

'I know.' She hesitated, and then made the plunge, color beating into her cheeks. 'Could Rod do anything with your father—if I could get him to try?'

'What makes you think you could get him to try?' he asked quickly, watching her steadily.

She began to arrange the dishes on the tray, to avoid looking at him. 'He's always been nice to me,' she said. 'I think he likes me.'

Ben was sensitive to atmospheres. It had more than once occurred to him that there was some undercurrent of emotion drawing these two together, perhaps in spite of themselves.

'And you like him,' he suggested.

'Well, he's my cousin, sort of, isn't he?'

'It couldn't be that you're in love with him,' he said, with an intonation that made the statement a question.

'No, it couldn't,' she flashed at him indignantly.

'Because Rod wouldn't be good for you. He's too like Father—too hard and too bossy. No woman—even if he loved her—could bend him an inch from the line he chose to follow. Rod has taken his stand on this matter. He's right in the front of the fight, and he wouldn't say a word to hinder Father. Fact is, I don't know anybody more likely to shoot down Sherrill than Rod. He'd do it openly, in a fair fight. No ambush stuff for him. Rod isn't afraid of any man alive.'

'Do they think they are God—Rod and your father?' she flung out in hot anger. 'Who made it their privilege to take other men's lives? Doesn't it ever strike them that they can be wrong too?'

'Maybe we're making too much of this, Lindy,' her cousin said. 'Maybe all they will do will be to burn Sherrill's ranch house.'

She changed the subject. What was the use of talk?

XVI

Though Bruce Sherrill never let it disturb the casual ease of his manner, he knew that he was walking through the valley of the shadow. From the earliest frontier days the cattle industry had been a violent and precarious one, its prosperity threatened by enemies that had to be overcome. Indians, rustlers, blizzards, drought, overfeeding, wild beasts, and poisonous plants had all to be whipped, depressions and bad markets to be roughed through. The ranchman had survived because he was an individual strong and rugged. Too often law on the high plains had been something written in a book, without force to give it practical application to the needs of the community. Cattlemen had fashioned their own law, and the moral value of it depended upon the character of the enforcer.

The homesteader had either to be accepted or to be fought illegally. Men like Jeff Randall and Ned Daly justified their highhanded methods on the ground that only terrorism would protect their rights. They had plenty of precedents to guide them. In Texas and Arizona, as well as in Wyoming, hired assassins known as stock detectives had shot down offenders from the brush.

Bruce had survived so far because he was not a rustler preying on the stock of the big ranches, and even though he was a far more dangerous enemy they had hesitated to sacrifice him. But he felt he had worn their patience too thin. The shooting of Ben Randall had been the last straw. By the nature of his business he was forced to live outdoors, and though he took what precautions he could he knew that he never swung to the saddle without the possibility of having a bullet whip across a hillside at him before he came home.

Ramrod worried over him as a mother does over a wayward son. 'I saw you riding the south prong yesterday,' he protested. 'A mark asking to be picked off.'

'I was looking for the heifer that got out of the big pasture,' Bruce explained.

'Are you the only man in this outfit can ride?' Ramrod asked in exasperation. 'What's the matter with telling Mark or Neal to go? Or me? I'm still able to fork a bronc.'

They were at breakfast. Neal walked over to the stove, got the coffee pot, and poured himself a cup. 'Anybody else?' he inquired.

Mark gulped down a last swallow and pushed his cup forward. 'Seeing you're up,' he said. 'And I think Ramrod is right, Mr. Sherrill. Leave us do the hill-ridin' for a spell.'

'I can't wrap myself up in tissue paper and mothballs,' Bruce explained. 'This is my scrap, not yours. Maybe the man in the bush with the rifle might not have good eyes and couldn't tell one of you from me at a hundred and seventy-five yards. He probably would not want to come closer to make sure. I'd feel fine passing the buck if he mistook one of you for me. It's been done before, you know.'

Ramrod was reaching for another slice of ham. He waited, fork poised, while he glared at the boss. 'Holy smoke! The boys are he men, ain't they? You don't have to tuck 'em up in bed nights. Anyhow, old Jeff isn't trying to collect him a two-bit cowpuncher. He's after big game—you, Bruce Sherrill.'

Neal backed the foreman's argument. He would be nineteen in a month, and he had done a man's work for three years. One thing he did not want was to be babied. 'That's right. Mark and I are just two spots in this game, but don't count us out.' He grinned, to make sure the others would know his next remark was a joke. 'We are two of the heroes at the siege of the Quartercircle D C where there was a pint of lead spilled and nobody hurt.'

'I wouldn't ask for better men,' Bruce said. 'But after all, as I told you before, this is not your fight. I advise you to leave. You are under no obligation to stay.'

Neal flushed angrily. 'How come you think we're quitters? I aim to stick around.'

'Same here,' Mark agreed. 'In pitch a deuce is sometimes good as an ace. When a guy shoots the moon a two-spot can knock him galley west.'[1]

Bruce was touched at the loyalty of his big broad-shouldered young riders, but he did not embarrass them by mentioning it. 'Fact is, we don't quite know where we are,' he commented. 'All the fireworks may have been to scare me and other homesteaders away. Nobody has been killed yet.'

His foreman snorted derisively. 'You sure take a lot of convincing. Rod told you his piece the other day, didn't he? And his father. Do you want an affidavit from old Jeff that he means business?—"To Whom It May Concern: I'm not foolin' when I shoot up Bruce Sherrill and attack his ranch and burn his haystacks and comb the hills to drygulch him and kill his horse. I mean to fill him full of slugs." Signed J. Randall.'

Mark glanced out of the window and reported a guest. 'Dave Gilcrest on his white mule Jenny,' he said.

Gilcrest bowlegged into the room and tossed two letters in front of Bruce. 'Picked 'em up in

1 In pitch, a card game played much in the cattle country, when one shot the moon he engaged to take high, low, jack, and the game or else be set. If an opponent held the two-spot he lost the bid.

yore mail box as I came along. How's everything on Bear Creek?'

'No complaints,' Bruce answered. 'Grass fine. How about Squaw?'

'About as usual. Pete Engle's house is finished and they have moved in.'

'Sarah all right?'

A grin touched the big man's homely puckered face, and he tugged at his long drooping mustache. 'Still worryin' some about me, but no more than usual. All I weigh is two hundred-odd pounds, and I'm strong enough to throw a yearling across the crick by its tail.'

'No new trouble with the cattlemen?'

'No. Couple of Pitchfork riders drifted up the crick yesterday and stopped to watch the Engles moving in. One of 'em was that fresh guy Wally Jelks. He made a sarcastic crack about what a nice little house it was and how he hoped it wouldn't burn down accidental like the other one. But there's another thing. Two fellows rode in yesterday with a pack outfit and set up a tent. Claimed they came to fish. Might be, but I got to sorta wonderin'. Folks don't usually pack a couple hundred miles just to fish.'

'Give their names?'

'Barnard and Sawyer. They dropped in to our place for milk. Asked a lot of questions about the trouble between us and the cattlemen. 'Course,

137

tenderfeet always are poppin' off with fool questions. That may not mean a thing.'

'But you think they may be stock detectives?'

'Yeah, or gunmen brought in for a showdown. We don't know what the hell old Jeff and his friends will do next.'

Bruce slit with a table knife the envelopes of his letters and read the enclosures. The first was not signed. Two sentences were written on a sheet of paper in a neat Spencerian style, probably by a woman. He thought he could give her name.

I am not your friend, but I don't want you murdered. For God's sake, if you have a lick of sense, get out in time.

The other letter bore a Washington postmark.

'Don't worry about the fishermen,' Bruce told Gilcrest. 'I'll ride over today and have a talk with them. I've a notion I know this Barnard. If he is the man I'm thinking of, he is all right.'

Bruce rode back with Gilcrest over the hogback to Squaw Creek. He found the fishermen's camp a mile above the Gilcrest place. The men were just tramping back in when he arrived. They carried rods and creels.

'Any luck?' he asked.

They showed him four fish, a very small take for a morning on a first-rate trout stream. A fair guess was that they had been fishing only as a blind.

'They weren't biting,' the older man explained. He was red-faced, bald, already beginning to carry surplus fat about his waist. But his eyes were keen and quick.

'Mr. Barnard, I reckon,' Bruce said, and gave his own name.

'We were going to look you up,' Barnard said. 'But you have beaten us to it. News must travel fast here. Mr. Sherrill, this is Mr. Sawyer, a Denver representative of our office.'

'A letter reached me from Washington today,' Bruce told them. 'But not before a rancher was in my house with word that strangers were on the creek.'

Sawyer was a lean thin man with a dark saturnine face. 'We are viewed with suspicion,' he said dryly. 'Nobody on this creek will say anything about the trouble with the cattlemen.'

'They are afraid to talk,' Bruce replied. 'Strangers don't come here to fish—too far from the railroad and a lot of good streams far nearer. The natives are afraid you might be men employed by the big ranches, cattle detectives or gunmen.'

'Do we look like gunmen?' Barnard asked.

'They don't want to take chances. Did you come by way of Bedrock?'

'Yes. We stayed there two days.' He added,

139

after a pause: 'We talked with a good many residents of the town. They express opinions more freely there than here.'

'Not in the danger zone,' Bruce said.

He did not ask them with whom they had talked nor what their reaction was to what they had heard. They were probably close-mouthed men and would give nobody a line on their findings before reporting at Washington.

'If people knew why you were here they would talk fast enough—both sides,' Bruce suggested.

'We've just decided to give out that information,' Barnard said. 'I can't see that it will do any harm.'

'You will have to take with a few grains of salt whatever any of us tell you,' the ranchman told him smilingly.

Bruce realized that as soon as the cattlemen learned that the campers were government men the two investigators would be invited to the big ranches and treated royally. This might have an important bearing on their findings, but it was something that could not be helped.

One good angle to the publicity would be a temporary cessation of hostilities. As long as Barnard and Sawyer were in the vicinity there would be no hostile actions committed by either faction.

Shots from Ambush

XVII

Bruce rode up a draw to the bench above. His wary gaze checked every shrub and land crease behind which an enemy could hide. Of late the price of life for him had been constant vigilance, and though by this time the big ranches must have heard that government men were in the neighborhood investigating, one of their overzealous riders might be irresponsible enough to cut loose at him.

Shadows from small clouds drifting in the deep sky tessellated the floor of the draw. The roan waded through blue and yellow flowers, and occasionally Bruce saw clumps of dainty columbines and a flash of red Indian paintbrush. His mount humped up the last steep rise to the ridge marking the boundary of the park.

From here the rider could look across an undulating stretch of wooded and open country to the snowclad peaks of the distant range. A thin silver thread back of a willow fringe showed him where the creek wound its way to the box cañon down which it would go tumbling over rocks and rapids.

Patiently Bruce scanned the country in front

of him through field-glasses. There were cattle grazing on a hillside half a mile from him, and though he meant to ride to them presently his immediate attention was concerned with any sign that might show a fellow-traveler on the tableland. What he looked for was a puff of dust or some moving object. He knew he could not make sure he was the only human being on this wide landscape. All he could do was to take what precautions he found possible.

He worked along the lip of the park toward the stock, searching carefully the broken terrain below him. When he was opposite the cattle he moved down the slope to get closer. If they carried the Quartercircle D C brand, he meant to push them out of the park to a grazing ground nearer his ranch. This was Diamond Tail range, no safe spot for his stuff, unfenced government land claimed as a priority right on account of long use.

A long look through the glasses assured him that this was his bunch, and he rode along the hillside to round up the animals. From a gulch not fifty yards away a man on horseback appeared. Rod Randall, with a rifle across the saddle hull in front of him. He was as much surprised as Bruce at the meeting, but he gave no overt sign of it. The men checked their mounts almost knee to knee.

'So you're pushin' your stuff onto our range,' Randall snapped.

Even then, with no certainty how far the man's reckless gusty temper would take him, Bruce took note of how well the Diamond Tail rider's appearance matched his arrogance. His long beautifully proportioned body showed at its best in the saddle. From the wide strong shoulders a well-poised head rose gracefully as that of the Praxitiles' Hermes.

'Driving it back to Bear Creek,' Bruce corrected.

'So you say.'

'If my fences hadn't been cut, they wouldn't have strayed,' Bruce mentioned.

The chill dark eyes of Randall flashed anger. 'You can talk yoreself out of anything, you damned sandlapper.' It was in the mind of Rod that this was no time to force a decision. Not with the government men here making an investigation. Moreover, he was more than half of the opinion that Sherrill was telling the truth. He would not run the risk of driving his stock up here to graze. The grass lower down was just as good. This logical conclusion annoyed Rod.

The watchful eyes of Bruce did not lift from those of his challenger. Except for a muscular hardening of the jaw there was no evidence of tenseness. The lean whipcord body was motionless. The fingers of the right hand resting on the thigh did not tighten. Rod Randall was a man of unpredictable impulses. He might let a blaze of passion fling reason overboard. Bruce had to be ready, yet appear to be at ease.

'Would I be fool enough to drive my stock up here and leave them at the mercy of your punchers?' he asked quietly.

Randall flung out a hand in an impatient frustrated gesture. 'Get 'em off of here,' he ordered.

Without another word Bruce swung his horse around that of Randall and started to circle the grazing cattle. He did not look back, and it was not until he turned to head a steer toward the rim that he caught sight of the Diamond Tail man again. Rod was watching him from the mouth of the draw out of which he had first ridden.

Bruce gave his attention to moving the cattle up the slope and was for a few minutes fully occupied. When he looked again Randall had disappeared. The stock were restless, half inclined to bolt. He edged them up gently, not urging the animals to travel fast. As soon as he had them over the lip of the park he knew they would be in a compact group and would accept guidance more readily.

The sound of a rifle shot whipped across the hillside. From a clump of young pines a small billow of smoke puffed. Bruce hung low in the saddle and raced for the shelter of a deep gully. The Winchester cracked again as the roan plunged into the water-gutted cut.

The gully led to the summit. Bruce followed it

without an instant's delay. The origin of the shots puzzled him. It was possible that Randall had ridden to the pines and fired from there. But that explanation did not make sense. He could have picked off his victim better from the entrance to the draw. If it could be done without too much risk, Bruce meant to find out who had tried to kill him.

The floor of the gully was filled with stones and rubble, and the hoofs of his horse advertised his progress with a clatter of shifting rock. The sound might not carry to the would-be assassin. In any case he had to risk it.

He came out of the gully at the rim of the park and took a swift survey of the ground in front of him. No other rider was in sight. He reasoned that if his ambusher tried to escape without being discovered, he would get out of the park as soon as he could, in which case he would appear on the rim in front of him within the next minute or two. There was a chance the fellow would elect to stay where he was until he thought it safe to move to another clump of pines deeper in the park. By following that plan he would probably get away without detection.

Bruce tied his horse to a stunted pine and went forward on foot, his senses keyed to the tensest wariness. Excitement hammered in his veins. He was the hunter, but it was in the cards that he might also be the hunted.

The sound of a rider moving up to the ledge reached him. He heard the sound of a hoof striking against a stone. Presently a cowpony clambered into sight.

The man in the saddle was Wally Jelks. He swung his mount in the direction of Bruce and pulled up abruptly. A rifle jumped to his shoulder and the roar of the gun crashed along the ridge. The sound of Sherrill's gun was close enough to have been the echo of the first shot.

The rifle dropped from the hands of Jelks. He caught at his left forearm with an oath and slumped forward against the horn.

'Hold it!' ordered Bruce, and stepped forward.

Jelks snatched at the reins, but under the menace of the lifted rifle stopped. The sleeve of his shirt showed a growing patch of crimson.

'Get down!' Bruce said sharply.

The cowboy swung from the saddle. 'You've busted my arm, damn it,' he complained angrily.

'Sit down by that tree,' Bruce told him. 'I'll look at it.'

The man sat down, still holding his arm. His surly face showed fear. 'All the blood in my body is drainin' out,' he yelped.

The Pitchfork rider watched Bruce draw the revolver from his holster and toss it into the brush before he made and set the tourniquet to stop the bleeding. The amateur surgeon was still at work when another rider came along the ridge.

146

Bruce looked up, to see Rod Randall swinging from his horse. He grounded the reins and joined the others.

'He shot me,' Jelks whined.

Rod looked down at the wounded man contemptuously for a moment before he gave judgment, 'You damned yellow-belly!' He had seen the first shots fired and could guess the rest of the story.

'I got to have a doctor quick,' Jelks pleaded. 'I'm bleedin' to death.'

Bruce stood up, his job finished. A cold anger burned in him. He spoke to Randall, his eyes stern and hostile. 'Take the assassin. He's yours.'

Dark blood poured into the cheeks of the Diamond Tail man. Anger sharpened the handsome face and brightened the eyes.

'No more mine than yours,' he flung back. 'I don't deal with bushwhackers. I can kill my own snakes in the open.'

Bruce thought of Quint Milroy, and a thin satiric smile rested on his lips. Rod might not be responsible for the man, but he was backing his father's campaign, and the chances were great that someday soon the old man would send the killer out on a murder mission. It was true, of course, that Jelks was not a Diamond Tail man. Probably he had not been commissioned to rub out Sherrill, but he had acted on the assumption that the big cattle interests would be glad to see him dead, a supposition that was one hundred per cent correct.

'You're easily satisfied,' Bruce said, contempt in the sneer. 'Take him or leave him. It's all one to me.'

He turned away, to walk back to his horse. Randall let him go a dozen yards before he called.

'Wait a minute.'

Bruce stopped and looked at Rod without answering.

'Get this, fellow,' Randall said. 'You're leaving this fool to die. You shot him, and you're not going to shift him on me.'

'You mean to ride away and leave him?'

'Just that. I've nothing to do with him.'

Jelks begged them not to go away and desert him. He was not much older than a boy, though he had trodden evil paths for years, and he was afraid.

If left alone the man would probably die, Bruce thought. He needed nursing, rest, and the attention of a doctor. To reach the Pitchfork he would have to travel a rough trail for more than fifteen miles. The Diamond Tail was even farther, and the nearest way there was down Bear Creek past the Quartercircle D C. Reluctantly Bruce admitted to himself the wounded puncher ought to be taken to his ranch. But he was not going to give in without a return concession.

'Looks bad for your friend,' he said callously, adding as if by an afterthought, 'unless you'll throw in for once with a damned nester and help save the scoundrel.'

'How?' demanded Randall.

'Help me get him to my ranch, and then send one of your riders for a doctor.'

Rod did not like any part of this. He did not want to join his enemy even on a humanitarian mission. But he had to admit that Sherrill was going more than halfway in offering to take in the man who had just tried to murder him. Hard though he was, young Randall had his own standards. He could not ride away and leave a wounded man to die.

'Let's go,' he said harshly.

They helped the wounded man to his saddle and rode with him between them. When they came to the upper stretch of the cañon the trail in places was too narrow for even two horses. Bruce turned his roan over to Randall and walked beside Jelks, lending a hand to support him when necessary. The cowboy thought it a hundred miles before they reached the ranch.

Ramrod came from the house to meet them, amazed at what he saw.

'You've read about the wolf and the lamb dwelling together,' Bruce said with a satiric smile. 'Here you have it. Nothing but loving-kindness in our hearts.'

'And smoking guns in our hands,' Randall added.

Rod stayed until after the wounded man had been put to bed. He wanted a word with Bruce.

'You understand that what I told you last time we met still goes,' he said. 'This happy little incident is over, and by my way of it you're still a one-gallus windjammer trying to be cock-a-doodle-do.'

Bruce had come out to the porch to remind him about sending for the doctor. He said, 'You're entitled to your opinion. I hope you won't forget to send for Doctor Bradley.'

'I won't forget,' Randall replied curtly, his dark stormy eyes on the other. 'When you know me better you'll find out I don't forget my promises.'

'That's too bad. Sometimes a hasty promise gets a man into trouble.'

'Or a hasty shot.' Randall's white teeth showed in a smile that held no friendliness. 'Afraid you've got yourself into a jam, Mr. Sherrill. These government men are guests at our ranch for a few days. It will break my heart to have to unload this story to them.'

'I'm sure it will,' Bruce agreed. 'You intend to edit the facts, I gather.'

'Slightly. I got on the scene just in time to see you drop Jelks while he wasn't looking, and I had to throw a gun on you to keep you from killing him. Then I made you bring him down here. Too bad, but we cattlemen can't afford to let wrong impressions get out just now.'

'You don't mind hitting below the belt, then,' Bruce suggested.

'Not in a free-for-all fight with nesters ruining the country.'

Bruce called to Ramrod and asked him to bring out to the porch his rifle and that of Jelks.

'Do you need rifles—right now?' Randall asked, narrowed eyes on his foe.

'For evidence.' Bruce turned to Ramrod. 'Examine both guns and tell us how many shots have been fired from each.'

Ramrod reported. 'Three from Wally's gun, one from yours, if the magazines were loaded to start with.'

'*If* is a big little word,' Randall sneered. 'How the hell you going to prove Jelks's rifle was full up?'

He walked to his horse and swung to the saddle. 'I'll send Doc Bradley,' he said. 'Don't throw any more slugs in poor Wally before he gets here.'

They watched him ride down the road, his straight flat back to them a symbol of insolent arrogance.

'He's got a lot of front window,' Ramrod said angrily.

'And plenty of goods to back the display,' Bruce replied regretfully. 'He's one tough *hombre*.'

151

A Difference of Opinion

XVIII

Ben had wandered down to the corral, had gathered the eggs for Linda from the barn, and was now lying on a stave hammock on the porch. He still tired easily, though he was improving daily.

Linda brought him out a glass of milk with an egg beaten in it. 'Drink that,' she ordered.

He drank it obediently. 'There's a guy riding up the road,' he said. 'Funny how many punchers come to ask you have you seen a stray buckskin pony with white stockings on the front legs, and seeing as I'm here, Miss Lindy, how about saving me a quadrille at the dance Friday night.' He tilted a grin at her over the edge of the glass.

She looked down the road at the approaching rider. 'The trouble with this country is that there aren't enough girls in it. There are so few of us that every goose looks like a swan to them.'

'How right you are about the first part of what you said.' He sat up at sudden attention. 'It's Rod.'

'I've known that for several minutes,' Linda said.

Rod swung from the saddle and dropped the reins. 'How you doing, Ben?' he asked after a word of greeting.

'Fine as silk. This girl's nursing could cure a dead man.'

'Thought you weren't allowed to come here,' Linda said, the sting of a fine whiplash in her voice. She was carrying a chip on her shoulder for Rod.

He laughed. The girl's sarcasm did not reach him. He knew it was not necessary to explain to her or to anybody else that he did not ask any man's permission to do anything in the world he wished.

'I couldn't be in the doghouse, could I?' he asked. 'You sound a little edgy, cousin dear.'

'How could I be anything but pleased to have you remember me?' she replied. 'With so many more important things on your mind.'

His spurs jingled as he came up the porch steps and found a chair. He leaned back and laced his fingers behind his head. 'About those more important things?' he inquired.

'Entertaining men from Washington. And saving Wally Jelks's life from a desperate ruffian.'

'Remarkable how fast news gets around.' He slanted an amused look at her. 'I still have time to drop in on my sick brother and his sweet-tempered nurse.'

Ben interposed with a question. 'What about that Wally Jelks business, Rod?'

His brother replied with a Yankee answer. 'What was it you heard?'

'We heard you stopped Sherrill from killing him after he was wounded.'

'Well. Don't you like that story?'

'Was that the way of it?'

'That's the official version.'

'I don't believe it,' Linda said flatly.

Rod gave her a long smiling scrutiny. 'Just between us, I don't believe it myself,' he agreed. 'Not exactly.'

'I knew it,' the girl cried.

'How did you know it?'

'I just did.'

'I see. Woman's intuition. You were right this time. Sherrill wasn't thorough enough to finish the job. What he intended to do was to walk away and let the man die. I wouldn't have it that way.'

'Were both men shooting?' Ben asked.

Rod took time to phrase his answer carefully. 'I'll say only this—that Jelks is a no-account skunk.'

'He started the shooting,' Linda said with sharp decision.

'Anyhow, he deserved what he got. Let it rest at that. The point that sticks out like a hurt thumb is this—Sherrill shoots a cowboy right while the government men are here investigating. He can't lift that load off his sore back.'

'Do you think that is fair fighting, when you know Wally Jelks started the shooting?' she demanded indignantly.

'Were you there?' Rod wanted to know, with mock deference.

'I said, do you think it's fair to hold back part of the truth?'

He gave her his point of view, with the tolerant patience a parent uses toward an unreasonable child. 'This isn't a sporting game we are playing. It's war. I play the cards dealt me, for all they are worth. I'm not such a jug-headed fool as to be soft with our foes. I'll hit them as often and as hard as I can, and I don't care a hang about the rules. When I slam a blow in it is meant to go where it will hurt the most.'

Linda objected to an assumption he had made. 'It isn't war—yet. But it will be soon if we don't come to our senses. Do you have to be so hard, Rod—to hate Bruce Sherrill so much?'

'You're wrong about that, girl,' Rod corrected. 'I don't waste my time hating him. If he weren't such a trouble-maker I think I could like him. The fellow has sand in his craw. But that's nothing. He's our enemy, trying to tear down all we have built up. I'll fight him to a fare-you-well, since that is what he wants.'

'Legally?'

He flung that aside with an impatient gesture. 'Any way.'

'With bullets?'

'If he hasn't sense enough to get out of our road.'

Her troubled eyes searched his unhappily. 'You are as mad as your father,' she said in a low voice. 'To kill a man does not prove him wrong.'

'It keeps him from pestering you anymore,' he said bluntly.

His dark intent look held steadily to her vivid face. He thought it beautiful, desirable for what it withheld as much as for what it offered. She was not like the bouncing daughters of other ranchmen in the neighborhood. In her there was the deep pride of reticent self-respect. Except when she was excited her voice was low and husky, rich with sweet undertones. The timbre of it excited him far more than the inviting giggles of pretty girls with come-hither eyes. She could be gay and friendly yet free in spirit, mistress of her own soul. He sensed in her a gallant courage she carried like a banner. This both attracted and irritated him. Her independence was an unconscious challenge to him. Women ought to accept the standards of their fathers or their husbands. The girl he married must merge her individuality in his and take his judgment as final, not critical of anything he thought or did.

'Yes, it keeps him from troubling you,' she

agreed, bitterly. 'God gives life—and any fool can destroy it.'

Both of them were trying to save the strong attraction, never put into words, that drew them together as a magnet does steel filings. They had to find a common ground or suffer the hurt of knowing there was a barrier between them they could not cross.

Ben guessed at the emotional stress lying beneath their words. He rose from the hammock, deciding that they could get along better without him. 'If you're going to discuss theology I'll take a walk,' he said lightly.

They watched him stroll away. Rod brought his gaze back to the girl.

'When a problem comes up a man has to make up his mind what to do,' he told her. 'It's not a woman's place to tell him. She must feel he is right and support him. It may be something he hates to do, and yet the job is there waiting for him. He can't shirk it, and nobody can stand between him and it, least of all the woman who loves him.'

'You think she should stay at home and pray that he will be successful and won't get killed himself when he starts out to be judge, jury, executioner, and God,' she cried.

'A man can't run away from facts that face him,' he replied, his tone still quiet but with no yielding in his stern face. 'Sherrill nearly killed

Ben. He wounded Jelks. His next victim won't be so lucky.' He stopped a moment, to choose words for his next point. 'There are worse things than killing, Lindy. Take Sherrill as an example. He was with the Rough Riders in Cuba. It was his duty to kill. If he picked off a Spanish sharpshooter, was he doing wrong?'

'That's not the same at all, Rod,' she protested. 'He was fighting for his country. There was no decision for him to make. He would be risking his life to do his duty. But if he kills somebody now for his own personal benefit he will be a murderer.'

'Meaning that I will be one if I am forced to shoot him. You use harsh words, Lindy—and think harsh thoughts.' He looked at her a long time, his grim eyes drilling into hers. 'I thought we were friends.'

'I thought so too.' She could not keep her voice quite steady. 'And now we seem miles apart.'

For the first time he put into words a recognition of the tie that had bound them. 'A woman must trust the man she loves, not judge him. She must understand that what he does is right for him and not oppose it. If she loves, she doesn't criticize.'

Linda knew there was no use arguing or trying to explain. They had come to a fundamental difference of viewpoint.

'I'm sorry,' she said dismally.

'Is that all you can say?' he demanded.

'I can't change the way I think, Rod. If I let a man I loved do what I thought wrong, because I was afraid to tell him so, I would despise myself.'

'You think nagging him would do any good?'

'No,' she admitted, her voice flat and hopeless. 'Nothing would do any good if their views were as far apart as ours are.'

He walked to his horse, swung to the saddle and without once looking back rode away. The girl watched him go, her eyes blurred with tears. She went slowly into the house and upstairs to her room. Linda had never wanted to marry him. A deep instinct warned her that she was too independent to live with a man like Rod. Clashes and frustrations would fret her soul. Yet she had come near loving him. Something warm and exciting had gone out of her life.

Conspirators Whisper

XIX

Bill Cairns tied at the far side of the Diamond Tail corral and walked around it as quietly as he could, keeping an eye alert to make sure no rider of the outfit saw him. The lights in the bunkhouse were already out. It was nearly eleven, and in the ranch country men go to bed early. The night was dark, neither moon nor stars showing, but on his way to the house he kept in the shadow of the out buildings as much as he could. He did not know why old Jeff Randall had sent for him, but his instructions were to keep from being seen if possible. The old schemer had some deviltry afoot, of course. He would presently find out what it was.

The big house was dark too, except for a lamp in the room Jeff called his office. Cairns tiptoed across the porch and knocked. When he opened the door he saw the ranchman's shapeless body slumped down on a chair. He had been reading the Redrock *Beacon* by the inadequate light of a cheap little kerosene lamp.

'Sit down, Bill,' the old man invited, and pushed a chair with his foot toward the visitor. 'Anybody see you?'

160

'Hell, no. It's the middle of the night.'

'Good.' Jeff shoved a bottle and a tumbler in the direction of his guest, who poured the glass half full and drained it. 'I see by the *Beacon* that Hal Bonsall announces he's going to run again for county clerk. He's a good man and deserves re-election.'

'Did you have me ride twelve miles to tell me that?' Cairns growled.

'Don't push on the reins, Bill,' his host said amiably. 'Rest yore weary bones and take another drink. We got all night before us.'

The Pitchfork foreman reached for the bottle and had another. 'Maybe you've got all night,' he complained. 'I've been in the saddle most of the day, and I've got to get back to the ranch while it's still dark. You've shot my night's sleep to pieces, but that makes no difference to you. When you whistle you expect us to come on the jump.'

'Nothing like that, Bill,' Jeff demurred. 'I've got a piece of business to talk over, and I thought it best not to tell the whole world. What people don't know won't hurt them.'

'All right. Shoot.'

Randall took a little time to come to the point. He thought he had Cairns sized up correctly, but if he was making a mistake it would be a very serious one.

'I'm giving you a chance to make a hundred

dollars, Bill, with very little trouble,' he said.

'That's fine,' jeered the foreman. 'Right generous of you.'

He knew that when Jeff Randall gave something for nothing, it would be time to be looking in the woodpile for what was concealed there.

'Fact is, we've got to do something to make these government snoopers see what skunks the sodbreakers are. Maybe you don't know it, but they are moving over to stay two-three days at the Pitchfork.'

'So I've heard. What about it?'

'My idea is to give them a sort of an object lesson, one they won't forget. Jolt them, kind of.'

'Talk turkey,' Cairns said impatiently. 'This ain't a guessin' contest, is it?'

Randall tapped the table with the edge of the folded newspaper. 'Let's suppose somebody slashed Pitchfork wires, then went in and shot down a bunch of cattle, say about a dozen. Wouldn't that convince them, so they would give hell to the nesters in their report?'

Cairns stared at the humped-up ranchman with unbelieving eyes. 'Goddlemighty!' he cried. 'I'm foreman of the outfit. You askin' me to do this?'

'I'm not suggesting you throw down yore boss, Bill. This would be the best thing in the world for him if you would do it.' The voice of the cattleman was suave and wheedling. 'What are

162

a dozen steers to a man who has thousands? It won't mean a thing to him. But it will mean a whole lot to Daly to have these two birds get the right idea about these nesters. You can see that.'

'Why don't you shoot some of yore own stuff?' Cairns wanted to know. 'You got more than the Pitchfork has.'

'It ain't in human nature, Bill, for a man to destroy his own stuff,' Randall explained, his manner making a virtue of it. 'I thought of it, but I just couldn't do it. But if I pay you a hundred dollars Daly and I will be bearing the loss together. That's reasonable, isn't it?'

'Ask Daly if he thinks so,' Cairns barked. 'You're proposing I sell my saddle—for a hundred plunks. I can lose that much at the wheel in twenty minutes. Every man may have his price, but I'm not going to throw down my outfit for chicken feed. You must figure me cheap.'

Randall moved noiselessly to the door, flung it open to make sure nobody was eavesdropping, shut it, and shuffled back to his chair. 'Keep yore voice down, Bill,' he admonished. 'I'm not advertisin' the contract for this job.' The old man leaned forward and wagged his thick forefinger at the Pitchfork foreman. 'Listen. If this report goes to Washington the way I want it there is going to be a new shuffle of the deck out in this neck of the woods. Quite a few homesteaders are bound to throw up their hands and quit. I don't claim to be a prophet, but it wouldn't surprise me if one or two of them weren't missing about that time, *if you know what I mean.*'

Cairns nodded. He knew very well. 'Go on,' he said. 'Finish sayin' yore piece.'

Randall's voice fell almost to a whisper. 'How would you like to own the Quartercircle D C? It's a fine little ranch. The right man could get along fast on it. He could run a nice bunch of cows and have plenty of feed and water for them.'

'I'd like it down to the ground.' The dull eyes of Cairns held fast to the gross face of the ranchman. 'But far as I know it isn't for sale.'

'It would be—if anything happened to Sherrill. He has no near relatives. It would be flung on the market and sold for a song.'

'And who would buy it?' Cairns answered his own question. 'Cliff Applegate, of course. He needs it bad.'

'It wouldn't suit me to have Cliff get it.' Randall's strong jaw clamped. There was a vindictive glare in his eyes. 'I'll see it goes to a man I can trust—like you. Don't worry, Bill. I know how to pull the strings to get what I want.'

The foreman did not doubt his last statement. The question was whether he would want Cairns to have the ranch. He had sons of his own he could put on it.

'How about putting it on paper, just as a sort of reminder to us both?' the Pitchfork man asked.

'That's a fool thing to say, Bill. Sherrill is still alive. You don't want to hang us both, do you?'

'Why don't you get Quint Milroy to pull off this cattle-killing?' Cairns asked suspiciously.

'A fair question. I'll tell you why.' The bull-necked old man's face was twisted for a moment to an expression of amused contempt. 'When Quint was a boy his father ran cattle. Now get this, Bill. The doggoned fool is sentimental. He likes cows. Rubbing out a man is just business, but pumping lead into a bunch of stock is gosh-awful. He isn't tough enough for that.'

Cairns rubbed his unshaven chin with the palm of his hand. It helped his slow brain to think. 'If there was a scoundrel who was dangerous to you, who went around dusting off men on our side, maybe Quint's conscience wouldn't keep him from doing a little drygulching,' he suggested.

'I think Quint could be persuaded,' Randall answered. His eyes were as cold as glacier ice.

There was no longer need to tell Cairns to keep his voice down. Both men were talking in whispers. Each looked at the other with unwinking eyes that searched for assurance. Neither trusted his fellow conspirator as far as he could throw a rope. But their interests marched together, at least for the present.

'Of course, like you say, I would be doing Daly a service if I helped bring this fight to a head in his favor,' the foreman said.

'Sure you would.' Randall realized the man wanted to be persuaded of this in self-justification. 'No doubt about it, Bill. You have to take a long view in a matter like this. Everybody but you and me would think the nesters had shot the stock.' An idea struck him. 'Why not build up some evidence of that? We could have Flack snitch us some personal thing Sherrill wears—his hat or pocketknife or anything that could be identified as his—and leave it on the ground near where the cattle are killed.'

Cairns thought that a good idea. He developed it further. 'You could have Flack warn us of the raid and I could lay a trap for the night riders. I could have some of our boys stationed near, and they could show up after the shooting. It would look as if Sherrill had to make his getaway so fast he couldn't stop to pick up the hat he had dropped.'

'Fine,' Randall approved. 'You could work that easy. There's no moon now. Not the least bit of danger for you.'

'Easy for you to say that, with you sitting here reading the *Beacon* while I pull off the job,' Cairns grumbled. 'Yo're always gettin' other fellows to pull yore chestnuts outa the fire. And coming down to cases, when would Quint get busy taking care of Sherrill?'

'Soon as it is safe. We'd better wait till those men go back to Washington and turn in their report. Don't worry about Sherrill. He's as good as buried right now.'

'I've heard that brag for some time,' sneered Cairns. 'But the cocky devil still struts around steppin' high as a bull elk in the rutting season. He has been the leader of these sod-busters from the first. If my guess is good—and it's the same as yours—he pulled the wires that got these snoopers out here. You and Daly and the other big cattlemen are the fellows he and his friends are putting the kibosh on. I'm just a hired hand, but so far I'm the only one in any of yore outfits has shown any fight. I'm the guy who put a slug in him, to keep him from finishing Ben. I hunted him down and would have caught him if Cliff Applegate's girl hadn't double-crossed me. At Redrock I killed his horse and would of got him only he stayed holed up in the sheriff's house till it was safe. You claim to be the big mogul around here. Why the hell don't you do something except load it all on me?'

In his excitement the foreman's voice had risen to a higher pitch than the whisper he had been using. The old man lifted his hand in warning to be more careful.

'You don't have to hire a hall, Bill,' he murmured. 'And you don't have to tell me what this scoundrel has done. I know it same as you do.' His narrowed eyes were slits of shining menace, his mouth a thin cruel gash in the large face. 'You've done well, but I'll do better. Just let me play my hand. I know when to wait and when to strike. It's not only getting rid of this fellow. We have to rub him out in a way that there won't be any come back on us. You do this chore and I won't ask anything more of you. And get this. If it's the last thing I do in this world I'll make sure Sherrill lies under the daisies in a wooden box.'

'Yeah, and what guarantee have I got that you'll fix it for me to have his ranch and not grab it yoreself?'

Randall showed distress at being mistrusted. 'I wouldn't do that, Bill.' He knew that a declaration of good faith would not be convincing and went on to give reasons. 'Fact is, I couldn't even if I wanted to. No use pretending the other cattlemen aren't jealous of me. I'm pretty aggressive. But a man can't hog everything in sight. It will be all I can do to see Cliff doesn't get the Quartercircle D C. I won't let him have it after throwing me down. I want a man on it who is on my side and owes me support. You're the one I have picked. Naturally if I buy it for you I'll have to put a mortgage on it, but you can pay it off on easy terms. We'll work together fine, Bill.'

Since Cairns wanted to believe this, he accepted old Jeff's reasoning. It was true there would be a lot of adverse criticism if he raked in the ranch for himself. To have there a man indebted to him would be wiser, since the other cattlemen resented greatly his greedy dominance.

They talked over in detail plans for the raid, after which they shook hands as allies. Cairns took another long drink and clumped out into the night. His mind was not quite easy, but he was not in a position to make surer that the old fox would play fair with him.

A Hat Is Found

XX

Ned Daly, owner of the Pitchfork, lay on a sofa and smoked a cigar, his eyes fixed on the visitor who sat uneasily on the edge of a chair. The ranchman was tied fast to the house by reason of a broken leg due to a fall from a pitching horse.

'You say they mean to pull this off tonight?' Daly asked.

'That's right, Mr. Daly. They're coming in through the north pasture.' Flack was not happy about what he was doing. He did not know the object of it. Since he was a timid man he liked to play safe, and he had a feeling there might be danger here for him somewhere. But he had his instructions from Jeff Randall and had to carry them out.

Cairns walked heavily into the room.

'I sent for you, Bill, to listen to a story this man has brought me,' Daly said. He waved his cigar toward the homesteader. 'Go ahead, Flack.'

What Flack had to tell was no news to the foreman, whom he had met in the willows by the creek less than an hour ago. He parroted the story old Jeff had rehearsed with him, that Sherrill had come to get him to join this raid on the Pitchfork.

Ramrod and another Quartercircle D C rider would be with them. And there was to be a fifth man. Sherrill had not decided who yet.

Daly did not doubt the story. There was no apparent point in this rat-faced spy coming to him with a cock-and-bull yarn that would prove untrue in a few hours. Yet it seemed strange for Sherrill to play into the hands of his enemies while the investigators were actually staying at the Pitchfork, or even while they were still in the district. Perhaps he was trying to get even because Wally Jelks had shot at him.

The owner of the Pitchfork was a big heavy-set man in his early fifties. Honest blue eyes looked out of a frank face tanned by wind and sun to a deep brown. He was an impetuous man, irascible at times, easily led, subject to strong prejudices.

'What do you think?' he asked Cairns.

'We've got the fool, sure as God made little apples,' the foreman exulted.

Daly looked at his watch. 'It's dinner time, Flack. I don't reckon you want to eat with the boys. It might not be too pleasant for you. Go into the kitchen and tell the cook I said for him to fix you up to eat there.'

As soon as Flack had gone, Daly flung out a question. 'Do you trust that treacherous skunk, Bill?'

'I've got no use for him,' Cairns answered. 'But he is in Randall's pay. He wouldn't dare try to

171

put anything over on us. I think his story is true. Don't you?'

'I reckon so. We'll have to fix up a trap for Sherrill.' He added fretfully, 'Too bad I've got this busted leg.'

'Don't worry. I'll get him.'

'No killing, Bill. Surprise them and take Sherrill prisoner. The others too, if you can. My guess is that they will come down the cañon and enter the pasture about where Bear Creek strikes it. If you keep the boys hidden in the willows they will ride right into you.'

'That's so,' agreed Cairns. 'There's no way for them to hit the north pasture except by the cañon.'

For an hour they discussed the problem. Daly was insistent that there should be no bloodshed. If Cairns could not capture any of the raiders without that he must let them escape. It was important that the cattlemen show clean hands just now.

Before the Pitchfork riders left that night, Daly had them into the room and made it clear they were out to capture the raiders but not kill them. Anyone disobeying this injunction would be fired at once and would get no help from the ranch if the law wanted him.

Barnard and Sawyer were in the room and heard the instructions given the men. Both of them were troubled at being caught in such a situation. They realized that it would have been better not to have visited the ranches, but the mistake could not be helped now. Barnard said a few blunt words. He warned the cowboys that the United States government had become interested and would not tolerate any lawlessness.

The night was dark and cloudy. The riders could see only a few feet in front of them, but Cairns knew every acre of the rough terrain and led his party with a sureness the younger men respected. They traveled an hour and a half before reaching Bear Creek. The foreman chose a spot with plenty of shrubbery on the bank of the stream and concealed the cowboys at strategic points, each man not too close to his nearest neighbor. He warned them that there was to be absolutely no talking back and forth. The success of the trap would depend upon the raiders being caught completely by surprise. Cairns chose for himself the place at the lower end of the line.

It must have been about twenty minutes later that a burst of firing startled the men in ambuscade. Eight or ten shots rang out, not more than a few seconds apart. They had been fired a few hundred yards below them, from around a bend in the stream.

The Pitchfork punchers came out from cover and gathered into two groups which presently merged into one. They milled around, uncertain what to do.

'Where is Cairns?' one of them asked.

None of them had seen him. A redheaded youth raised his voice and shouted the name of the foreman. Two more shots sounded.

The voice of Cairns reached them. 'This way, boys,' he shouted. 'Hurry up!'

They found him, his horse beside him, looking down at a dead steer. Two others had been shot and lay on the ground not far away.

'I got a crack at one of the scalawags,' he said. 'But they were lighting out fast as they could. Don't think I hit him.'

'We didn't get a crack at one of the whole doggoned bunch,' a puncher cried, slapping his hat against his leathers in vexation.

'How about giving them a chase?' another asked.

'Might try it.' Cairns's voice sounded very dubious. 'Not much chance. They were getting outa here hell-for-leather. Listen.'

No sound of horses' hoofs came to them. Evidently the raiders had made a clean escape. There would be small chance of finding them, since they could ride in almost any direction.

'They've killed two steers and a heifer,' one lad announced. The moaning of a wounded animal came to them.

'Hit in the head,' a cowboy called out after he had knelt and examined the steer. 'Have to kill it, I reckon. Take a look, Cairns.'

The foreman's gun cracked and the head of the steer fell down.

'Look what I've found,' a man shouted.

He joined the others, an old white wide-brimmed hat in his hand. Cairns took the hat and stared at it. 'It must of fell off one of their heads, and he dassent stop to pick it up,' the foreman said.

He handed it back to the man who had found it. 'We'll keep that, Jack. It might be evidence.'

'How?' someone asked. 'The fellow ain't gonna advertise in the *Beacon* he has lost a hat.'

Jack gave an exclamation of excitement. 'His initials are stamped in the band. See here.' He struck a match to read them. 'B. S. Why it's Bruce Sherrill's hat.'

They crowded around. Somebody struck another match. The initials were stamped on the sweatband plain to read.

'He's left his calling card,' Jack cried jubilantly. 'I'll bet he's sweatin' blood right now wondering who will find the hat.'

'Mr. Sherrill was sure careless,' Cairns said. 'But you'll see he will have some kind of an explanation. Maybe he sold his hat some time to one of you boys.'

Cairns congratulated himself on the smooth way he had worked this. He had let one of the boys find the hat and identify its owner. There had not been a slip-up anywhere. The whole affair had been pulled off with perfect timing. There was not a possibility he could be suspected.

They rode back to the ranch house and reported. Late though it was, Daly and his two guests were still up. They had been too interested and too anxious to go to bed. In an expedition of this sort there was always a chance that somebody would be killed. Even though no raider had been captured, Daly was more than satisfied. The hat found on the scene was a mute witness Sherrill would find it hard to refute.

At the Pitchfork

XXI

Cairns carried the news himself to the sheriff. He was not going to lose the opportunity of exulting over him. Humphreys was disturbed to hear of the raid and particularly to learn that there was evidence implicating Bruce Sherrill. But when he took the story home to his wife Jessie scoffed at his fears.

'Bruce isn't such a fool,' she told him stoutly. 'And I wouldn't believe a word that scoundrel Bill Cairns says, not after he stood out among the trees there and shot Bruce's horse. I wouldn't put it past him to have done it himself just to get Bruce into trouble.'

'That's possible,' the sheriff agreed. 'But Bill Cairns did not find the hat, he says. The boy who found it was Jack Peters. He seems to me a nice straightforward lad. I think I had better ride out to the Pitchfork and look around. Daly too has the reputation of being an honest man. I don't think he would cook up evidence. I would like to talk with him.'

'What about Bruce?' she asked. 'He is in town. As he passed an hour ago he waved at me. Are you going to tell him?'

'I think so. If he has a defense I want to hear it before I meet Daly.'

The sheriff found Bruce at Doan & Devon's store. He drew the ranchman aside and told him what he had heard.

'Looks like a frame-up,' Bruce said at once. 'I didn't leave the ranch Thursday night.'

'Can you prove that?'

'Only by Ramrod. Mark and Neal went to a dance and didn't get back till morning.'

'That's bad. They claim Ramrod was with you. And what about that hat they found? Could it be yours?'

'I don't see how it could. There's an old hat of mine around the house. But how could Cairns get hold of it?' Bruce came to a swift decision. A gleam of mirth sparkled in his eyes. 'You say you are going out to the Pitchfork. I'll side you and be your deputy, Tim.'

Humphreys reminded him that he was under suspicion. 'You can't laugh this off, son. It's a serious charge.'

'Can't I whistle in the dark?' Bruce wanted to know. The smile was wiped from his face. 'Fact is, I can't let a lie like this stand without facing it, not with Barnard and Sawyer out at Daly's ranch having the wool pulled over their eyes.'

The sheriff understood the urge of Bruce to clear himself. He was not sure whether Bruce had been involved in this raid, though it did not seem in character. He was bold enough to do anything, but Tim had thought him too wise to prejudice the case of the homesteaders by such a piece of folly. Nor was Sherrill the kind to shoot down cattle wantonly, unless his friend's judgment of him was wholly wrong. It was possible of course that another of the raiders might have done the killing before he could be stopped.

It would not be a bad idea to let Bruce confront his accusers. Sometimes in the heat of talk the truth slipped out unexpectedly. But there was another angle to this. Cairns was not the only Pitchfork man who had made threats after the wounding of Wally Jelks. According to the story told the riders Wally had been shot without warning. If they believed Bruce the leader of this raid, they would think of it as an outrageous defiance of the ranch.

'I don't think you had better go out to the Pitchfork now,' the sheriff said. 'It has quite a score piled up against you. Some of its warriors are a little quick on the trigger.'

Bruce brushed the danger aside as negligible. 'Like Wally Jelks,' he said dryly. 'When I am not looking for trouble. Out in the open all they will do is scowl.'

'Aren't there any buildings or ditches at the Pitchfork from which a man could take a crack at you?' Humphreys asked.

Sherrill chuckled. 'I'll be under the protection of the sheriff. When do we start?'

'All right. All right.' The sheriff threw up his hands in surrender. 'Be ready to start in fifteen minutes. Meet me in front of my office. And don't forget that Cairns is in town. At least he was an hour ago.'

The mention of the name was like a stage cue. The foreman straddled into the store and ordered a cigar. His glance picked up Humphreys and Sherrill.

'You arresting that scoundrel, sheriff?' he demanded.

'Take it easy, Bill,' Humphreys advised. 'When the time comes for an arrest I'll make it.'

'I wonder,' Cairns replied insolently.

'Now, gentlemen. If you please. Let us not have any trouble here.' The placatory voice was that of Clem Doan, one of the owners of the store.

Bruce said nothing. This was the sheriff's business, and he judged him competent to handle it.

'There won't be any trouble, Clem,' Humphreys said quietly. 'Bill is one of my constituents and wants to be sure I do my duty.'

He turned his back on Cairns and walked out of the store with Bruce beside him. Ten minutes later the two men were jogging out of town.

Near the summit of Wind Break Pass,

Humphreys looked back over the zigzag trail they had followed and caught sight of a horseman a few hundred yards behind them.

'I believe it is Cairns,' he said. 'On his way to the Pitchfork.'

Bruce nodded. 'I think we'd better stop and admire the view, Tim,' he proposed. 'I'd rather have him in front of us than behind.'

The foreman did not draw up, but as he passed he flung a jeer at the officer. 'You make a fine front, sheriff, for criminals to hide behind.'

'I gather you don't approve of me, Bill,' Humphreys answered blandly.

'What do you care, since the crooks who elected you do?' Cairns snarled. 'I judge a man by the company he keeps.'

He rode past them, his thick body stiff in the saddle. At intervals they caught sight of him in front of them every mile of the way to the ranch.

They reached the Pitchfork in midafternoon. The ranch house lay in a circular bowl slashed by openings through which a small stream ran in and out. From the rim, before the road dropped, the valley was a checkerboard of brown and green, the pattern set by pasture lands of native grasses and alfalfa fields. The big house, as the main building was called, stood out of the cluster of structures huddled beside the creek in a grove of cottonwoods. Except for a wide porch extending across the front and one side, it was plain and unadorned.

A man came out of the bunkhouse and caught sight of the two riders moving down into the valley. He watched them until they were close enough for identification before waking to excited activity. He shouted something through the door behind him, then broke for the big house at a run and disappeared in it. Men poured out of the bunkhouse like seeds squirted from a squeezed orange. The sound of their voices drifted to the approaching horsemen. One gave directions and the men scattered to posts at different parts of the yard.

'Mr. Cairns has been fixing up a welcome for me,' Bruce drawled. 'Where do we go from here, sheriff?'

Humphreys held his pony to an even road gait. 'To the front porch. Cairns isn't with them. I don't think they will start anything, at least until he shows up. Not with me here.'

'Nice to have the law so close,' Bruce said, his smile a trifle stiff. 'Hope none of the boys forget who you are.'

'Don't make any cracks,' Humphreys warned. 'I'll do any talking that's necessary.'

'I'll be quiet as an undertaker,' Bruce promised.

A man stood at a corner of the blacksmith shop, two at the stable, a fourth in front of the bunkhouse. An older man, baldheaded, had moved to the house porch. Bruce noticed that all of them watched him steadily. That they had itching trigger fingers he felt sure.

The sheriff waved a hand in greeting and dismounted. Bruce was careful not to hurry, not to let an alarmed glance sweep the yard.

'Howdy, Baldy,' Humphreys said evenly. 'You head of the reception committee.'

'What's that killer doing here?' the baldheaded man demanded.

'You mean Sherrill. Why, he's here with me. Don't make a mistake.'

A slim girl of about fifteen with long dark-lashed eyes came out of the house, quite unaware that this was an explosive moment. 'Father says for you to come in,' she told the visitors, and looked with shy curiosity at Bruce. His friendly smile surprised her. It did not match his hoof-and-horns reputation.

The self-invited guests followed her into the big room where her father was lying on a lounge. The foreman stood near him bristling at Sherrill, his shallow bleak eyes filled with venomous hostility.

Daly said angrily, 'You have yore nerve to come here, Sherrill, after what you did the other night.'

'I brought him with me, Mr. Daly,' explained Humphreys. 'Thought we ought to get both sides together and figure out the right of this.'

183

'Goddlemighty!' the cattleman exploded. 'What do you mean figure on it? Has he a right to shoot down my stuff?'

'Sherrill claims he did not leave the ranch that night.'

'He's a damn liar. Probably he'll claim he didn't shoot Jelks either.' Daly turned to his daughter. 'Janet, ask Mr. Barnard and Mr. Sawyer to come here. And don't come back yoreself.'

The government men joined the party. They had met and talked with the sheriff during their stay at Redrock.

'First-off, Humphreys, let's get this clear,' challenged Daly. 'Is this fellow yore prisoner?'

'I haven't made any arrests. I'm here to investigate this raid. I've wondered how your men happened to be on the ground just as it was being pulled off.'

'Can't tell you that,' Daly answered bluntly. 'We were warned. That's all the information you'll get from me on that point.'

'Warned that Sherrill was leading a raid on your place?'

'That's right.'

'You can't leave it that way, Mr. Daly,' the sheriff remonstrated. 'If you have evidence against him you'll have to come clean with it. He has a right to demand that.'

'I don't care what he demands. I'll tell what I please. Bring me that hat, Bill.'

Cairns brought him a hat from the table and Daly handed it to the sheriff. 'One of my boys found it right near where the cattle were killed.'

The officer looked the hat over, read the initials stenciled on the sweat band, and handed the Stetson to Bruce.

'This yours?' he asked.

Before the hat reached his hands Bruce knew that it was his. 'Yes,' he said.

'Any idea how it got here?'

'No.' Bruce looked for a long moment at Cairns. His gaze shifted to Daly and shuttled back to the foreman. 'But Cairns can tell you.'

'You're right I can,' the wagon boss replied, heavy triumph in his voice. 'Jack Peters picked it up thirty yards from where you killed our stock. I was cutting loose at you, and you couldn't stop to pick it up when it fell.'

'You recognized me?'

Cairns hesitated. His original story had not included this detail, but he had slid in later that he felt sure one of the retreating raiders was Sherrill.

'Practically.'

'How far was I from you?'

'Not more than thirty yards.'

'And on a black night, without moon or stars, you indentified me at thirty yards.' Bruce turned contemptuously away. He addressed his words to Barnard. 'This is a frame-up. I don't

185

know yet how Cairns got my hat, but I am sure he planted it where one of his boys would find it. Do you think I would be so foolish as to raid this ranch while you are here investigating this trouble?'

'Somebody raided it, Mr. Sherrill,' Barnard said.

'I think it was an inside job, done to prejudice you against the homesteaders. The story smells to high heaven. I have ridden for years and never saw a cowboy lose his hat unless he was on a pitching horse or there was a heavy wind blowing. My boys will tell you that I haven't worn that old hat for months.'

'How do you think it reached the place where the cattle were killed?' Sawyer asked.

'Cairns can tell you that. He must have got somebody to smuggle it out of my house to him.'

The Pitchfork foreman exploded angrily. Barnard raised a hand to stop his profane denial.

'There's another charge against you, Mr. Sherrill,' the government man said. 'Only a few days ago you shot a cowboy.'

'After he had fired at me three times.'

'That's not the way we heard it from a bystander.'

'Randall told me he was going to doctor the facts to suit him. I don't know whether you commissioned Jelks to kill me, Daly. If so, don't blame him. He did his best. While we're on the subject, I wish you would send a wagon to pick up your killer. Doctor Bradley says he can be moved safely. I don't want the fellow around my place any longer.'

Daly flushed angrily. 'With Rod Randall on the spot as a witness you'll have trouble getting anybody to swallow your lie that Jelks was my killer. You've got so much gall you think you can talk yoreself out of anything.'

The sheriff cut into the quarrel. 'Thought I was to do the talking, Bruce,' he said.

The accused man nodded. 'All right, Tim.' He knew he had lost ground with Barnard and Sawyer. The weight of evidence was against him. 'I'll say just one thing more. If the Pitchfork expects to prove I was leading a raid against its cattle, Daly will have to uncover the witness he claims brought him warning of it.'

'Right,' agreed the sheriff. 'Now if you are all through I'll take charge. I want to talk with each one of the boys who went out to stop the raiders. I'll do all the questioning. You and Mr. Sawyer may be present, Mr. Barnard. Also Daly and Sherrill.'

'You're trying to cut me out of it,' blustered Cairns. 'I won't stand for it.'

'I want only one man on each side present,' Humphreys said. 'If you would rather leave and let Cairns stay, Daly—'

'I'll stay,' Daly interrupted. 'You can go, Bill. That's fair enough. Get the boys in soon as you can.'

Cairns left, sulkily. Humphreys talked with the cowboys one at a time. He got from each one his story of the night's adventure. Before he had finished certain facts stood out. None of them had at any time seen any of the raiders. Nor had they heard the sound of their horses. The only evidences of their presence, outside of the hat, were the sound of the shots and the dead cattle. One other material point came out. When the shots were heard, Cairns had not been with them. They found him a short time later at the scene of the shooting.

After the testimony had all been heard, Daly flung an angry question at the sheriff. 'Are you trying to prove, Humphreys, that I got Cairns to shoot my own cattle?' he demanded.

'I'm trying to get at the truth,' the sheriff replied. 'But I'll say this. Cairns could have killed the stock before the boys got there. If he did, I don't think you had a thing to do with it.'

'That's a crazy idea. Why would Bill do that?'

'I don't say he did it. He might have done it— to prejudice these gentlemen against the home-steaders.'

'No decent cattleman ever did such a thing,' Daly protested.

The sheriff agreed that was true. Neither did any decent homesteader.

'You are not going to arrest Sherrill?' Daly said.

'Not unless you will let me hear the story of the man who warned you of the raid,' Humphreys told him.

'He'd be in danger of getting shot if I did,' the cattleman urged.

'Not if you let me talk with him privately. He would not be known.'

'I'll see if I can fix it,' the cattleman said.

Bruce had a suggestion for the sheriff's ear alone. 'Come over to the ranch and talk with Jelks. Bring these two men with you.'

Humphreys thought that would be a good idea.

XXII

Cairns made it his business to see Jeff Randall the night of the day the sheriff visited the Pitchfork. He was getting disturbed at the course of the investigation into the raid. It had not occurred to him that he would fall under suspicion. Flack was the danger spot. Rumors had reached him that the homesteaders distrusted the man. Sherrill was no fool. He knew that somebody had brought the hat to the Pitchfork, and it would not take him long to decide on Flack as the man. Under pressure the spy would break. The foreman had no doubt of that. If the fellow confessed to his part in the conspiracy, Cairns knew he would be through, not only at the Pitchfork, but in this whole district. A man could not throw down his own outfit without being ruined.

From Randall the worried man got at first small comfort. The owner of the Diamond Tail was concerned only for his own safety. If the truth came out, it would be very damaging to him. Not only would it influence the report of Barnard; his position as leader of the cattlemen would be lost forever.

'You've sure made a mess of it,' Jeff snarled. 'I

might of known you'd put yore clumsy foot in a hornet's nest.'

Cairns flared up. '*You* botched this job. It was yore idea. It was foolproof, you claimed. Flack is not my man. You picked him. I'll say this right now. If they hang the raid on me, you'll be in it up to yore neck.'

Randall did not waste any time arguing this. His mind moved directly to a consideration of the obvious way out. He sat slumped in a chair before the office table, his thick fingers making circles on a cheap pad with the blunt point of a pencil stub. Before he raised his flinty washed-out blue eyes to the Pitchfork foreman, he knew exactly what he meant to do.

'Leave this to me. I'll take care of it.' In his voice there was the rasp of harsh command. 'Keep yore chin up. Daly won't suspect you. He's the kind of fool who would never believe one of his own men would throw him down. If anything comes up, stand pat on the story you have told. Don't give way an inch.'

'What are you going to do?' Cairns asked.

'None of yore damn business.' There more than a touch of contempt in the old man's manner. 'And for God's sake don't get goosey. I'll see you through.'

After Cairns had gone, he sat for a long time huddled in the chair, no expression in his gross hard face. At last he rose and shambled over to the cabin where Quint Milroy slept alone. He tapped on the door, gently. The gunman's voice answered almost at once.

'Who is it?'

'Jeff Randall. Want to talk with you, Quint.'

'In a minute.' Milroy had been asleep, lightly as usual. He rose, put on his trousers, and buckled the belt around his waist with the butt of the forty-five close to his hand, after which he lit a lamp and opened the door, standing well back of it as he did so.

Randall walked in. 'Sorry to waken you, Quint,' he said. 'Something has come up unexpected.'

Milroy closed and bolted the door. He waited in silence, cold eyes fixed on his midnight guest. Long ago he had learned to be sparing of words. More than one of his victims had talked themselves into a grave. No curiosity and no questions showed in his dark saturnine face. He could be as patient as an Indian.

The old man sat down and motioned the other to a chair. 'I've got a job for you, Quint,' he said bluntly.

Still Milroy waited, silent, watchful.

Old Jeff lowered his voice almost to a whisper and talked for several minutes. When he had finished, the killer made one comment.

'It will be five hundred dollars,' he said.

The ranchman's face showed a pained protest. 'Have a heart, Quint. You never had an easier job. No danger and no possible come-back. Everybody will think the homesteaders did it for throwing them down.'

'If it is so easy and safe, do it yourself,' Milroy suggested, his low voice studiously polite.

'Now—now. You know I can't do that, Quint. For you it is just like shooting tame trout in a pond. You are an expert. There isn't a man living I would trust to do this quick as I would you.'

'The price is still five hundred dollars,' Milroy mentioned gently. 'Payable in advance.'

Randall threw up his hands. 'You win. One thing, though. This has to be done quick.'

'How quick?'

'I'd like it done tonight. I know that's rushing you, but it is a hurry-up job.'

Milroy rose from the chair, his lithe slender body straight as a ramrod. 'Get the money while I saddle,' he said.

The old-timer shuffled to the door, then turned for another word. 'You'll have time to get back before morning. It won't do for you to be seen— or to be away at breakfast time.'

The gunman said nothing. He did not need any advice from amateurs.

XXIII

Flack finished washing the dishes and drew the window curtain. Nobody lived within three miles of him. There was not a chance in ten thousand that anybody would be watching him, but he was a careful man and did not believe in taking avoidable risks. After bolting the door he pushed aside the cot, removed a loose board in the floor, and from a recess underneath took a tin box. This he carried to the table and opened. Inside it were a cheap notebook and a small number of bills with a rubber band around them. Most of these were ones, but there were a few fives and two tens.

Out of a hip pocket he drew several more crumpled bills, Lovingly he smoothed them out and put them with the others. He opened the notebook and jotted down a memorandum.

> *July* 16. That old fox J. R. has trapped B. S. Looks like they have got B. wriggling in a cleft stick.

He replaced the box and its contents in the hiding-place, then settled down to read a two-weeks-old *Beacon* by the light of a small coal-oil lamp.

The house in which he lived was a one-room log cabin and a good deal of the furniture was home-made. But the place was meticulously neat. Though he was living in the cheapest possible way, Flack was no careless housekeeper. He liked to know that everything was in its place ready for use when he wanted it.

He looked twice at his fat silver watch, and at exactly eight-thirty rose to make preparations for bed. By nine o'clock he was sound asleep. He dreamed that the tin box was bulging full with bills, many of them of one-hundred-dollar denomination. When he took them to the bank at Redrock, the president, Dean Kilburn, told him they were all counterfeit and that he would send the sheriff to arrest him. Hardly had he reached home before Humphreys came knocking at the door. He could hear that knocking now, not loud but persistent.

To the sound of that knocking he woke up.

Flack sat up in bed, not fully restored from the unhappiness of his dream. 'Who's there?' he quavered.

'Quint Milroy,' a voice answered. 'I'm bringing a message from Jeff Randall.'

'From Jeff. What's he want—at this time of night?'

'He wants you to take a little trip for him.

195

Something has come up unexpected, he told me.'

Flack put on his trousers and opened the door. 'Come in, Quint,' he said.

Milroy entered and delivered the message. It roared from the barrel of a forty-five and the homesteader collapsed to the floor. The killer struck a match and made sure another shot was not necessary. From a vest pocket he took a paper and pinned it to the nightshirt of the dead man. On the note some words were printed roughly by a pencil.

The messenger rose, looked at his victim for a long moment, and left the cabin. He closed the door behind him, then walked to a small pine where his horse was tied.

He had earned his five hundred dollars.

The Sheriff Reads a Diary

XXIV

When Sheriff Humphreys talked with Wally Jelks in the presence of the two government men, the cowboy had nothing to say except a repetition of the statement that he was not going to talk. He had been in a sullen, suspicious mood ever since reaching the Quartercircle D C. It was not pleasant to be staying in the house of the man he had tried to kill. His first fear of retaliatory violence had subsided. He could not complain that his physical needs were not met. What irked him was the cold contempt of the men who waited on him. If Neal brought him breakfast, he put the food down and walked out without a word. Any necessary speech with him was made as brief as possible. Though he was now able to sit down at table with the others, he was served alone. 'Like I was a skunk or a rattlesnake,' he told Ramrod bitterly, and for once got an answer. 'A rattler gives warning before it strikes,' the foreman replied scornfully. This treatment of him, as though he were something vile, had got under his skin. He found some slight compensation in acting mulish with the sheriff.

His attitude raised a doubt in the minds of

the government agents. An innocent man did not armor himself in sullen stubbornness. Rod Randall was a prejudiced witness, and it was possible he had not told the truth.

From the ranch on Bear Creek, Humphreys crossed the ridge to Squaw Creek. He wanted to see Flack. Daly had given him the man's name, under a promise that he would not let the homesteaders know the fellow was acting as a spy for the cattlemen.

The sheriff dropped down from the top of the hogback to Squaw and followed the trail toward its headwaters. It was a rough path and grew worse the farther he went. A cañon brought him to the park where Flack had homesteaded. He looked down from the lip of the saucer on the cabin, stable, and mountain corral of the steading. No smoke was rising from the chimney, but the nester's big bony horse was in the corral.

Humphreys rode down, tied to a sapling, and walked to the cabin. It was probable that Flack was not at home, but he could leave a note for the man. He knocked on the door, and receiving no answer opened it.

What he saw shocked him. Flack was lying on the floor, face up, arms flung wide. A crimson stain above the heart showed that he had been shot. Since he was wearing a nightshirt and was barefoot, the presumption was that he had been killed before daybreak. On his breast a paper had been pinned. Without touching it, the sheriff knelt and read the words written there.

The dirty spy was betraying us and got what was coming to him.

There was no signature. That he had been rubbed out because he had become involved in the feud was clear. The implication of the note was that the homesteaders had shot him in revenge for his betrayal of them.

Though no detective, Humphreys was an experienced man of strong common sense. He was glad he had discovered the body instead of arriving after a dozen others had tramped down any evidence the assassin might have left. Without knowing in the least what he was looking for, he made a thorough search of the cabin. If Sherrill was right in his suspicion, Flack probably had money hidden. There was no sign that the murderer had looked for this. The homesteader's new suit and hat were hanging in the home-made closet. His old leather trunk had apparently not been disturbed. The papers and clothes in it were neatly arranged.

Humphreys went through it carefully and gathered no information of value. He knew some of the ways of solitary men and searched the rafter angles without success. The crevices between the logs of the walls concealed no hidden cache. His eyes scanned the floor foot by foot for a loose board. Not finding one, he pushed the cot to one side. All the planks seemed to be nailed down, but by testing them he found that in one shorter nails had been used that did not reach the two by four supporting the floor. In the space below he found a tin box. The key to it was in Flack's pocket.

The box contained bank bills and a notebook that had evidently been used as a sort of diary. Flack had jotted down data that seemed important to him, the high spots in the monotonous life of a homesteader. The first pages Humphreys skimmed over rapidly. They dealt with his taking up the land, the shifts he was put to in stocking his place and getting enough food to keep alive. There were stretches when he had nothing to eat but beans and oatmeal, except for the fish he caught and the game he shot. Sherrill's name appeared several times. Once he had brought him a side of bacon and a pound of Arbuckle's coffee. A week later he had loaned Flack five dollars, to be turned over to Prop Zang a first payment on a horse he was buying on time. In February he had been to Redrock and persuaded Doan & Devon's to let him have a load of groceries on credit, Sherrill having guaranteed payment. His muley cow had strayed, but at a later date mentioned that he had found it grazing on Slab Hill with Malloy's stuff.

Under date of April 3 the sheriff found an item he thought significant. On the valley road the hillman had met Jeff Randall driving a buckboard. To his surprise the old man had stopped to talk with him and had made a proposition. Flack had not set down what it was, but there was a comment that showed he was justifying to himself his future course. *When a fellow is pushed to the wall he has to look out for himself.*

From that time only initials were used to represent the leading characters in the story that was developing. Days and weeks were skipped with no record. An entry dated June 7 read:

Got $15 on acc't from J. R.

The fortunes of the nester improved after this. The sheriff read:

June 12. Saw J. R. and Bill C. at the Cross Roads store. Gave them tip of wirecutting and got $25 for the info.

The raid in which Ben Randall was wounded occurred on the night of the twelfth, Humphreys recalled.

June 26. Met B. S. at Redrock. I hadn't ought to of bought the suit yet, but think

201

he swallowed my story. Notified J. R. I saw him.

July 15. From J. R. $40 for story to D. and for swiping hat to give Bill C. Am not easy abt this. The boys on the creek look funny and quit talking when I show up. Malloy bawled me out yesterday. Was afraid he would jump me. He made threats.

July 16. That old fox J. R. has trapped B. S. Looks like they have got B. wriggling in a cleft stick.

There were no more entries. The last one must have been made a few hours before the death of Flack. The man had evidently begun to get anxious lest his treachery be discovered, but he had not guessed that retribution was so near. The sheriff knew that his visit to the Pitchfork had precipitated the murder. It had developed the fact that somebody was betraying the homesteaders. Suspicion had fallen on Flack. Perhaps his neighbors already had evidence implicating him and this had been the last nail in his coffin.

Humphreys had spent the night at the Quartercircle D C. Sherrill himself had not left the ranch unless it had been after midnight, but one of his riders might have crossed the hogback with word of Flack's treachery. It had to be that way, if the killing had resulted from his share in the conspiracy to discredit the homesteaders by faking a raid. Unless Daly had sent them word who his informant was—a supposition absurd on the face of it—nobody but Sherrill had been present at the Pitchfork investigation who could have spread the news, except himself and the government men. The sheriff did not like the conclusion to which this was driving him, but he could find no escape from it.

Cal Malloy was named in the diary. He might be the actual killer. Malloy was a plump tubby man with a round moon face, well thought of by his neighbors, ready to divide with any of them what he had. But back of his amiable kindliness there was a steely nature with a vindictive streak. He gave loyalty, and he expected it in return. How far his anger would take him Humphreys did not know, but at present the sheriff made him his number one suspect.

Back of the murder—the real cause of it—ran the sinister plotting of Jeff Randall. That was quite clear to the officer. The old schemer could not be touched by the law, but if he had not been trying to get the better of his enemies by foul means, Flack would still have been alive. The diary would have to be offered in evidence at the trial of the man or men against whom proof of guilt piled up. Whether it hurt them or not, it would certainly ruin Randall's influence with the cattlemen whom he now led.

Bruce Asks a Question

XXV

Brand Applegate brought the news to the Bar B B that Flack had been found dead in his cabin by Sheriff Humphreys.

'Who did it?' his father asked.

'They don't know yet. Some of his own crowd. There was a note pinned on his breast saying they had shot him because he was betraying them.'

Linda was dishing up the potatoes for dinner. She stopped, to ask a question of her father. 'I suppose Flack was the one who told in advance of that raid when Ben was shot,' she said.

The cattleman nodded. 'No harm in your knowing now. That was the way of it. The little scoundrel was selling his saddle.'

'And they found out?'

'Must have. Those things get out in the end. You can't keep a secret known to half a dozen people.'

'Who does Tim suspect of killing him?' she asked.

Brand took the dish of potatoes from her and helped himself liberally. 'He doesn't say. But it came out while he was at the Pitchfork that somebody was giving information to Uncle Jeff.

Bruce Sherrill was the only one of the other side there.'

'So they think he did it?' Linda inquired quickly.

'Search me,' her brother answered. 'He might have passed the word on and had somebody else do it.'

'Or he might not be guilty at all.'

Brand agreed. 'I can give you a dozen names to put in a hat. Pick out any one, and it might be right.'

Nonetheless Linda's heart was heavy with dread. Sherrill had been in the raid. That was known, by reason of his hat found on the scene. It was logical to think he must have had something to do with the killing of the man who had betrayed them.

After dinner Ben saddled two horses and Linda rode with him to the Cross Roads store. A few supplies were needed at the ranch, not enough to justify a trip to Redrock.

'Do you think Bruce Sherrill killed this man?' she asked her cousin after a long silence.

'He might have,' Ben replied. 'A man does crazy things. Look at how I came close to killing Pete Engle.'

'Yes, but this is different. Whoever did this went up to the man's cabin to murder him. It was a cold-blooded killing.'

When they rode up to the store half an hour

later, a man came out of the building to the hitch rack where his horse was tied. Linda felt a queer excitement pulsing through her body. The man was Bruce Sherrill. He waited for the cousins to dismount, uncertain of the greeting he might receive.

Ben nodded to him, stiffly, but did not speak. He answered silently with a slight bow.

Linda said, her eyes drilling into his, 'I hear a friend of yours has been killed.'

He retorted quietly, 'No friend of mine.'

'An enemy, perhaps,' she challenged.

He brushed aside indirection. 'What are you driving at, Miss Applegate? Say it plainly.'

She knew the urgent impulse in her had carried her too far, but she had to go on now. 'Do you know who killed this man Flack?'

His steady eyes mocked her. 'No. Do you?'

'He was a spy. Somebody must have found it out. He was killed in revenge.'

'You're wrong.' His voice was hard and cold. 'He was killed because somebody was afraid of him.'

'Afraid of him?' she repeated, not understanding what he meant. 'Why would people fear him?'

'He knew too much, and under pressure he would have talked. He had to be destroyed before he told what he knew.'

She shook her head. 'That doesn't mean anything to me. What did he know, except that he was betraying his side?'

'He knew there was no raid on the Pitchfork pasture Thursday night, that he had been paid to tell a cooked-up lie to Daly—and to give Cairns an old hat of mine to show I had been there.'

'But there *was* a raid,' she flung back. 'Several Pitchfork steers were killed.'

'By Cairns probably—to prejudice the government men against us homesteaders.'

Linda turned puzzled eyes on her cousin. 'Does that make sense to you—that Mr. Daly would kill his own stock?'

'I know Daly wouldn't,' Ben told her. His hostile eyes fastened on the owner of the Quartercircle D C. 'He's up against it, Lindy, and has to find a story that will shift the blame to our side. So there wasn't any raid, and his friends weren't sore at Flack for double-crossing them, and it was the Pitchfork that was in a jam and rubbed out the spy. He didn't think up a good enough yarn to get away with it. That one is too thin.'

Bruce knew the facts must be as he had said. He had been up and down the creeks and talked with every homesteader within a range of a dozen miles. That none of them had anything to do with the murder of Flack he was convinced. But he realized that unless proof of guilt was established elsewhere few would believe in the innocence of the small settlers. The obvious explanation of the spy's death was that he had been blotted out by some of his angry neighbors in punishment for what he had done.

It was of slight importance to Bruce what Ben Randall thought of him, but the desire was strong in him to set himself right with Linda Applegate. He put a blunt, sharp question to her.

'Do you think I murdered Flack?'

The words, the stern eyes, the clean pride of the man shown in the fine set of head and shoulders, were a challenge not only to her judgment but to her emotions. A heat flamed up in her as when a match is put to tow. There was a sudden gladness in her, the quick music of joy bells ringing in her heart. She knew, beyond any need of evidence, in spite of any testimony that might be piled up against him, that good was in him and not evil.

She said, her low husky voice a little tremulous, 'I'm sure you didn't.'

Her answer took Sherrill as much by surprise as it did her cousin. She had been a great deal in his thoughts since she had come into his life at its most dangerous hour to save him from imminent death. The girl was a lovely creature, slim and tall, with a light free step that reminded him of the meadowlark's song in spring. What was it in a woman's eyes and lips, the turn of her head, the powdered freckles beside her nose, that set her apart from all others of her sex? And deeper yet, what was that electric spark which drew a man and a girl together, in close kinship of the spirit, regardless of their will to hate and of circumstances that made them enemies?

Ben said, with flippant irony, 'Flack probably shot himself by accident while he was cleaning a gun, then after he was dead went out and flung the gun in the creek.'

'Or it might be this way,' Bruce suggested. 'The man who hired him as a spy was afraid he might not stay hired and thought it a good idea to get rid of him before it was too late.'

'Maybe you would like to name this man who hired him and later killed him,' Ben prompted, his voice low and even.

Bruce shook his head. He knew that he and young Randall were thinking of the same man, but he did not intend to go out of his way to start premature trouble. 'Not now,' he replied. 'All I could do is guess—and my guess might not be any better than yours.'

'Or as good,' Ben told him scornfully. 'Come on, Lindy. What are we waiting here for?'

Linda looked at Bruce, trust and trouble in her shining eyes, then turned and followed her cousin into the store.

Bruce Argues His Case

XXVI

Tim Humphreys went to Merritt Charlton, the county prosecuting attorney, with the information he had gathered about the killing of Flack. Charlton listened to the story and read the diary. He shook his head. There was no evidence pointing to the actual murderer, though it was a fair guess that one of the creek settlers had shot him on account of his spying. The sheriff had looked into the threat made by Malloy. Two or three men had been present at the time, and they agreed that it had been a warning rather than a threat.

'It may be one of his neighbors killed him, but I don't see how we are going to find out who unless those in the know start talking,' the lawyer said.

'I asked Sherrill to drop in to your office,' the sheriff said. 'He ought to be here any minute.'

'Does he claim to have evidence?'

Humphreys told what he had found out about the raid while at the Pitchfork. The assertion of Bruce that there had not been any raid was backed up by what Flack had written in the diary. If this was true, Bill Cairns had a potent reason for closing the mouth of the man who might have ruined him. One of the ranch riders had mentioned casually, with no idea of the fact's possible importance, that on the night of the sixteenth he had seen the foreman slip into the corral, saddle, and ride away. The cowboy had supposed he was going to see a woman.

Bruce walked into the office, greeted the men, tossed his hat on the table, and sat down. He grinned cheerfully at Charlton. 'Not guilty, Mr. Prosecutor,' he said.

'Can you say as much for all your friends?' the attorney asked bluntly.

'I'm sure I can,' Bruce answered. 'We wanted Flack alive very much. Inside of twenty-four hours we could have proved by him the raid on the Pitchfork was a fake. They beat us to him and rubbed out our witness.'

'You say he was your witness. That may be just a bluff. If the other side had him in their pay, why would he go back on them?'

'Because when we got after him he would not have had the sand in his craw to stand out. Flack was a weak sister.'

'Can you prove Flack was a spy?'

Bruce had to agree he could not. But he believed that Daly would admit it now the man was dead. In point of fact he had to be a spy or the contention of the cattlemen that the creek settlers had killed him in revenge fell to the ground.

'He was a paid spy,' Humphreys admitted. 'We have evidence of that, and we feel sure that you suspected it.'

'I did. But he was not worth killing. We shut him out of our confidence. Think this through, Charlton. This last raid was a frame-up to get us in bad with the government men. When Tim began making inquiries about the raid, somebody got frightened for fear the truth would come out. There was one way to prevent that, by getting rid of Flack.'

That might be true, the prosecuting attorney assented, but on the other hand the homesteaders had a grievance against Flack and one of them might have taken this way to settle it. Bruce pointed out that these covered-wagon settlers were not violent people. They had come from communities where law prevailed. They did not carry guns, as many of the cowboys did. Nor were they used to making their own law, as cattlemen had been forced to do in earlier days and to some extent still did. Living in older districts as tenant farmers had tamed their insurgent impulses.

Charlton shrugged his shoulders. He had observed that the most subdued man in the world was sometimes capable of murder. Blandly he suggested that Bruce was at that moment carrying a six-shooter.

'I belong to another breed of cats,' Bruce told him.

'That's not a fair argument, Charlton,' the sheriff said. 'The cattlemen feel very bitterly toward Bruce, and their riders hold this feeling too. While we were at the Pitchfork the other day some of the boys from its bunkhouse very nearly got to shooting. Bruce would be foolish not to carry a gun for protection.'

'I'm not accusing him of killing Flack,' answered Charlton. 'Fact is—not for publication—I would pick a man on the other side. But that's only a guess.'

'You mean Bill Cairns,' Humphreys prompted.

'I'm not saying his name.'

'If you happen to be looking in the direction of Cairns, you might take a glance at the Big Mogul behind him,' Bruce said. 'At the man who pulls the strings and makes his puppets jump.'

Charlton leaned back in his chair and gazed at the ranchman wearily. 'Give me some evidence and I'll look at him.'

Bruce turned to the sheriff. 'It might be interesting to find out if Quint Milroy has a good alibi for the night Flack was killed.'

'If he were to tell me he was asleep in his cabin, would you have any way to prove it wasn't true?' Humphreys asked.

'Just a shot in the dark,' Bruce admitted. 'He may be innocent as Mary's little lamb.'

The owner of the Quartercircle D C had not expected the sheriff to welcome Milroy as a suspect with any enthusiasm. Tim would do his duty. If there was any lead pointing to the man, Humphreys would look into it thoroughly, but he was not going to antagonize Milroy on an unsupported guess.

The prosecuting attorney raised a point. 'Could Flack have got your hat without anybody seeing him around your place?' he asked.

'Easily,' Bruce told him. 'We are often all away from the house hours at a time. Not far away. Say down in the pasture. He could have slipped in without being seen.'

Humphreys rose. 'Well, I've got to get back to my office. By the way, Bruce, Mr. Barnard wants to see you before he leaves. He is starting for Washington tomorrow. He'll be at the hotel here tonight.'

'Has he given you any line as to how he feels?' Bruce inquired.

'No. He is close-mouthed. I had a long talk with him today. He asked a lot of questions about Jeff Randall. You might as well know. Flack left a diary. He was Randall's man and got forty dollars for stealing your hat and telling Daly you were going to raid his ranch.'

'That helps,' Bruce said eagerly. 'It helps a lot. Randall is in this now. He has a motive for killing Flack.'

Charlton spoke a word of caution. 'The diary doesn't say Jeff Randall. It says J. R.'

'Same thing. Does Barnard know about the diary?'

'Yes. He and Sawyer have read it. Would you like to see it?'

'Very much.' Bruce read what was written in the notebook and returned it to the prosecutor. 'Thanks a great deal, Charlton.'

'I don't know that I ought to have shown it to you,' the lawyer replied. 'But I don't think you had anything to do with this killing.'

Bruce had a long talk with the two government men at the hotel that evening. They questioned him closely on every angle of the trouble between the cattlemen and the homesteaders. What they wanted were facts, and they offered no opinion of their own. One point struck Bruce as favorable. A great many of their queries had to do with Jeff Randall, his relation to the other cattlemen and his attitude toward the small settlers as shown by his actions.

XXVII

The decision of the administration at Washington was a stunning surprise to those of the cattlemen who had fenced government land. It came in the form of an order to take down within thirty days all fences enclosing land belonging to the federal state. Messages flew back and forth between the offending ranchmen and their congressmen. Senators called on the President and received no satisfaction. Jeff Randall went back himself, met the man in the White House, and did not help his standing with him by getting into a passion in which he said bluntly he would be damned if he would take down his fences. He had a title to the use of the land established by long custom and he was not going to be euchred out of it.

Jeff came home in a towering rage. It did not improve his temper to discover that Daly, Applegate, and the other stockmen who had been his allies in pre-empting illegally were busy tearing down barb-wire in obedience to the order. To find them very cool to him was a shock. Humphreys had shown them the notebook left by Flack. They had long resented the ramrod ways of the owner of the Diamond Tail, and it was more than they could stomach to learn that he had killed a friendly neighbor's cattle and hurt rather than helped their cause with the authorities. He realized that his influence over them was gone and that now he was practically a lone wolf in the community.

Cairns showed up at the Diamond Tail the day after Randall's return. He had been discharged by Daly after a severe tongue-lashing and had spent the time while Jeff was at Washington in heavy drinking at Redrock. The two men quarreled bitterly, but ended by burying their resentment and entering into a treaty of offense and defense. Each of them needed the other, since both were in bad odor. So the former foreman of the Pitchfork went on Randall's pay roll.

Rod remonstrated with his father about the hiring of Cairns. He knew the old man was bent on revenge and that Cairns would egg him on to folly that might ruin him.

'You can't afford to take Bill on,' he urged. 'The fellow is completely discredited. It is generally believed that he murdered Flack. Why tie him around yore neck when you are in bad yourself?'

'I'll take on anyone I like,' Jeff stormed. 'You may be a quitter like your brother Ben, but I'm going through to a finish.'

'What's the sense in being bullheaded when you know you're licked?' Rod asked. 'No man can fight the United States government. And to hire Cairns now is like waving a red rag in front of a wild bull. All the neighbors will resent it.'

'Let 'em. I don't care a cuss how they feel.' He glared at his son. 'Or anybody else.'

Rod was one man on the ranch who was not afraid of Jeff. He said, casually: 'You can't quarrel with me, because I won't have it that way. And when you get hell-in-the-neck like you have now I'm not going to pussyfoot and tell you it's fine. That man in the White House is just as tough as you are. Knuckle down before it is too late.'

'I wouldn't give up if I knew he was going to send me to the pen for the rest of my life,' the old man roared. 'I'll not pull down a single rod of fencing. If he doesn't like it he can lump it.'

'He'll like it fine,' Rod said dryly. 'All he'll do is sic the law on you. I like a good fighter, but I don't see any sense in one trying to butt his head through a stone wall.'

But old Jeff was beyond caution. If he could not rule he would ruin. He felt that even his own family had turned against him. He could not settle scores with all those who had fought him and those who were now deserting him, but at least he could destroy the one whom he thought the originator of all his troubles.

The bitter bile so filled him that he wanted his enemy to know the destruction of all his hopes, the defeat of his plans, before the man went out himself in the crash of his fortunes. Jeff was no longer sure of all his men. Even tough reckless cowboys became sensitive to the pressure of public opinion. His hatred of Sherrill they could understand and respect. What they could not forgive was the raid he had engineered on a friend's stock. One of his riders had quit. Two or three others were sullen and critical. He would have to move adroitly to involve them in his schemes. Quint Milroy he could depend upon. The man had a dour loyalty to the one that paid him. And since Cairns now had nobody else to whom he could turn he would go through if he could do so without too much danger. There was a big brutal quarter-breed called Rudy who would do anything for money, and a sidekick of his named Fox who always followed Rudy. Jeff could not count his son Rod in to obey orders. That young man's reactions were unpredictable. He was violent enough. Given what he considered sufficient cause, he might stand up and shoot it out with Sherrill. But he had standards he would not violate. It did not make Jeff any happier to know that Rod's code had been his once, before the lust for power had grown stronger than his principles.

One afternoon Rod met Linda and her brother Brand in the hills driving a bunch of strays back to Bar B B range. The girl was wearing old Levi's, high-heeled boots, and a dusty sombrero droopy with age. But the boy's clothes she wore could not conceal the grace of her slim, lithe figure or the beauty of her vivid face. Rod had not seen her since the day he had broken with her at the Applegate ranch. It gave him a stab of pain to find her so lovely, but no sign of this touched his immobile countenance.

They stopped to chat. All talk in this cattle country now came shortly to the one absorbing topic, the order of the government to tear down fences illegally built.

'I hear Uncle Jeff is standing pat,' Brand said.

'Yes, he's hell-bent to get into a federal prison. No arguing him out of it.' Rod smiled, ruefully. 'I don't know whether he thinks he's too big a man for the law to make an example of, or whether he is just so bullheaded he is going to ram-stam it through. He has got the idea that all the rest of us are quitters. Since I told him what I thought he doesn't talk with me about it anymore. He and that scoundrel Bill Cairns sit with their heads together cooking up trouble.'

'What kind of trouble?' Linda asked.

Rod looked at her. 'He did not tell me what kind.'

Her heart sank. 'It's too bad he has taken in Cairns,' she said. 'Folks think the fellow killed that man Flack.'

He lifted his shoulders in a shrug. 'Does it

220

matter who killed Flack? He was selling his friends down the river.'

'Whoever did it is a murderer. That matters, doesn't it?'

Rod agreed. 'Yes. That was no way to kill a man. But since Flack was what he was, I'm not going to get into a sweat about who rubbed him out. He's better dead.'

He spoke with sharp decision. Linda did not argue the point. He might be right. In any case there was no profit in disagreeing with him.

She and her brother picked up the cattle again and pushed them down to their own range. She was worried. With Cairns beside him to whisper revenge in his ears Jeff was not likely to sit with folded hands waiting until the government made him a prisoner. He would settle the score with at least one man first.

The day was hot and the air filled with the dust stirred up by the moving cattle. Linda had offered to help Brand because she felt restless. It was sometimes a relief to get on a horse and face the sweep of the wind against her body. But today was an exception.

After a long silence she said, 'I'm glad Rod stood up to Uncle Jeff.'

'Rod is all right.' Brand added an explanation. 'Uncle Jeff is like an old bull who has been boss of the herd a long time. He starts snorting and pawing up the ground when competition shows

221

up, and nothing will convince the old-timer he isn't still tops but a whale of a licking. That's what Uncle Jeff is pointing for right now.'

Linda realized this, but the worst of it was that before the old man was made harmless he could do damage beyond repair.

The Applegates See Red

XXVIII

Linda swung from the saddle and handed the reins to Brand. 'I'm so hot and dirty I'm going down to the swimming hole,' she said.

'You're in luck,' he replied. 'I won't have time till dark.'

She went into the house and got a towel and soap, after which she found fresh underwear, a petticoat, dress, and shoes. These she carried with her. The swimming hole was about three hundred yards from the house. Before undressing she ran up a white flag to the top of a pole her father had put there. When the flag was flying, all the men on the ranch knew that Linda was using the pool and gave it a wide berth.

She dived from a big flat rock into the cool water and swam leisurely across to the trunk of a dead tree on the opposite side of the creek. Here she relaxed, taking it easy. Holding to the stub of a branch, she splashed water with her feet. Not far away a meadowlark was flinging out its full-throated song. She floated lazily, and peace began to flow into her soul.

The sound of a breaking twig startled her. The girl's glance swept across the stream. Bill Cairns was stepping onto the big rock from which she had dived.

His tobacco-stained teeth showed in a wide lewd grin. 'In case you don't know me, I'm Bill Cairns, the fellow you have never thought about,' he said.

From her brothers she had heard the man had been drinking hard ever since his disgrace, and she could see that though he might not be drunk now he was under the influence of liquor.

'You had better go away quickly,' Linda said. She was holding to the broken branch of the tree, sunken in the water up to her throat.

'Why, I've just come, my dear,' he jeered. 'Rode a long way, and got a nice eyeful. If you want to hit me again, come right out and do it. Remember last time I was here? Lookin' for that wolf Sherrill, and you having him hid in yore bedroom all the time. You ain't got him under the water there now, have you?'

'Go, you fool!' she ordered. 'You know what my father or my brothers will do if they come.'

He sat down on the rock, fingering her clothes with his hairy hands. 'But they're not coming,' he exulted. 'We're here alone, you and the man who isn't good enough for you to spit on.'

'If you don't go I'll call for help,' she warned.

'I wouldn't do that,' he mocked. 'I'm toting a gun, and they'll come running without any—if they hear you at all.'

'Haven't you any sense? Don't you know you'll be hunted down like a coyote and shot on sight if you don't stop bothering me?'

'Now let's talk that over. I haven't lifted a finger to you. I'm just sittin' on a rock by a creek enjoyin' the beauties of nature. It's a free country. A fellow can go and come as he pleases.' He broke off, struck by the change in her. She was looking past him at something that held her eyes fixed. 'What's the matter, girl?' His eyes slewed around, and his jaw dropped.

Brand Applegate was standing not five yards from him, a revolver pointed at Cairns.

'Don't kill him,' Linda cried.

Her brother's eyes were hard and ice-cold. 'I'll teach him to play his dirty tricks on you,' he said. 'Get up, you rat, and keep your hands away from that gun.'

'He's drunk, Brand,' the girl urged. 'Remember that. Don't shoot him.'

Brand stepped forward, drew the man's revolver from its holster, and flung it into the creek. 'I won't kill him this time,' he promised. 'I'm going to hammer him with my fists till he can't stand. Get going, fellow. We're heading for the house. You haven't a thimbleful of brains, or you wouldn't have left your horse where I could run on to it.'

Cairns was frightened. 'I wasn't aimin' to hurt

her any, Brand,' he wheedled. 'You know that. Jest havin' a little fun.'

The forty-five prodded into his back. 'Don't talk!' Brand snapped. 'Get moving.'

As soon as the men had gone, Linda swam back to the rock and dressed hurriedly. She left the discarded boots, Levi's, and shirt where they lay. Cairns was a big muscular fellow, twenty pounds heavier than her brother, and a notorious bruiser. He might beat Brand badly and shoot him with his own gun. She ran toward the house.

While she was still a hundred yards away, she caught sight of the fighting men. They were not standing toe to toe slogging it out. Brand was too wise for that. He was a good boxer, and he was making the most of it. Though not as strong as his foe, young Applegate was hard as nails. He had not flung away his stamina in dissipation. Hard punishing blows sank into the bully's belly and made him grunt. Slashing right- and left-handers bruised his face and cut it. Cairns was breathing fast, his wind already gone. His flailing fists went wild, landing mostly on Brand's arms and shoulders.

Linda had to pass near them to get into the house. Since she was no longer worried about her brother, she had stopped running. But only for a moment. Cairns broke away from the fight, to get Brand's revolver lying on the porch. The girl beat

226

him to it and whipped the gun from the floor as she ran.

The big man turned, to meet Brand crowding close.

'I've had enough,' he bawled. 'I give up.'

The younger man's fist struck his nose and set blood trickling. 'I haven't started yet,' Brand told him.

Cairns covered up to protect his face. The jarring blows pounded his stomach. His knees bent and he sank to the ground.

'Get up,' Brand snarled.

Nothing less than an earthquake would have brought the beaten man to his feet. He lay there cowering. Brand glared at him disgusted.

Linda caught her brother's wrist. 'No more, Brand—please.'

'All right.' He pushed the toe of his boot into the fallen man's ribs. 'Get up and light outa here. Don't ever show your face on this ranch again.'

As Cairns rose heavily to his feet, Cliff Applegate and his younger son rode into the yard. The ranchman's gaze took in the ruffian's battered, bleeding face, his cowed manner, and the harsh anger of Brand. He swung from the saddle and moved forward, a quirt dangling from his wrist. His eyes demanded an explanation from his son.

'Lindy went down to the swimming hole after

we got back,' Brand told him. 'I found him sitting on the rock deviling her.'

'She was in swimming?' Cliff asked.

'Yes. I brought him back here and whaled him.'

'He's just leaving, Father,' the girl said hurriedly. 'I think maybe he was drunk.'

'Go into the house, Lindy,' the cattleman ordered, his strong fingers closing on the handle of the quirt.

Linda turned and went into the house, closing the door behind her. She heard the frightened protest of the victim, followed by a howl of pain, and she hurried to the back of the house to escape the sounds of the whistling quirt and the yelps of the unhappy wretch enduring it.

Presently there was silence. She looked out of a window. Young Cliff was bringing the horse of Cairns from the place where he had left it. The beaten man stumbled to the horse and clung to the horn to support himself. He tried two or three times to lift his foot to the stirrup and could not make it. When at last he got his boot into it, he had hardly the strength to drag himself to the hull. Slowly he rode away, shoulders bowed and both hands fastened in a tight grip to the pommel.

Linda went into the kitchen and sank down into a chair beside the table. She knew by the surging inside her that she was going to be sick.

Bud Wong noted her white face and colorless lips. 'Missy not feel well,' he said.

Through a window he had seen the last part of the fight and the subsequent quirting. He guessed that somehow she was involved in the trouble.

'I'm sick,' she told him. 'Go away, please.'

She was moving to the sink as he vanished.

After a time she felt better physically, but the whole incident was something dreadful to remember. She was unhappy and much distressed. The picture of the coarse scoundrel fingering her clothes and gloating over her nakedness sent waves of shame through her. Why were men such beasts? And why did her father and brother feel it helped to beat the fellow into a state of whimpering cowardice?

She knew that Cairns had got off lightly according to the code of the frontier. If Brand had shot him down few would have censured him. There was no sympathy for the fellow in her thoughts, only a sense of somehow having been soiled.

Old Jeff Sympathizes

XXIX

Cairns lay on a hillside above the Diamond Tail ranch house until long after dark. He waited until the light in the bunkhouse went out and only one was left in the main building. Everybody had gone to bed except old Jeff. He could go down now unnoticed.

He was very stiff and sore. The least movement would send pains jumping through his body. When he had looked at his legs a while ago, he had been sorry for himself. They were ridged with purple wheals where the quirt had wound around them like a rope of fire.

Though the clothes rubbing against his flesh made walking painful, he could not face the torture of getting into the saddle again. Leading the horse, he went down a draw to the house. From the back of the root house he watched to make sure nobody would see him. His vanity could not endure witnesses to his humiliation. He would have to let old Jeff see him, but nobody else.

Jeff was muddling over his accounts when Cairns opened the door of the office. He looked up, and was startled at what he saw.

'Great Caesar's ghost!' he exclaimed. 'Have you been tangling with a panther?'

'Gimme a drink,' Cairns said hoarsely.

Jeff got a bottle and a glass. The battered man poured out and drank enough for three men.

'Who in Mexico did that to you?' Randall asked.

Cairns lied. 'The Applegates jumped me, all three of them. They pounded me till I couldn't stand, then the boys held me while the old devil wore himself out quirting me.'

'What for?'

'I happened to drop down to the creek while that little vixen Lindy was taking a bath. Brand covered me with a gun. He made out I was down there spying on her. After he got me to the house they all jumped me.'

Randall took the story with several grains of salt, but he did not intend to say so. He was going to be a Good Samaritan and tie the humiliated man to him by sympathetic kindness.

'They're a high-handed bunch of lunkheads, Bill.' He shoved a chair in the direction of his visitor. 'Sit down and tell me about it.'

'I can't sit down,' Cairns explained angrily. 'My thighs hurt like hell. I'll have to go to bed and stay there for a week.'

Jeff suppressed a chuckle. 'Too bad. I've got some ointment might help them.'

'I'm not going to the bunkhouse. You'll have

231

to let me stay at the house.' Cairns ripped out a furious oath. 'This has got to be kept quiet. I won't have your riders getting funny with me. I'll gun any one of them that does.'

'I'll fix that,' Jeff said in a soothing voice. 'You can have the room next to ours. Nobody will need to see you except Mary and me. Better tell me all about it now, so that if anything gets out I'll know what to say.'

Cairns went into details, suppressing some and inventing others that would put him in a better light. The ranchman nodded his head, a sly wise smile on his face.

'She could have saved you, Lindy could, if she'd had a mind to do it. All she needed to say was that you had dropped down to the creek to wash up, account of its being so hot a day. And why didn't she? Because you made that crack about Sherrill in her bedroom. Now don't misunderstand me. The girl is straight as a string. But I've heard she is crazy about that fellow. You made her mad, and she let her men folks beat you up. You can blame Sherrill for that.'

'I don't have to blame anybody but the Applegates, and you bet I'll take care of them someday,' Cairns replied with bitter venom.

'You're not lookin' at this right, Bill,' the older man told him. 'The Applegates aren't going to spill a word of what happened, account of it might embarrass Lindy to have folks talking. But if you do any one of them a meanness the whole story will come out. You know how popular the girl is with all the young fellows. One of them sure would fix your clock. Listen. You want to pay her back for what she let them do to you, don't you? There's one sure way. Hit her through the man she is in love with.'

Randall did not stress this any further at the moment. He had sown a seed in the man's mind that later might germinate. Cairns was a jealous cantankerous brute, and also revengeful. The old man thought he could prod the fellow's urge to kill in the right direction.

Cairns was up and about in two days but he looked, as one of the boys in the bunkhouse said in an aside, 'like a harrow had run over his face.' The sarcastic comment of his neighbor was that it was an improvement at that. Bill was too overbearing to be a popular citizen. Jeff had given the boys as an explanation of his new employee's plight the story that he had been thrown by his mount in rocky ground. The Diamond Tail riders had accepted this in skeptical silence, broken by a big tough fellow called Rudy. His comment was, 'I reckon his bronc must of picked him up again after it throwed him and then jounced him up and down on the other side of his face.'

One of the cowpunchers asked Cairns which horse in his string had piled him, but Bill flew to anger so swiftly that others decided not to try questions with a sting to them. Of late they had revised their opinion of Bill. The fellow had thrown down his outfit and they felt contempt for him. But he was a big cranky bully who could use his fists and there was no use inviting trouble with him. The men at the bunkhouse knew that somebody had given him a terrible beating and they discussed among themselves who it could be. 'If I knew who he was the guy would be right popular with me,' Rudy drawled. 'Maybe he has got Mr. Cairns so tame I won't have to knock his ears down myself.'

Rod returned from Redrock and reported to his father a rumor he had heard. A fellow had told it to him just as he was leaving town. There might be nothing to it. The country was full of all sorts of wild guesses these days. This might be just a pipe dream. The story was that the sheriff had uncovered a witness who had actually seen Flack murdered.

While he repeated the rumor Rod watched the old man, for there had been moments when he suspected his father of knowing too much about the killing of Flack. But the old man did not bat an eye. He made a casual comment, then asked his son how the market for beef stuff was standing up.

But inside of the hour Jeff was having a private talk with Quint Milroy. The killer told him not to worry. He was satisfied that nobody had seen him either going or coming. Any fool could start a story of that sort to make himself momentarily important. Jeff agreed that was true, but he could not keep a small worry from gnawing at his mind.

Sherrill and Applegate Ride Together

XXX

Prop Zang came to Sheriff Humphreys with an odd story. He had recently employed to help him at the corral a young cowpuncher named Sim Tepley who had been riding through this country on the chuck line. An old-timer who did odd jobs when he was not drunk had been sleeping in the hay at the barn of the Elephant one night and awakened to hear voices in one of the stalls below. One of the two in conversation was Tepley, the other a range rider he had known in Montana. Next day old Libby came to Zang and told him what he had heard.

In strict confidence Tepley had let out to his friend that he felt sure he had seen the murderer of Flack a few minutes after the killing. The night of the crime he had camped on the creek a couple of hundred yards below Flack's cabin. He had been riding all day and reached the park late. Before he reached the house, the light went out. He decided to wait until morning, then drop in on whoever lived there in time to join him at breakfast.

Later in the night he had been awakened by

the sound of a horse's hoofs on the trail a few yards from him. The traveler was heading for the cabin. Tepley was not interested and settled himself to go to sleep again, but before he could do so the sound of a pistol shot startled him. He heard presently the noise of an approaching horse, probably the same rider returning. The itinerant cowboy was curious. He was not exactly disturbed, but he was at least interested. He crept close to the trail and crouched back of a thick clump of bushes. The mounted man passed within four feet of him.

When it ought to be breakfast time, Tepley saw no smoke rising from the cabin chimney. The owner might be a late riser. After a time, warned by his stomach that he needed food, the puncher rode closer and halloed the house without result. He opened the door and found a man lying dead on the floor.

It did not take Tepley long to get out of the park, and not only the park but that part of the district. He was a stranger and might easily become suspect. The best course was to keep his mouth shut. This he had done until the night he met an old friend upon whom he could rely.

The sheriff and the prosecuting attorney put Tepley through a stiff questioning. At first the cowboy denied the whole tale, but after he had made sure they held no thought of his own guilt, he threw up his hands and admitted its truth. He had been close enough to get a good look at the man who was probably the killer and thought he would recognize him if they met again.

Humphreys decided to tour the district with Tepley and give him a chance to look over the inhabitants. But first he had to make sure this new development was kept secret. Five men in addition to Tepley had heard the story. That was too many. The weak link in the chain was Libby. The sheriff considered flinging him in jail for a few days as a vagrant, but he could not bring himself to hurt the harmless old fellow's feelings. He warned him earnestly not to tell anybody what he had learned. Unfortunately the old toper drank too much that night and babbled his story to a roomful in a saloon. It was the first time in years he had been given a chance to be important.

With Tepley posing as his deputy, Humphreys had left town that afternoon and did not find out that Libby had broadcast all he knew. The two men talked with every homesteader on Squaw Creek and crossed over the hogback to the Quartercircle D C. There they spent the night. In the morning they rode to the Bar B B, in time to see its riders before they set off to work. Nobody they had yet met was the horseman Tepley had seen riding from Flack's place.

The Applegates were pleased to have Humphreys drop in and Linda insisted he and his companion stay for dinner. The sheriff was sorry he had not time. They had to get on to the Diamond Tail to talk with Randall. It was more than an hour after they had left that Bruce Sherrill rode up to the house on a horse that had been ridden hard.

Linda came to the door. 'You!' she cried, surprised.

He had scarcely time to say good morning before blurting out, 'Is the sheriff here?'

'No, he left a little while ago,' the girl told him. 'Has something happened?'

'It may, if I don't reach him in time. Can I get a fresh horse?'

Linda's father came to the porch from the house. 'Why don't you come at night?' he asked. 'Then you could take one without a by-your-leave, as you did last time.'

'I'm sorry, Mr. Applegate,' Bruce answered. 'This is urgent. I'm afraid there will be a killing, unless I can head off Humphreys.'

'What do you mean—a killing?' the ranchman demanded. 'Who is going to get killed?'

'Maybe nobody. Maybe I'm worried about nothing. But I don't think so. An hour ago a man just back from Redrock dropped in at the ranch. He says the talk is buzzing all over town that the young man Humphreys has with him, the one he claims is his deputy, is a witness to the killing of Flack. They have been all up and down Squaw and Bear creeks, over to my place, and then here.

239

This Tepley claims he would know the man again if he saw him. That's the story they are telling. Tim is giving him a chance to look us all over.'

'What's wrong with that?' Applegate wanted to know. 'It will suit me fine if they find the scoundrel and arrest him.'

'They won't arrest him. They'll be shot down. Humphreys doesn't know it has got out that Tepley is a witness to the killing. He'll be knocked off without a chance for his life—he and Tepley too.'

'You're assuming he'll run across the guilty man,' Applegate differed. 'Chances are ten to one he won't.'

Bruce looked at him hard and long. 'He'll find the man if they go to the Diamond Tail. The murderer has to be one of two men—Bill Cairns or Quint Milroy. Do you think either one of them would let Tepley get back to Redrock alive if it is true he can identify the killer?'

Cliff Applegate's eyes held fast to those of the younger man. He was thinking this out, and Bruce could see he did not like the thoughts trooping through his mind. The ranchman had read the diary Flack had left. He knew that the latest raid on the Pitchfork had been framed by Cairns and Jeff Randall, that Flack might easily become a dangerous witness against them. Cairns was the kind of man to commit a cowardly murder to save himself, but it would be like him to involve somebody else in it too if he could. Applegate no longer had any dealings with old Jeff, but after all the man was his brother-in-law. It shocked him to think Randall might have let himself get trapped in so evil a business. If Quint Milroy had any part in this, it had been at the instigation of the man who employed him.

The cattleman spoke to his daughter sharply. 'Tell Grant to saddle Buck for me. I'm going over to the Diamond Tail. Have him rope Nugget for Sherrill.'

He went into the house for his Winchester. Bruce walked beside Linda to the stable, leading his spent horse.

She said, 'Do you think Uncle Jeff had anything to do with this?'

'I don't know,' he answered. 'I believe the killing was hatched at the Diamond Tail, but if Cairns did it he might have played a lone hand.'

'I hope you catch Mr. Humphreys before he reaches the Diamond Tail. It isn't safe for you there, or for Father either.'

Bruce told her he did not think old Jeff hated Cliff Applegate that much.

'It's not Uncle Jeff. It's that Bill Cairns.' Embarrassment brought a deeper color to her cheeks. 'Something happened here the other day. The man—overstepped himself. Father gave him a terrible beating. We weren't going to talk about it, but—I wish he weren't going to the Diamond Tail while the fellow is there.'

'I'll keep an eye on Cairns while your father is around,' Bruce promised. 'With so many of us about he can't do anything.'

'Thank you.' Her face still flushed, she tried to explain away the appeal she had not quite put into words. 'I don't know why I ask this of you, since you have so many more enemies there than he has. And anyhow, you are not one of us. I have no right to expect you to watch out for him.'

He said, his voice low and gentle: 'Not long ago a girl looked out for me, an enemy of her family. She saved me from my foes, who were ready to pounce on and kill me. She fought for me against her father and her brothers. She dressed my wound and she nursed me. And more than all that she believed in me when others didn't.'

Linda felt a queer sense of weakness, of stilled pulses, followed by a clamor of the blood, by a warm gladness flooding her bosom. She did not dare to look at him. When she spoke, her words were an evasion, the first irrelevant ones that came to her lips.

'I'm glad we have two horses in the corral and won't lose time running some up.'

She watched the two men ride away. Her father's manner was still stiff toward Sherrill, as though he wanted it understood that they might be allies for the moment with no friendship involved. But at least Applegate no longer cherished bitter enmity. The situation had changed, and he was adapting himself to it. Linda thought perhaps he held a reluctant admiration for Bruce, a feeling he certainly would not admit.

What Linda felt was a little frightening. When Bruce looked at her she had a sense of being drawn to him irresistibly. Her will became fluid. Probably if he whispered 'Come' she would run to him. When she was alone at night she chastised herself for being such a fool. But she knew the truth, that if anything happened to him the light would go out of her life.

XXXI

Humphreys gave his pseudo-deputy instructions as they came down the hill to the Diamond Tail ranch house.

'Listen, Sim,' he said. 'If the killer is either of the fellows I think it is, he is too dangerous to arrest here. I wouldn't get away with it. One in particular is a notorious bad man, a dead shot and chain lightning on the draw. Don't let him know you have ever seen him before. I'll get him to town somehow and arrest him there. You can let me know he's the one we want by giving that bandanna round your neck a pull to straighten it.'

The moment Jeff Randall saw them the bleached blue eyes in the weathered face narrowed warily. Not an hour earlier a messenger had reached him with a story confirming what Rod had been told and adding that the sheriff and the new witness, a wandering cowboy named Sim Tepley, were traveling through the district to identify the guilty man.

Quint Milroy was out in the big pasture helping to drive home a bunch of calves, but he might get back at any minute. It was very important this Tepley should not meet him.

'Have to excuse me just a minute, Humphreys,' the cattleman said. 'I got to tell one of my boys how to fix up a horse got cut by bob-wire. Be back in a minute. Make yourselves at home.'

The sheriff was suspicious of this explanation, but he could see no ground for his mistrust, even when he saw through the window the old man talking with Cairns.

Randall rejoined them and suggested a drink. Humphreys declined. He was a teetotaler. Tepley took two fingers of whiskey and washed it down with water.

The ranchman asked how the Flack case was coming on. Had the sheriff made up his mind who had shot the man? Not yet, the officer admitted. There was not much evidence on which to go. Randall said his best guess was that scoundrel Sherrill. He was a bad character and had plenty of reason to want to get rid of the spy.

From his seat the sheriff saw Cairns ride out of the yard and wondered where he was going. His mind was not easy. They discussed the fencing order.

'Mine stay up,' the cattleman announced bluntly.

'Afraid you'll have trouble,' Humphreys commented. 'I think the President has his dander up and means to go through.'

The door opened and Quint Milroy walked into the room. He had a bunch of mail in his hand.

'Didn't you see Bill?' Randall asked sharply.

'No. Is he looking for me? I swung across the pasture to pick up the mail as I came back.'

Tepley was busy adjusting the bandanna around his throat. The sheriff said: 'Quint, meet Sim Tepley. Sim, this is Mr. Quint Milroy.'

Taken by surprise, the cowboy stared at the newcomer unhappily. It was disturbing to discover that the man whom his testimony might send to the gallows was the most notorious gunman in the Northwest. To find this out sent a shock of alarm through him. If the killer became aware of what he knew, his chances of living long would be slight. He made a gesture as if to step forward and shake hands, but Milroy did not meet the advance. The killer never shook hands. Once he had seen a man shot down by another while his right hand was held fast.

'Tepley is the sheriff's new deputy,' Randall explained.

With the still hard-eyed wariness that distinguished him, Milroy looked the young man over. Tepley was probably only a cipher in his life, but since he was a law officer he was worth attention. There was always a chance that they might come into conflict. It amused him to see how the mere mention of his name had startled the young fellow. He was used to that look on the faces of those who met him for the first time. His reputation inspired awe. They did not talk with him casually and freely, but chose their words carefully in order not to give offence.

'New in this neighborhood, aren't you?' Randall asked Tepley.

The young man said he was, and privately thought it would be a good one to leave. He added that he had been working on the 3 D ranch near Miles City, Montana.

'But you thought you'd rather come here and be a deputy sheriff,' the old man suggested.

'Well, it wasn't quite thataway,' Tepley answered. 'When I got to Redrock I was riding the chuck line. I happened to meet Mr. Humphreys and he took me on for a tryout.'

'I see.' The old man rubbed his unshaven chin with the palm of his hand, faded eyes fastened on the unhappy youth. 'And do you like being a man-hunter?'

The sheriff smiled. 'That's a kind of big word, Jeff, for a little job. Nine tenths of a sheriff's work is just routine. I brought Sim along on this jaunt so he could get the hang of it.'

Randall tittered. 'Not to get the hang on someone here, I hope.'

Humphreys laughed obligingly at the pun. 'Well, I reckon we better be drifting, Sim,' he said.

The cattleman had other ideas. 'You're going to stay for dinner,' he announced flatly.

This left the sheriff no choice. The custom of

the ranch country was that anybody dropping in before a meal time stayed to eat. Without discourtesy he could not decline.

While Milroy and the two guests were washing up for dinner a half-hour later, using the tin basins on a bench outside the house, Cairns came into the yard at a road gait. He pulled up to stare at them in surprise. Before he could say a word, Jeff called him sharply to the porch. The man swung from the saddle and joined his employer. As Humphreys dried his face, he noticed that Randall was giving Cairns murmured instructions.

Cairns gobbled his dinner fast and left. A few minutes later Milroy also departed. There was nothing unusual about this. Riders in the ranch country went to the table to eat and after they had finished withdrew from the room. Dining was not a formal function. But Humphreys felt a bell of danger ringing in him. It was time to get away from here, he thought, if not already too late. Yet his mind could give him no justifiable reason for this apprehension.

While the sheriff and his companion saddled, they saw nothing of Cairns and Milroy. Over a hill trail Rod dropped down to the ranch. He had been checking the feed on the bench land above with a view to pushing some more stock up from the valley pastures. The presence of the departing guests surprised him. He exchanged

248

greetings with Humphreys and took a long look at Tepley.

'Tim's new deputy,' Jeff explained. 'Just giving their ponies a workout.' His son caught the sarcasm in the old man's words.

Rod did not answer. His eyes had shifted to the road that ran down from the ridge to the ranch house. Two riders were descending it.

'Looks like Uncle Cliff,' he said. Astonished, he cried a moment later, 'And the man with him is that fellow Sherrill.'

'Sherrill! What's he doing here?' Old Jeff's voice held the rasp of anger.

'I reckon we're going to find that out,' Rod said quietly.

The riders drew up at the porch.

'Nice to see you again, Cliff,' Jeff snapped ironically. 'I see you brought a friend with you.'

'No friend of mine,' Applegate dissented. 'He had a little business with the sheriff, and I thought maybe I'd better come along.'

'Brought yore rifle in case you met a bear on the way,' Jeff snorted.

'I don't know exactly why I brought it,' Cliff replied, 'except that fireworks seem to go off when Sherrill is around.'

Rod said to Bruce, 'Your business with the sheriff to give yourself up for gunning Flack?'

Bruce retorted, looking him steadily in the eye, 'Private business.'

Jeff exploded. 'Don't bring yore private business here, damn you, unless you want yore head shot off.'

The sheriff interposed. 'We're just leaving, Bruce. Unless you want to stay, you can ride with us.'

'That will suit me fine,' Bruce said.

'It will suit us too,' Rod added.

Jeff was searching the reason for this visit and the effect it might have on plans he had made. His brother-in-law and Sherrill had come, of course, to help the sheriff in case any protection was needed. Word must have reached them that Tepley was the witness who had seen the killer of Flack, and they believed that the murderer was connected with the Diamond Tail outfit. It pleased Jeff to have Sherrill ride back with Humphreys. Given good luck, the men lying in wait for Tepley would get him too. But he did not want Applegate to be one of the party. If Cairns had a chance, he would certainly shoot Cliff down too. For two reasons that would be bad medicine. The owner of the Bar B B was too big a man in the community. His death would stir up a tremendous row. And though Jeff had been angry at Cliff, still was in fact, his anger did not run to a deep hatred. He expected some day to patch up the quarrel with him.

'Since you are here, Cliff, you'd better get off

and rest yore saddle,' Jeff said. 'I haven't had a chin with you for a long time.'

Cliff was surprised at this invitation. It was as near an apology as one could expect from Randall. But Cliff was stiff-necked, with a proper sense of pride. He felt that Jeff had grossly insulted him, and he did not intend to show any eagerness to resume cordial relations. He was not going to let Jeff get the idea that he could be kicked out and picked up again easily.

'Some other day, Jeff,' he said with some constraint. 'I'm too busy to stop now.'

'You weren't too busy to ride all the way over here with this scalawag Sherrill,' Jeff told him, bristling.

'I didn't want him to come alone,' Cliff said bluntly. 'If your invitation holds we'll come over some other time.'

'Don't bother,' Jeff flung out angrily. 'It's now or never.'

'Just as you say.' Cliff turned to the sheriff. 'If you're ready we'll start, Tim.'

Jeff watched them go, then turned abruptly and shambled into the house. Half an hour later he hunted up Rod.

'Boy, slap a saddle on yore bronc and ride after your uncle,' he said. 'I'm scared something will happen to him. Bill Cairns may have seen him come and be watching to get him. Cliff gave him a terrible quirting the other day and he's hell-bent to get even.'

'Why didn't you tell me sooner?' Rod demanded, heading for the corral.

'I kept gettin' more worried, thinkin' it over. Likely there's no sense in worrying. Still, if that fool Cairns did take a crack at him there would be hell to pay.'

Five minutes later Rod rode out of the yard at a gallop.

A Two-Way Trail

XXXII

Sheriff Humphreys waited till they had topped the ridge at the lip of the valley and were out of sight of the ranch house before he burst out with the indignant question he had been holding back.

'What have you to say to me, Bruce, so danged important it brought you busting in to the Diamond Tail where you are as welcome as a hydrophobia skunk?'

Applegate answered for Sherrill. He was annoyed because he had let himself be stampeded into going to his brother-in-law's place when there was no need of it. 'He got goosey for you, Tim. Word came from Redrock that yore new deputy is an important witness in the Flack case, and that you had brought him along to identify the killer. He was so het up I got to worrying too. I ought to have had better sense.'

Bruce explained, apologetically. 'I was playing a hunch, Tim, that the fellow who killed Flack lives at the Diamond Tail. If he does—and if word had reached him that you were bringing Tepley to identify the murderer, I thought you two wouldn't be good insurance risks.'

The sheriff stared at him, but his eyes were looking at details that began to piece themselves together in his mind. The whisperings of Randall and Cairns. Bill riding out to intercept Milroy and missing him because he had detoured to get the mail. The look on old Jeff's face when Milroy walked into the room. His keeping the two visitors for dinner. The hurried departure of Cairns and Milroy.

What had been a vague sense of danger sharpened to a certainty. Somewhere on the road to the Bar B B, gunmen were now lying in the thick brush to close forever the mouth of the witness.

Humphreys said sharply, 'You're right, Bruce. If you hadn't warned us neither Tepley nor I would have reached the Bar B B alive.'

'Now you've gone crazy with the heat too, Tim,' scoffed Applegate. He did not want to believe a cold-blooded killing could have been planned at the Diamond Tail.

'Tell him your story,' the sheriff said to his deputy.

The cowboy repeated what he knew. He was willing to take oath that Quint Milroy was the man he had seen riding from Flack's cabin just after the shot had been fired.

Applegate was unhappy. He did not doubt that Tepley was telling the truth, and he was sure that if Milroy had killed Flack, it had been

254

done at Jeff's order. He understood now why Randall had tried to detain him at the ranch. Even though he had quarreled with Cliff, he did not want him to be trapped in an ambush set for others.

'If they mean to bushwhack us, what spot would they pick?' Humphreys asked.

'The only good place would be at the gulch the other side of Tucker's Prong,' Applegate answered. 'The ground is hilly, with plenty of brush, and a trail winds up the gulch by which they could get back to the Diamond Tail without being seen.'

'That trail leads two ways,' Bruce drawled.

The cattleman caught his meaning. 'So it does. If we strike it above us here, it will take us to the gully where they are lying, assuming that it is true they are out to get you and Tepley, Tim.'

'You mean we could surprise them and capture Milroy now,' the sheriff said.

'That's what I mean,' Applegate replied. His eyes were hard and chill. There was a cold lump in his stomach. What he was going to do might bring disaster to a man who was a relative by marriage and had once been his close friend. But he had to find out the truth. Mingled with his heartache was anger. He was not going to condone the drygulching of a friend.

'I'll have to swear you in as deputies,' Humphreys said.

Bruce remembered his promise to Linda and regretted his suggestion.

'Three of us will be enough,' he said. 'I don't think Mr. Applegate need go. Randall will regard this as a personal fight on him, and we don't want to start trouble among relatives.'

Cliff turned on him, resentful antagonism in his bleak eyes. 'If you will kindly let me run my own business, sir,' he said.

Bruce had nothing more to say. He knew his attempt to exclude Applegate had been crude, but it was the best he could think of at the moment. The ranchman was justified in thinking it presumptuous.

They passed through a gate into a Diamond Tail pasture. This they crossed, ascending by a grade that got steadily sharper to the plateau above. After leaving the pasture, they struck a trail and followed it. This was ground that Applegate had covered fifty times. He knew it as a man does the palm of his hand. It was still open range, and his cattle mingled with the Diamond Tail stock to feed on it.

They rode for miles along the rim of the plateau, at times close to the edge from which they could look down into the valley below and across at the sandstone cliffs that defined the opposite limit of the floor, and again farther back in the rolling park country they were traversing.

Applegate drew up in a cluster of pines and

swung from the saddle. They were on Tucker's Prong, which jutted out into the valley from the adjoining rock rim like a folded thumb from the knuckles of a fist. The other three dismounted, tying their horses to young trees as Cliff was doing. He led them into the upper neck of the gulch that dropped down to the road below.

'No talking,' he ordered. 'And don't make any noise. When we get far enough down so that I can see them, I'll give you a signal. The gulch opens up near the bottom. There's a lot of brush. You'll have to be very careful how you move. We'll spread out. Lie low till you hear me give the order to Milroy to drop his gun. I don't know how near we can get to them without being seen.'

The sheriff added a word. 'We are here to capture Milroy. If we can do it without any shooting, fine. We must not hurt either Milroy or Cairns, except in absolute self-defense.'

'If they make a break to escape when I throw down on them, don't kill them,' Cliff said. 'Shoot their horses.'

Though his eyes scanned the cañon below him carefully, Applegate took the first quarter of a mile at a steady walk. As he got lower he moved more slowly. One of the Diamond Tail men might be stationed higher than the other, to make sure a chance range rider did not drift down on his way to the road. At a bend in the gulch he raised a hand in warning. The others joined him. Below

257

them the cañon opened to a greater width, the floor of it covered with a thick tangle of bushes. If their guess about the ambushers was correct, the men were concealed somewhere in that deep carpet of vegetation.

'We'd better separate here,' the sheriff directed. 'You creep down close to the left wall, Tepley. I'll be next you, with Sherrill on my right. Then Applegate. We must try to keep abreast of one another. We're going to have a heck of a time getting through the brush without being heard.'

The shrubbery was thicker in the center than it was closer to the walls. Bruce knew they were near the mouth of the gulch and that the road could not be far below them. Somewhere in the next hundred yards they would sight the ambushers. He moved very carefully, not taking a step without scanning the terrain in front of him. Each time he set down a foot he had to be sure a dead branch did not snap, and as he parted bushes to make way for his rifle and his body he had to know there would not be a rustling to betray his presence.

Back of a rock slab projecting from the wall he caught sight of horses. A guard was with them. Bruce recognized the man, Mose Fox, a Diamond Tail cowboy. Since he was here, the rider of the fourth horse was probably his pal Rudy.

A rifle crashed, and the echo of it went roaring down the gulch. The trigger of Sim Tepley's rifle had caught on a twig. There was an agitation in the bushes below, the parting of branches as men scurried through the thicket to reach better cover.

Cliff Applegate rose from back of a rock, rifle in hand. 'Stay right where you are, Milroy,' he ordered. 'I've got the drop on you.'

The head and shoulders of the sheriff appeared above the scrub oak. 'Don't make any trouble, boys,' he shouted. 'The law wants Milroy.'

It flashed through the mind of Bruce that this was a foolhardy thing for both of them to do, though he realized that Humphreys' hand had been forced by the cattleman, who in turn had been pushed prematurely to show himself by the accidental discharge of the deputy's gun.

The challenge brought the Diamond Tail gunmen to activity. A bullet from a Winchester whipped up the gorge. Applegate swayed on his feet and went down back of the boulder. Bruce fired at the spot from which the smoke came. A man running low dodged from the brush and made for a pile of rocks near the wall. As Bruce raised to fire again he recognized Cairns. The man flung himself back of the boulders, apparently not hit.

The cañon was filled with the sound of gun explosions beating against the cliffs. Bruce caught a glimpse of Applegate's head and rifle lifted above the sandstone outcrop behind which

259

he crouched and heard the smash of the slug against stone.

Tepley cried, 'I'm hit.'

A voice, shrill with panic, shouted, 'We'd better get outa here.' Cairns, Bruce decided. A moment later he saw the man edging among the rocks toward the horses.

Applegate fired. A horse gave a shrill whinny of pain and sank to its knees. The other ponies, wild with fear, tore through the brush toward the road. Cairns caught the bridle of one, swung to the saddle, and crouched low on the neck of the animal as it galloped through the slapping scrub oak.

Fox ducked out from the pocket formed by the rock slab to follow Cairns. A bullet from the sheriff's rifle stopped him. He stumbled and fell.

'I give up,' he cried, repeating the words several times.

Bruce became aware of bushes rustling to the left, not far from the wall. The foliage moved. Somebody was creeping up to reach Tepley, somebody who wanted to finish a job he had started, one very important to him.

Sherrill wormed his way back of the sheriff, traveling on hands and knees, hitching the rifle forward as he went. He was in a hurry.

Humphreys murmured, 'They've got Applegate and Tepley.'

'One of them is coming up to make sure of Tepley,' Bruce answered in a whisper.

A bullet whistled past him just as he reached the cowboy. Since he could not see the fellow who had sent it Bruce guessed the man had fired on the chance of a hit.

'I'm wounded,' Tepley said.

Bruce nodded. 'He's on the way up now to get you. You hit bad?'

'I dunno. In the side. Don't leave me.'

'I won't. We'll get to that big rock.'

Tepley edged along, supported by Bruce. Another bullet whined through the shrubbery. Bruce did not fire but kept going. He did not want the sharpshooter to know their exact location.

The cowboy slumped down, exhausted, back of the boulder. Bruce waited, crouched beside him, his rifle half-raised.

There was a lull in the shooting, broken by a shot from the draw, not far above the road. That would be Rudy, Bruce guessed. Cairns was galloping away from the danger zone, Fox was wounded and out of the battle, and Milroy was crawling up through the underbrush to destroy the witness who could hang him. Since there had been only four horses, there could be only four of the ambushing party. Tepley alive was a danger to one of them, and that one was Quint Milroy.

Bruce Takes a Prisoner

XXXIII

A heavy screen of foliage burgeoned out beside the rock that gave cover to Sherrill and the wounded cowboy and through this Bruce could check on the man stalking Tepley. Once or twice he caught sight of a part of an arm or leg. Yet he did not fire. He was convinced that Milroy did not know he had joined Tepley and had not spotted the exact position of his victim.

An idea was buzzing through the head of Bruce. The gunman was moving directly toward their rock. It might be possible to capture him alive. Bruce whispered to his companion not to make the least sound. The enemy was scarcely forty feet distant.

Humphreys saw the moving bushes and flung a bullet at what they might conceal. The desperado must have realized the brush was not dense enough to give him cover. He fired once in the direction of the shot and made a dash for the boulder.

Bruce could have killed him, but he waited. Milroy was delivering himself into his hands. The Diamond Tail gun fighter clawed his way up a short steep bank below the rock and flung himself on hands and knees behind it. For one startled fraction of a second horror stared out of his eyes. Before he could lift a finger the barrel of a rifle crashed down on his head. The limbs and body of the man relaxed instantly. He was out. Bruce took the bandanna from his throat and tied securely behind his back the hands of the captive.

He called to the sheriff, 'I've got Milroy.'

Humphreys came across the hillside, looked down at the unconscious man, and then at Bruce.

'You had a chance to kill him,' he said.

'Thought you said you wanted him alive.'

'So I do, but I said that before they shot up our friends . . . How is Sim?'

'I haven't had time to look.' Bruce knelt beside the young man, took off his coat, and unbuttoned his shirt. Luck had been with Tepley. The bullet had made only a flesh wound. It had struck a pipe in his pocket, been deflected, and plowed through muscular tissue without piercing the rib.

'I'll leave you to take care of him, Tim,' Bruce said. 'Want to get across and see how Applegate is.'

'Go carefully,' the sheriff warned. 'One of them may still be down there ready to plug you.'

'Better take a look at Milroy before he wakes up. I may not have tied his hands tight enough.'

Humphreys drew handcuffs from his pocket and fastened them on the prisoner.

No shots from below interfered with the

passage of Sherrill across the gulch. It was probable that Rudy had either caught one of the horses or was making his escape on foot.

Bruce found the cattleman sitting behind his rock shelter, the rifle across his knees. 'Hell in Georgia for a while,' he mentioned grimly. 'Tim and his deputy all right?'

'Tepley was hit. In the side. A glancing bullet. He ought to make it all right. How about you, sir?'

'One in the shoulder, kindness of Cairns, I think.'

'Yes. I took a crack at him as he ran for the rocks, but I don't think I hit him.' Bruce suggested he had better look at the wound.

'All right. That fellow Fox is down just below us. Every time he hears a shot he yells for me not to kill him.'

While Bruce examined the shoulder he told Applegate that they had captured Milroy.

'Wounded him first, I reckon?'

'No. He got too close to where I was hidden and I knocked him out with the barrel of my rifle.'

A voice hailed them from the road. It asked if Cliff Applegate was there.

'Reinforcements, for our side or theirs,' Cliff decided. 'Ask him who he is and what he wants.'

The man below replied that he was Rod Randall. His father had got worried and sent him.

'Tell him I'm here, and for him to come up if he is alone,' Cliff said.

Bruce shouted the message. Voices from the road drifted to them. Rod called up that he had been alone, but the Applegate boys had just joined him.

'You all right, Father?' someone asked.

'That's Brand,' the cattleman told Bruce. 'I reckon Lindy got worried and sent the boys when they got home.'

The three young men came up through the mouth of the gulch and joined them.

'You're hurt,' Brand cried, after one look at his father.

'I'll make the grade,' the cattleman told him. 'This fellow patched me up fine. There's a Diamond Tail rider near the rocks who has been shot up some. One of you better look after him.'

'Do you know who these scoundrels attacking you are, Uncle Cliff?' Rod demanded angrily.

The ranchman looked at young Randall with no friendliness in his frosty eyes. 'I know three of them and can guess at the fourth,' he said sourly. 'If you want to make sure who he is, better ask Jeff.'

Rod said, 'You ought to know Father wouldn't try to do you any harm.' He added, to back his claim. 'When he found Bill Cairns missing, he was scared the fellow meant to waylay you and sent me to warn you.'

'Good of him,' the cattleman told Rod bitterly. 'I'm certainly grateful to him. Did he send Milroy and this crybaby Fox with you?'

Bruce cut in. This was no time for angry argument. 'We have three wounded men on our hands—maybe four—two of them prisoners. First thing is to get them out of here to some place where a doctor can look after them.'

'The Bar B B is nearest,' Brand said, looking doubtfully at his father. 'But we're not prepared to take care of that many.'

'You won't have to,' Bruce explained. 'Tim can take Milroy to town with him in a wagon—and Tepley too. I don't know how badly Fox is hurt.'

'He has been making enough fuss,' the cattleman said scornfully. His gaze fastened on Rod. 'If he has a friend here he had better go look after the fellow.'

Rod answered stiffly. 'I'm particular who my friends are. I don't include drygulchers any more than you do. But I'll take a look at him.'

Randall turned and walked to the wounded cowboy. He was both angry and unhappy. The explanation his father had given him did not cover the situation. Cairns might have lain in ambush to attack Cliff Applegate, but the other three men would not have been with him without orders from old Jeff. He understood why his father had sent him to warn Cliff. Warped though his standards had become, he could not let his

266

former friend, the uncle of his children, walk blindly into a trap set for others.

What was he to do? Milroy would probably keep his mouth shut, but if pressure was put on Fox he might tell all he knew. Rod had to save his father if he could. The first thing he must find out how deeply Fox could implicate Jeff.

The cowboy was shot in the right thigh. There was a good deal of blood around the wound, but no arteries had been cut. While Rod was giving first aid, he questioned the man. He learned that Jeff had not talked with Fox before the party set out to intercept the sheriff. Rudy had got him to come, and Rudy's instructions had reached him through Quint Milroy and not direct from the boss. It might be worse, Rod reflected. If Cairns and Milroy did not blab, the old man might have an out, though of course he would be suspected.

One detail in the story Fox told him gave Rod a gleam of hope. The first shot had come from the sheriff's party. Rod drilled into the wounded man the point that this was an anchor post upon which to tie the defense. His party had been pushing Diamond Tail stock down the gulch when somebody began shooting at them. This had started the battle. He must stick to that regardless of the pressure put upon him. If he held fast to that, Rod promised to see he had a good lawyer and money to fight the case. If he did not, the ranch would cut loose from him and leave him to his fate.

After Rod had done what he could for Fox, he crossed the gulch to have a talk with Milroy. The gunman would expect the Diamond Tail to get him out of this trouble and Rod wanted to assure him that it would stand back of him. There was a better chance to see the prisoner alone now than there would be later. Young Cliff had gone up to the top of the Prong to bring down the horses left in the grove. Brand was on his way to the Bar B B to get a wagon. He noticed that Sherrill was hovering around their father, perhaps to protect him against the possible return of Cairns, with an occasional eye directed toward Fox to prevent any attempt at escape.

Humphreys asked Rod how badly wounded were Applegate and Fox. Randall thought they would both pull through and inquired about Tepley. The sheriff and Tepley had been lucky.

Rod thought all the wounded were fortunate. 'About a pint of lead spilled and not a coroner's case in the lot,' he said, and then pointed a question at Humphreys that was meant to make a suggestion to the prisoner. 'How come you to start shooting at our boys while they were driving stock down the gulch?'

'So that's going to be your story,' the sheriff replied.

'Am I wrong?' Rod persisted. 'Didn't you fire first?'

'One of our guns went off by accident.'

Rod's skeptical smile was grim. 'By accident? That sounds to me, sheriff. You start shooting and four men are wounded. Then you claim an accident. I say it's a damned outrage, and to top it you have Quint handcuffed. For defending himself, I reckon.'

'Milroy is under arrest for the murder of Flack,' Humphreys answered. 'Before anybody was hurt, I told your men I had a posse to capture him. That started the fireworks. Cairns shot down Applegate.'

'If Cairns did that, he is through at the Diamond Tail. But I'll have to get more than your word for it, Humphreys.' Randall spoke with a cool arrogance that admitted no doubt. 'And as for that nonsense about Quint shooting Flack, no unbiased person will believe a word of it. I don't suppose Quint ever spoke ten sentences to the man.'

'Not five,' Milroy corrected, his voice even and low. Inside, the man was boiling with rage, but this showed only in the bleak deadly menace of the eyes. His anger was at Sherrill, who had brought him to this humiliating pass.

He knew that Rod was giving him assurance of support at his trials, but this was not enough. He did not intend that there should ever be a trial.

Long before that he meant to be free and out of the country.

'Like to have a word alone with Quint,' Rod said to the officer.

Humphreys had expected this. He nodded consent. 'Walk over to that fault in the wall—after you have left your gun here, Rod. No shenanigan. I'll drill a hole in Milroy if you make one false move.'

'I'm not a fool,' Rod retorted irritably, and laid his revolver on a rock.

He walked beside the prisoner the seven or eight steps to the cliff. The two men spoke in whispers.

'I'm not going to lie cooped up in jail,' Milroy said flatly. 'Tell Jeff he has got to get me out right away.'

The words were a threat. Rod realized that. If Jeff did not rescue him he would talk.

'We'll get you out, if I have to tear down the jail,' Rod promised.

'See you do,' Milroy ordered. 'Soon as I'm free I mean to kill that devil Sherrill and light out from here.'

Rod did not comment on that.

XXXIV

Rod slammed an ultimatum at his father straight from the shoulder. 'You're in one hell of a jam,' he said. 'You're bucking the government, and the law at home here. All your friends have quit you. The homesteaders have got it in for you, and the stockmen won't support you an inch of the way. I don't want to hear how deep you are in the Flack killing. But I can tell you this. You've come to the end of your rambunctious bullheaded course. The rest of your life will be spent in the penitentiary—unless you show some sense. Either you do what I say or I fork my bronc and get out of here for good.'

Jeff looked at his strong reckless son and knew he dare not let him go. The old man looked ten years older than he had a few weeks earlier. Everything had gone wrong for him. He could no longer find comfort in his family or his possessions. The position he had held in the community was lost. The doors of a prison were opening for him. His nerves were jumpy, and he could not sleep nights.

'What do you want me to do?' he asked.

'First, kick Bill Cairns out and tell him never

to show his face on the place again. Next, give orders to the boys to begin tearing down the fences on government land tomorrow. You have only a week left to get them down.'

'You give them the orders,' Jeff said. 'I just can't do it. If I've got to back water let me save face. But what about Quint? You know I've tried to get them to let me go bail, and they won't do it.'

'I'll take care of Quint.' Rod looked through the window and saw Cairns crossing the yard. He leaned out and called the man. 'Come here, Bill.'

Cairns stood in the doorway. 'Want me?' he asked.

Rod looked the man over contemptuously. 'Pack yore things, then come and get your time. You're through here. Get out and don't ever come back or I'll set the dogs on you.'

The big ruffian's face turned purple with rage.

'You boss of this outfit?' the man demanded, and slid an ugly look at the old man.

'Don't talk back,' Rod ordered. 'Get going.'

'Jeff can still talk, can't he? He hired me. It's up to him to fire me, if that's what he wants.'

'I told you to let Cliff Applegate alone,' Jeff snapped. 'But you were hell-bent on getting even with him for the quirting he gave you. When a man works for me, he can't grind his own corn in my mill. What Rod has told you goes.'

'Fine,' Cairns retorted bitterly. 'I do yore dirty

work for you and lose out at the Pitchfork. I'm to get the Quartercircle D C ranch after you have bumped off Sherrill. Instead I get the boot. You're a fine character, Jeff. By God, you would double-cross yore mother. But you won't get away with this. I'll spill everything I know—and that's plenty.'

The big man backed away hurriedly as Rod advanced toward him. 'Don't you!' he cried. 'Don't you dare touch me.'

He was close to the edge of the porch when Rod's fist lashed out and caught him just under the chin. His head snapped back, and he went off the porch, shoulders and buttocks hitting the ground together. For a few moments he lay there, jarred and shaken, before he got heavily to his feet. He glared at his assailant furiously. The man's fingers almost touched the revolver butt at his hip. Rod was not wearing a coat. Cairns could see he was unarmed. Now was the time to send a slug into the flat stomach of the arrogant fool.

But Cairns could not do it. Not with the fearless eyes fixed on him scornfully. And presently the urge to kill subsided. It would be a crazy thing to do. He would never get off the ranch alive.

'I'll remember this, Jeff,' he said to the ranchman grinning in the doorway back of his son. 'You can't do this to me and get away with it. Sure as God made little apples I'll fix you for this.'

He turned and walked to the corral. Fifteen minutes later he rode out of the yard. A bilious hatred boiled in him, of Jeff far more than of his son. Rod did not owe him anything. What he had done had been for his father. But the old man was in his debt plenty. In serving Jeff he had lost a good job and become an outcast. Now the ranchman was repudiating him to save his own skin.

Cairns did not go to Redrock. If he hung around there on a drinking spree, Humphreys would probably arrest him. He went to a hog ranch he knew twenty miles down the river where he could get drunk without interruption and plan revenge.

Rod decided not to tell his father what his scheme was for freeing Milroy. He meant to play a lone hand, and it was safer to take nobody into his confidence. After breakfast the day following the departure of Cairns, he left for Redrock on a bay horse he had recently bought, one that did not carry the Diamond Tail brand. His first call was at the office of the sheriff, to get a permit to visit Milroy with a view to discussing with the prisoner the retaining of an attorney for the defense.

To this Humphreys could not very well object, though he told Randall he would have to search him to make sure he was not carrying a weapon. They decided that since it was a little late Rod should see Milroy the following day.

The sheriff walked with Rod to the jail next morning and personally took the young man to the cell where Milroy was confined. He did not offer to unlock the cell, since the men could talk as well with the bars between them. But he did leave them alone for a private talk.

Milroy let Rod do most of the talking. He fixed his dead heavy-lidded eyes steadily on the young man and listened.

'It ought to work,' he said at last.

'Looks to me almost foolproof,' Rod answered. 'Cairns would probably find a way to bungle it if he was in your place, but you won't. It is safe and easy. You get out without hurting the jailor. That's important.' The eyes of Randall held steadily to those of the bad man. 'Schmidt is married and has three kids. If you kill him you are sunk. I'll help see you never get away alive. But there needn't be any shooting. He'll give up soon as you cover him.'

'Don't threaten me, Rod. I won't take it.' Milroy spoke in a soft even voice like the purr of a cat, one as chill as a blizzard-laden north wind.

'Use your head, Quint,' Randall said impatiently. 'I know your record. What I said was for your sake as well as for Schmidt.'

'I don't get jumpy and kill when it isn't necessary,' Milroy reminded him.

Rod opened his vest and unwound from his body a long length of string. He handed it through the bars to the prisoner, who at once concealed it under the mattress of his cot.

'The best time for the break would be tomorrow morning early if you can make it then,' Rod suggested. 'There aren't many folks around before church time Sunday.'

'Schmidt brings my breakfast about seven. That would be all right with me.'

'Good. The horse will be in that clump of cottonwoods about a hundred yards south of the jail. You'd better make straight for the Colorado line, Quint.'

The deadpan face of the killer was blank of expression. 'I'll consider your advice,' he said.

Humphreys came back into the room. 'You boys finished your talk?' he asked amiably.

Rod grinned at him with friendly impudence. 'We're going to get Tom Black of Denver to defend Quint. He'll knock hell out of your case, Tim.'

'It's not my case, Rod,' the sheriff corrected. 'I'm through when I make the arrest.'

It was nearly midnight when Milroy heard the hoot of an owl outside. He rose from the cot and went to the barred window. Neither moon nor stars lit the night. A man was standing below. Quint lowered one end of the string that had been given him. Presently there came a tug. He drew up the string carefully and took from it a revolver.

Before he put it under his pillow he discovered

that there were no cartridges in the cylinder.

The early morning sun was shining through the window when Schmidt arrived with his breakfast. While the tray was still in the jailor's hands the prisoner covered him with the revolver.

'Take it easy,' Milroy warned. 'Don't shout. Don't try to run. Put the tray on the floor and unlock the door.'

Schmidt did as he was told. Milroy tied his hands behind him with the string and gagged him, using the man's own handkerchief to stuff into his mouth, then locked him in the cell.

The prisoner walked out into the pleasant sunshine and across to the cottonwoods. Two men were moving down the street toward him less than a hundred yards distance. He did not hurry. If they showed any interest in him, he could get to the saddled horse in plenty of time. When he reached the grove he tested the stirrups to make sure they were the right length. The men passed the jail without giving him a second look. He rode from town through its struggling outskirts into open country. But the road he took was not one that would lead to Colorado. Unfinished business in Wyoming claimed his attention before he hit the long trail.

Near the point where Squaw Creek ran into the valley, he met a young Diamond Tail puncher named Dick Spears. The cowboy opened his eyes at sight of Milroy.

The gunman stopped his question. 'Never mind how I got out, Dick. Point is, I'm here. I want you to take a note to Jeff Randall.'

'Sure,' Dick said.

Milroy knew he was dependable, but after he had scribbled a few lines he stressed the need of secrecy. He was to give the note to nobody but Jeff and was to keep his mouth shut afterward.

Looking into the man's cold eyes, Dick knew he would do no talking.

A Debt Is Paid

XXXV

Before Jeff Randall reached the line cabin he knew that somebody was there or had been recently. A thin trickle of smoke rose from the stovepipe. Likely it was Jim West, one of the Diamond Tail riders. The old man jogged forward and pulled up in front of the shack. He lowered to the ground the sack of provisions he was carrying and started to swing his ungainly body from the saddle.

'Stay where you're at,' a harsh voice ordered.

Bill Cairns stood in the doorway, a rifle in his hands. It was plain that he had been on a long hard spree. He was unshaven, red-eyed, and slovenly. The expression on his face shocked Randall. The usual sullen ugly look had sharpened to one of cruel triumph.

A cold knot of fear tied up the old-timer's stomach. He knew that never in his long turbulent life had he been in greater danger. Hatred of him was surging up in this fellow's heart. The week's debauch had blurred his judgment. But Jeff never had been a coward. There was no change in his granite face, none in his slumped figure. He had to talk fast, and what he said had to be good.

'Nice to meet you again, Bill,' he replied, his voice cool and even. 'I wasn't expecting to see you here.'

'You didn't come then to kick me off yore ranch again?' Cairns jeered.

Jeff played for time. 'I reckon I was a little hasty, Bill. We can fix everything up fine, you an' me.'

'Sure. You can fix anything, damn yore lying tongue. You fixed for me to have the Quartercircle D C. Just leave it to you. You fixed me out of a good job and then double-crossed me. I was sittin' pretty till you fixed it to ruin me.'

The voice of Cairns rose almost to a scream. He was working his nerve up for the kill. Jeff realized the passion of the man was getting out of hand. Death was crowding close to him.

'I aim to satisfy you, Bill,' he said, still apparently confident that they were going to arrive at a friendly understanding. 'No reason why we should fuss after all these years. Now listen. I've got a plan—'

'Take it to hell with you,' Cairns interrupted furiously. 'You've come to the last step of yore last rotten mile.'

The rifle roared. Jeff's gray head fell forward. Slowly the heavy body slid to the ground. Cairns moved toward him. He drew a revolver and fired it into the huddled mass at his feet.

Cairns stared down at what he had done, fear

already beginning to seep through him. Even though he got away at once, Rod would suspect him. He told himself that nothing could be proved, not if he escaped unseen. Far up in the range was an old trapper's cabin. Few knew of its existence, since cattle never ranged so high. He still had left half a jug of whiskey. By stuffing a few more provisions in the gunny sack he would have food enough for a week. After that he could light out for parts unknown.

From a draw where he had left his mount he brought the animal and saddled it. Panic was starting to rise in him. He must get from here at once. His hurried glance swept the cabin, to make sure he was leaving no evidence that would betray him. Those who found Randall's body would know somebody had eaten a meal here, but they would have no way of telling who it was. He tied his roll and the sack of food back of the saddle and climbed into the hull.

Not until he had disappeared into a draw leading to the foothills did the crawling fear inside his belly subside. Give him another mile or two and he would be deep in the folds of the land waves. He came out of the draw to the ridge above, and a wave of sickness swept through him. Linda Applegate, on horseback, was watching him as he came up from the gully. After the murder was discovered, she would be a witness to prove he had been on the spot.

His first crazy impulse was to kill her. He had his Winchester half-raised before caution stopped him. She probably was not alone. His second thought was to turn and run. But this would convict him if he ever came to trial. Slowly he rode forward, his fear-filled eyes stabbing right and left in search of any companion she might have.

The girl remained where she was, motionless. He tried to smile, and his mouth twisted to a horrible grimace. His throat was so dry that when he spoke the words that came were a croak.

'Are you alone?' he asked.

The look on his face warned her. Back of the fawning smile was something dreadful and cruel. She knew he had started to kill her and had stopped.

'Of course not,' she answered, her gaze holding fast to his. 'My brothers are just over the hill rounding up strays. Do you want to see them?'

His frightened eyes swept the brow of the hill. 'No, miss. I jest happen to be here—on my way to the Diamond Tail. Came up from down the river.'

Linda felt sure he was lying and could see no reason for it. She still had an urgent sense of imminent danger, unreasonable though it was. He reminded her of a wild beast ready to pounce, held by some restraining fear. Her heart died within her. She had to fight down a rising terror.

She must not let him know she was frightened.

'You'd better go,' she warned him. 'If my brothers see you it will be too late.'

The lids over his eyes narrowed. 'You wouldn't lie to me.'

She had to go through with her bluff. 'I don't have to put up with this,' she told him contemptuously. 'I'll call them.'

'Don't you!' he snarled, and tried to cover the threat with an apologetic grin. 'I'm kinda out of sorts, Miss Lindy. Been traveling without food all day.'

Linda turned her horse up the hill and rode away. She did not look back, though she was dreadfully afraid he would shoot. As soon as she was over the brow she put her horse to a gallop. To deceive the man she tried to shout 'Brand— Cliff!' but no sound came from her frozen throat. The horse was wet with sweat when she pulled up at last, a clammy perspiration on her forehead.

If she had known it, Cairns was driving his mount just as fast in the opposite direction. He cursed the luck that had brought her here just at this moment. He would stay at the trapper's cabin overnight, but no longer.

The fugitive moved in and out among the hills, working steadily toward the blue range at the horizon's edge. When he reached the cabin Pierre Renaud had built twenty-five years before, darkness was beginning to settle over the hills.

He dismounted before the door, now sagging from its leather hinges, untied the sack, and went into the cabin.

While his eyes adjusted themselves to the semi-darkness, he stood near the door. Some stir of movement startled him. A pack rat, no doubt. But a wave of terror swept over him. The dim figure of a man was taking form.

He dropped the sack. 'Who is it?' he cried, nerves jumpy.

'Take it easy, Bill,' the answer came low and cold.

An instant relief swept away his panic. 'Goddlemighty!' he yelped irritably. 'That you, Quint? What's the sense in scaring the living daylights out of a fellow? How come you here?'

'I'll ask the questions,' Milroy said curtly. 'That grub?'

'In the sack. That's right.'

'You didn't know I was here? So Jeff didn't send you.'

Cairns hesitated. He had to be careful what he said. 'I haven't seen Jeff for a while. You expecting a message from him?'

Milroy did not intend to give out information till he knew where Cairns stood. 'Why haven't you seen him? Isn't he at the ranch?'

'I reckon he is. I been on the dodge. Humphreys got to crowdin' me, account of my wounding Applegate.'

That sounded reasonable enough, but there was an unease in the manner of Cairns that told Milroy he was concealing something. He never had trusted the big bully and he was full of doubts now. Was it possible Cairns had turned traitor and was buying his own safety by betraying Quint?

'Where did you get the grub?' Milroy demanded.

'Bought it at the Cross Roads store as I came up. Figured I would hole up here till I could make a getaway.' He dallied with the impulse to tell the truth, but decided against it. Milroy evidently still had a tie-up with the Diamond Tail.

Quint pushed his suspicion into the background of his mind. There was nothing at all fishy in the story of Cairns. Yet he meant to be on his guard every minute.

'If you have grub enough for two-three days it will save me a trip to the south boundary cabin,' he said. 'Since you are here, you had better fix us up some supper.'

Milroy mentioned that he was a little short of ammunition and helped himself to a dozen cartridges from his visitor's belt. After he had loaded his revolver, he read a copy of the Redrock *Beacon* the former foreman had brought with him. With one watchful eye on the cook he read the story of the Tucker's Prong battle and an editorial praising Sheriff Humphreys. When Cairns called 'Come and get it,' he moved to the table. As they ate they sat opposite each other.

'Seen or heard anything of that fellow Bruce Sherrill?' asked Quint.

'No, and I don't want to,' answered Cairns sourly.

His companion's reply was soft but chill. 'Different here.'

When the meal was over and Cairns had washed the dishes at his host's suggestion, Milroy mentioned that they would have separate bedrooms in order not to disturb each other by snoring. He would stay in the cabin and Bill could choose any place he liked under the starry sky.

Cairns grumbled at this, but did not press the opposition beyond saying that Quint was acting mighty funny. They both kinda had their tails in a crack and had ought to trust each other and pull together.

He picketed his horse at a grassy spot back of the house. For his own sleeping camp he chose a place nearly a quarter of a mile away from the house. He did not know of any reason why Quint should have a chip on his shoulder, but since he felt that way a fellow had better fix it so the killer could not pump lead in him while he slept.

XXXVI

Rod was sitting on the hotel porch sunning himself when Tim Humphreys and his wife passed on their way to Sunday School. Randall lifted his hat to the lady and fired an innocent question at her husband.

'What's this I hear about a prisoner walking out on you, sheriff?'

Deacon Humphreys lost his temper and temporarily his religion. 'For a thin dime, you blasted scamp, I'd throw you into jail to take Milroy's place,' he exploded. 'I ought to have known better than to trust a hellion like you out of my sight. I don't know yet how you did it, but I'll find out and when I do—'

Rod was as grave as a judge. 'What have I done, sheriff? He was in prison, and I visited him. Isn't that what your Bible teaches you to do?'

Jessie Humphreys giggled at the young man's effrontery. Her husband flung a withering look at her, and decided not to discuss the issue at present with the jaunty reprobate on the porch. He was afraid that if he stayed any longer he would not be in the right frame of mind to teach his Sunday-School class.

Randall strolled down to the Elephant corral and hired Prop's flea-bitten gray. As he swung to the saddle he was still smiling at his passage with the sheriff. He did not get many laughs nowadays, and this prison break was a double-jointed joke. One on the sheriff, and one on Milroy when he broke the revolver and found no cartridges in it.

On his way home he turned in at the side road leading to the Bar B B. He wanted to find out how Cliff was getting along and to drop a hint for relay to Sherrill.

A rider cutting across the pasture waved a hand at him. He pulled up to wait for Linda. She had been down to the box to get the mail, she said, and had ridden a few miles farther for the fun of it.

'Have a good ride?' he asked.

After a second's hesitation she told him it had been all right. She did not want to tell him or any of her family that she had met Bill Cairns and had a harrowing experience with him. The last meeting before this one had nearly resulted in the death of her father.

They found a horse tied at the hitch rack in front of the house. Linda recognized the pony and her pulse began to quicken.

'Mr. Bruce Sherrill paying a neighborly call,' Rod drawled. This suited him, since his visit had to do with the owner of the Quartercircle D C.

Cliff Applegate was lying on the sofa in the parlor talking with Bruce when they came into the room. Linda said, her voice casual, 'I think you know Rod, Mr. Sherrill.'

'We have met,' Rod said dryly.

Bruce laughed. 'We have what you might call a shooting acquaintance. Every time we meet, his friends are making a target of me.'

'Not friends of mine,' Rod differed, eying Sherrill with cool insolence. 'My friends fight in the open. Not that I'd wear any mourning if one of these brush skunks shot straight for a change.'

Cliff Applegate brought his fist down on the seat of a chair standing beside the sofa. 'It's time we ran the scoundrels out of the country, Rod. This fight about the fencing is over. We lost it when the government made its decision. These bushwhackers are paying off private grudges. The good citizens of the country won't stand for it. Either these assassins quit or we hunt them down like wolves.'

Rod's next remark seemed on the surface to bear no relation to what Applegate had said. 'By the way, there was a jail break this morning at Redrock,' he mentioned.

Though he tossed the news out lightly, all of those present guessed its significance.

'Quint Milroy?' Linda asked.

'Right first time,' Rod answered.

Bruce was not much surprised. He had not

expected the man to be a prisoner long. 'How did he pull it off?' he wanted to know.

'Threw down on Schmidt with a six-shooter when he brought him his breakfast. Somebody must have slipped him a gun. He locked Schmidt up, walked out of the jail, and found a saddled horse waiting for him in some cottonwoods near. Maybe somebody rode in to go to church and just happened to tie it there.'

'Five blocks from any church,' Bruce commented.

'Same fellow who gave him the gun left the horse,' Cliff said with decision. 'Whose horse was it?'

'Horse not yet identified.' Rod smiled blandly. 'Glad I'm in the clear. I dropped in on Quint yesterday to talk over getting him a defense lawyer to fight the silly charge he killed Flack. Humphreys is a suspicious soul. He searched me before he would let me see Quint.'

'Surely nobody would suspect you,' Bruce said, without a smile.

'Does anybody know where Milroy went after he got away?' Linda asked. 'He wouldn't come back here, would he?'

Rod rolled and lit a cigarette. 'When I talked with him the day before the getaway, he didn't mention his destination.' The dark eyes slanted toward Sherrill. 'But he did say something about unfinished business in this district.'

A cold wind blew through Linda. 'What did he mean?'

'That's anybody's guess,' Rod answered. 'What do you think he meant, Sherrill?'

'How would I know?' Bruce replied, his gaze locked to that of Randall. 'I'm not in his confidence.'

'No, I don't suppose you are.' The smoker let out a fat smoke wreath and watched it drift to the ceiling, thinning as it moved. 'He's a little annoyed at you for some reason. Maybe he doesn't like being slammed over the head with a rifle barrel. Quint is a proud man. Nobody ever got the best of him before. It got under his skin to be lugged off to jail like a drunken cowboy. He doesn't blame Humphreys. That is what a sheriff is paid for.' Rod took another drag at the cigarette and said, as if he were meditating aloud, 'I don't think I would like to be the man he has it in for.'

'If I were the man I would be grateful to the one who had told me,' Bruce said carelessly.

'If you were the man,' Randall returned, his voice as casual as that of Sherrill, 'it would be a good idea to stay under cover until Quint had said a permanent good-bye to this part of the country.'

Linda knew that Rod would not take the trouble to warn Bruce unless the danger was urgent. In spite of the fear his information had drummed up in her, the girl wondered at Rod. He had of course contrived to free Milroy, yet he had stopped to get her father to warn Bruce of his peril. The man had unpredictable impulses. She guessed some instinct for fair play in him had been the motive. If he had been a little different—if it had not been for the occasional willful streak of ruthlessness in him, she might have fallen in love with him.

Instead, she had given her heart to this man who had been an enemy of them all. The two men were much alike. Both were strong and fearless and independent. Each followed his own way of life with little regard to what others thought. Neither of them was cut to a pattern. But there was one essential difference. In spite of his recklessness Bruce was dependable, knew right from wrong and made the better choice.

Bruce rose and said he must be going.

'I'll ride with you far as the junction,' Rod suggested.

Cliff would not hear of it. 'You'll both stay for supper.'

While they ate, Cliff proposed that Sherrill remain at the Bar B B for a few days and help with the stock. One of the boys could ride over and tell Ramrod he would not be home.

Bruce shook his head. He was sorry, but he had to get back to the ranch. He had ridden over to find out how Applegate was getting along, but just now they were too busy at the Quartercircle D C for him to be gone long.

This was the answer Linda had expected, but

she could not let it rest as final. She made a chance to be with him alone.

'Why don't you stay with us?' she asked. 'You know Rod wouldn't have said what he did if he weren't sure this Milroy means to kill you.'

' "The best-laid schemes o' mice and men gang aft a-gley," ' he quoted. 'Milroy is just a man, the same as I am.'

'He's a terrible man. He won't give you a chance. If you stayed here you would be safe.'

'Safe and shamed,' he said.

She flung up a hand in a small gesture of impatient despair. 'You men are all alike. As if you were little boys being egged on to fight. You are afraid someone will think you afraid.'

'Maybe,' he agreed. 'But I can't skulk here in hiding from any man and keep my self-respect.'

'Why not?' she urged. 'You have given proof you are not a coward. To set yourself up for a mark to be shot from ambush isn't bravery. It's foolhardiness.'

'What would you think of your brother Brand if he crept into a hole because somebody thought perhaps a desperado was looking for him?'

'There isn't any perhaps about this, Bruce. Milroy told Tim Humphreys he would get you soon as he was free. He must have told Rod that too. They say he has killed a dozen men. He'll sneak up on you like an Indian. Don't go and let yourself be killed.'

They were standing on a vine-covered porch in the vague light of those few minutes when dusk is giving way to darkness. The fine planes of her face, the fear in the dark shadowed eyes, gave her the ethereal look that in the semidarkness sometimes makes even a plain woman beautiful. And Linda had never been to him anything but lovely. He had an absurd conviction that if he held her close, if he kissed those tremulous lips, their souls would fuse and become spiritually one.

'I'm not going to be killed,' he promised. 'I never had as much to live for as now.'

His hand found hers in pledge of what he said, and the pulse of her fingertips went through him like a drink of strong wine. The throbbing life in them was a symbol of the vitality of her slim warm body and vivid personality. He could remember afterward that when he drew her to him she gave a little contented sigh as her arms went around his neck.

It might have been a minute later, it might have been ten, when young Cliff's voice brought them back to earth.

'Where is Sherrill at?' he asked. 'Rod is ready to go.'

His father answered, 'He and Lindy stepped out somewhere.'

Still in her lover's arms, Linda whispered quickly, 'You won't go now.'

'I've got to go,' he told her.

'Not now that we have just found each other,' she pleaded.

'I don't like it, but this is the way it has to be. I'll be careful. You needn't worry.'

Her fingers bit into his arms. 'I won't have it,' she cried softly, passion in her voice. 'You can't go. It's senseless—and insane. All he has to do is wait in the brush and shoot you.'

'I'll be watching for him every minute.'

'I thought you loved me,' she protested. 'If you do, you are part of my life. I have a right to help decide what you will do.'

'Even you can't come between me and what I think right,' he told her, his low words asking for understanding.

Her fear was accented by what she had gone through a few hours earlier. 'Listen, Bruce,' she urged. 'I didn't mean to tell you, but I must. This afternoon I met Bill Cairns on the ridge above the south line of the Diamond Tail. He raised his rifle to kill me—and didn't fire because he was afraid I wasn't alone. I told him my brothers were just over the hill gathering strays. That saved my life. But nothing would save yours if Milroy got the drop on you.'

He stared at her, greatly disturbed. 'He must have been bluffing, unless he has gone mad. Why in God's name would he hurt you?'

'I don't know why, except that Father and

Brand gave him a terrible beating. But he wasn't bluffing. I read murder in his awful face.'

He could feel her body trembling in his arms.

'Don't ever leave the ranch until I've settled with him,' he ordered hoarsely. 'Stay near the house. Never go riding.'

'I won't, if you'll stay here too until Milroy is captured.'

'I can't do that. Don't you see I can't, Linda? No use talking. I've got to go.'

Her anxiety, the futility of its demand, broke loose in anger. 'I'm to do as you order, but it doesn't matter how much I worry when your silly pride tells you to go out and be murdered.'

She walked down the porch and into the house. Without a moment's hesitation Sherrill repeated to her father what Linda had told him of her afternoon's danger. He could feel the girl's anger beating on him for the betrayal of her confidence.

'You knew it was a secret,' she said in hot scorn.

The shocked horror of Applegate found a vent in temper. 'A secret when a villain threatens your life! Are you crazy, girl? It's our business to see he never gets another chance. It would have been a fine how-d'ye-do if Bruce had left without warning us.'

After Rod and Bruce had gone, Linda turned on her father, a stormy challenge in her eyes.

'I suppose you think it's right for him to strut

around and get killed and wrong for me to stick my nose out of the house,' she cried.

Cliff looked at her gravely. He guessed her emotions were involved and wondered how deeply.

'Sherrill is a man and you're a girl. He has to play his cards the way they are dealt. Out in this country a man has to fight his own battles. He can't call in the police to protect him. With a woman it is different. It's our job to see she is safe.'

Linda went upstairs to her room, bitterly resentful. A woman was of no importance. She must take orders like a forty-dollar-a-month cowboy. If she married, she must be her husband's slave for life. When he came home, having nothing more interesting to do at the moment, she must be a good contented squaw and meet him with a smiling face. He would let her make decisions about when to set the hens and buying a new dress. But if it was anything that counted, his will must be law.

She paced the room, eyes bleak and heart troubled. Her distress lay far deeper than her anger, which was for the hour only and not too serious. Not long ago she had argued with Rod that when a woman loved a man she must make him see what was right to do. Now she realized that she could not be a conscience for Bruce Sherrill any more than for Rod Randall. A strong man would be guided by his own code and standards, not by hers.

And as she thought it out, she discovered that did not matter vitally, if the principle that governed him was decent and honest. She would have to trust her husband's integrity. The real ache in her heart was the fear that she might never see him again alive. Somewhere she had read that to part is to die a little. How true that was if the parting was with somebody one loved as wildly as she did Bruce! For the first time she understood how the women in the Civil War days must have felt when their lovers and husbands went gaily to the battlefields.

Rod Finds a Charred Envelope

XXXVII

Bruce Sherrill and Rod Randall jogged down the valley not too comfortable in each other's society. They had been enemies and still felt a sharp animosity. Scarcely more than a month ago Rod had warned Bruce to mend his ways or be shot. But since that time the feud had been stopped by the intervention of the government. Though they would probably never be friends, in their feeling was a mutual substratum of respect and even admiration.

Upon one subject they were agreed. Bill Cairns must be run out of the country or killed. Neither of them was sure that he had really intended to shoot Linda. He was a bully who liked to see others afraid of him. He might have been trying only to frighten her. Since he had evened the score with her father by wounding him, there did not seem to be any point in the wanton murder of Cliff's daughter. But whatever his intention it would not do to let him ride around terrifying women.

At the Cross Roads they separated, Bruce to take the foothill trail and Rod to continue to the Diamond Tail.

Rod noticed there was no light in the office of his father. Usually the old man spent his evenings there working out his accounts. When Ned came out of the house to meet his brother, Rod flung at him a careless question.

'Where's the old man?'

Ned explained that he had ridden down to the south boundary cabin in the morning with a sack of provisions and that he ought to have been back before supper, but had not arrived. It was odd, Rod thought, that his father had taken the supplies himself instead of sending one of the riders. It might be because he wanted to get away from the house, where he could see his men tearing down the wire on the government land above the valley. To see this tangible evidence of his defeat galled the stiff old-timer's pride.

Out of the gloom a saddled horse without a rider moved toward them.

'It's Nig!' Ned cried. 'Father was riding him.'

He ran forward and caught the bridle of the horse. To quiet the animal he laid a hand on its neck in reassurance. The boy looked at his hand, eyes dilated. There was blood on the palm and fingers. He stared at his brother, the heart pounding fast against his ribs.

'There has been an accident,' he said, with a catch in his throat.

Rod's mind worked in flashes. This was no accident. If his father had been flung from the horse there would be no blood on Nig's neck. What he saw in imagination was old Jeff shot while in the saddle, probably in the head. His body must have fallen forward, face against his mount.

The older brother snapped out crisp orders. 'Tell Yorky and Cash to saddle for a ride. Have Bud hitch the wagon, put some straw in the bed, and drive to the south boundary cabin. Say for them to be quiet about it. We don't want to worry Mary till it is necessary.'

Ned got a six-shooter from the house and saddled a pony for himself. His brother made no objection. In a few minutes they were on their way. Bud would follow with the wagon.

They found Jeff Randall's body lying in the dust outside the cabin. He had been shot through the forehead just above the eyes. There was a second wound in the body, from a revolver fired at close quarters into the heart. He had been dead a good many hours.

Yorky lit a lamp in the cabin and the brothers carried the body inside and put it on a cot. Ned covered the face with a handkerchief.

The hut was one used by line riders caught by night too far from the ranch. It was kept stocked with provisions for them. Somebody had eaten a meal there that day. Unwashed dishes and scraps of food littered the table. On the stove were a greasy fry-pan and a coffee pot half filled.

'Father must have fixed him a dinner,' Ned said.

'Not Father, somebody else,' Rod differed. 'The man who ate here saw him coming and killed him before he got off his horse.'

Ned, white-faced and shaken, looked at his brother. 'While I was driving the calves up this morning I saw a fellow riding across the pasture. The horse was a bay. It was heading this way.'

'Could you tell who the man was?'

'No. Too far away. I kinda thought the horse was one I knew. But I guess not.' He would have said more, but his brother was not listening.

Rod had picked up a paper, burnt at one end. It was part of an envelope twisted into a spill, no doubt to light a pipe. Part of the address was still on the charred paper, the letters at the right-hand side.

ns,
nch,
oads,
ming.

The young man frowned down at the scrap of writing, trying to complete the words. 'Someone on a ranch who gets his mail at Cross Roads,' he murmured. 'What ranch, do you reckon? Might be ours.'

Ned peered around his shoulder. 'One of our boys might of left it a week ago.'

'Yeah, so he might.' Rod spoke slowly, thinking aloud. 'Or the killer might have left it today. Dick Spears slept out here night before last. You know how neat he is—always cleans up before he leaves.' A startled look jumped to Rod's face. The letters had made words in his mind. 'Whose horse was it you thought was crossing the pasture?' he asked.

'I sort of thought for a minute it was that big bay of Bill Cairns's,' Ned replied. 'But I might easy have been wrong.'

'You weren't wrong,' Rod told him, his face harsh and grim. 'The man was Cairns, and the murdering fool has left his calling card to tell us he was here.' From his pocket Rod took a letter, and on the back of the envelope wrote an address:

Mr. William Cairns,
Diamond Tail Ranch,
Cross Roads,
Wyoming.

Cairns had probably lit the spill after he had eaten, before the arrival of Jeff. He had stamped it out and dropped it. At that time it did not matter whether anybody knew he had stopped here for a meal. The custom of the country was that a traveler helped himself to food at a line cabin and chopped enough wood to replace what he had used.

But after Cairns had shot the ranchman from his horse, it became vitally important nobody should know he had been in the neighborhood. Rod had no doubt that the fellow had been in a panic to get away without being seen. The charred spill escaped his mind entirely.

The gunny sack with the provisions had vanished. The killer must have taken it with him. If he was getting out of the country he would want to travel light, yet have supplies enough to get him far out of the district without having to ask for food at a ranch house. He might strike south for Colorado, but Rod did not think he would head for a fairly thickly settled farming country. More likely he would try to reach the Hole-in-the-Wall where a nomadic population of outlaws still skulked between raids in unknown mountain pockets. A fugitive could lead a furtive life there for months untouched by the law.

Rod knew now that Linda had not exaggerated the danger when she met Cairns. He had wanted to kill her because he had not dared to let her stay alive, a witness who would testify he had been on the spot where the murder was committed. Only the girl's quick wit had saved her. Everybody knew that Linda sometimes rode with her brothers after stock. If they were near he dared not shoot.

After Bud arrived with the wagon, they took the body of the ranchman back to the Diamond Tail. Rod sent riders to the adjoining spreads with the news of the crime. He did not wait for the sheriff, but armed and saddled his men as quickly as he could. His mind was made up to shoot Cairns down as soon as he could find the ruffian.

Before they started, Mary brought out to Rod a note she had found in the coat pocket of her husband. Evidently it had been left by a messenger. It read:

> Jeff, I'll be at the old Renaud cabin tonight. Bring me grub and cartridges for my .45. Do this yourself or send Rod. If you can't make it to Renaud's leave the stuff at the south boundary cabin. Keep mum about my being here. I'm not forgetting the job you want done. Burn this.
>
> Quint.

This was the explanation, of course, for old Jeff's trip to the line cabin. Rod had another angle in the tragedy to worry over. Had Quint Milroy been a party to the killing? If so, by setting the killer free, Rod had helped seal his father's doom. The note might have been a decoy. He could not see what Milroy had to gain by the death of a man bringing him food to assist in his escape, but there might be factors in this Rod did not know.

He was inclined to acquit Milroy of complicity. Since his father had wanted to get food to the man, he felt he ought to carry out the old man's wishes. Rod decided to take some to the Renaud cabin himself and have a talk with Milroy. That might clear his mind as to the fellow's guilt. It had been fifteen years since his father had shown him Renaud's Roost while they had been hunting. It was in a wild and not easily accessible region, but he felt sure he could find the place again.

As Rod rode into the hills with his men, a sentence in Quint's note jumped more than once to his mind. *I'm not forgetting the job you want done.* He wished he could forget that. It was not a pleasant memory of his vindictive father to carry through the years. Rod was quite sure he knew what the job was.

At the Old Trapper's Cabin

XXXVIII

Bruce had not been asleep an hour when he was awakened by the barking of the dogs and the voice of somebody outside calling to him. Through the window he saw a man on horseback, who turned out to be Dick Spears from the Diamond Tail. He was rousing the settlers on the creek to tell them to be on the alert for Bill Cairns who had murdered Jeff Randall at the south boundary cabin. The cowpuncher brought a special message from Rod to Bruce. It was that the killing must have occurred just before Cairns met Linda on the ledge above the cabin. Bruce drew the same deduction that Randall had. Linda had missed death by a hair's breadth. The miscreant had been afraid the sound of a shot would bring her brothers over the hill to avenge her.

'Rod thinks Cairns will make for the Hole-in-the-Wall,' Dick explained. 'We're combing Squaw Creek and the country north of there. He thought you might cover Bear and its headwaters. Bill took enough grub from the cabin to last him several days.'

The assignment suited Bruce. He decided to

take Mark and Neal with him, leaving Ramrod at the ranch. While they were loading a pack animal with supplies, he consulted with the old-timer as to where the fugitive was likely to hole up. Ramrod thought that was anybody's guess. The fellow might have got over the passes already, or he might be lying low until the hunt for him spent itself. If he had crossed the divide, it would be up to Humphreys and other sheriffs to cut off his retreat, but if he was still on this slope there was a good chance of one of the posses jumping him up. He would have to be within reach of water, and in a place where he could find concealment for his horse. The foreman suggested several likely spots for a camper on the dodge, among others Renaud's Roost.

Bruce had heard of the old cabin, but did not know exactly where it was. On a piece of wrapping paper Ramrod drew a map for him. When he reached the fork he was to follow the branch known as Sunk Creek till he came to a small park into which a grove of aspens ran down from a draw at the northeast corner. This draw led to a walled cañon. Near the upper end of the gorge was a break in the south wall. If he followed this defile it would bring him to a rough region of wild and rocky scarps. He would see three bunched pines standing alone to the left of the rim. The cabin was in a hollow back of them. Ramrod had never been there but once, and then he had been guided to the spot by Cairns, who had mentioned casually that it would be a good hide-out for a fellow in a jam.

Though there was no chance of running across Cairns during the night, the Quartercircle D C men traveled for hours, working deeper into the high hills back of the ranch country. There was a sliver of a moon, and the stars were out. Even in the rough country over which they moved, the ponies were surefooted as cats.

About three o'clock Bruce called a halt. They lit a fire, thawed out, and rolled up in their blankets. When they awoke, the sky was lightening with the promise of coming day.

Bruce thought there was only a slender chance of finding the hunted man at Renaud's Roost, but he felt he ought to check on the place rather than by-pass it. He left the two cowboys, arranging to meet them later near the headwaters of Bear Creek. Neal suggested that perhaps he ought to go with Sherrill, but Bruce vetoed the offer. He did not think two men ought to waste hours on a detour of so little promise.

He struck Sunk Creek at the fork and followed its winding course through the hills to a grassy meadow from the yonder end of which aspens marched up a gulch to the rim. He skirted the edge of the grove and rode into a box cañon. It brought him to a gorge that slashed through the south wall to the floor of the ravine. Up to this point in the journey Ramrod's memory had served him perfectly.

The gorge was steep and narrow. Its bed was filled with rubble and with boulders flung from above through many centuries. He emerged at the upper entrance, to see in one sweeping glance a tangle of tossed-up hills in the hollows of which a hundred men might have hidden. The three twisted pines Ramrod had promised were bunched on the rim of the mesa a few hundred yards from him.

To one of the pines he tied his horse. From the rim he looked down into a pocket out of which ran four or five draws. A small stream from the mesa watered it and disappeared in one of the outlets. On the bank of the brook was an old log cabin. Screened by bushes, Bruce watched that cabin and its surroundings for several minutes. He could see no sign of occupancy.

In the near end of the cabin there was no window. Bruce moved down cautiously, keeping to the fringe of bushes bordering the stream. A man in the house could not see him unless he came to the door and looked up the creek. If anybody had appeared in the doorway, Bruce would have been greatly surprised. His opinion was that there was not another human being within miles of him.

Yet he did not take a step without scanning the terrain closely. Though he was coming up on the blind side of the shack, Cairns might be crouched back of the sagging door watching him through the wide crack between it and the jamb from which the hinge had broken loose. He covered the dozen yards between the creek and the blank wall at a run. When he peered around the corner there was still no movement about the place. On tiptoe he stepped forward and crouched back of the rotting door. A moment later he was inside the cabin. Nobody else was in the room.

But what he saw startled him. On the home-made table were cans of tomatoes, a slab of bacon, a package of Arbuckle's, and a small sack of flour. A skillet and a can with coffee grounds in it stood on the chimney hearth. The ashes in the fireplace were cold. Whoever was staying here had not yet breakfasted this morning. But it was an easy guess that the owner of the provisions would be back soon. He took a step toward the door—and stopped abruptly. Somewhere in the stretch of space outside a pistol shot rang out, and two more before the sound of it had died.

XXXIX

Half an hour before Bruce reached Renaud's Roost a man came out of a draw and walked toward the cabin with breakfast in mind. The man was Bill Cairns. He stopped abruptly. His eye had fallen on a horseman coming down from the rim. Quickly he ducked back into the land fold from which he had emerged. The one man in the world he least wanted to meet was Rod Randall.

A hideous fear welled up in him. He was trapped. His horse was picketed back of the cabin, and he could not reach it without being seen. A fugitive afoot in this wild country was as good as dead. He did not know what had brought Randall straight to the spot where he was hiding, but it was sure that he would not be in the hut three minutes without learning from Milroy that Cairns was here. His best chance was to get Rod now, while he was not expecting trouble. It took all the nerve he had to announce his presence, even by a shot from ambush. If he missed, that young devil Randall would probably succeed in rubbing him out.

Rifle in hand, he came out of the draw to try his

luck. The distance was about two hundred yards. Rod had dismounted and grounded his reins. He was moving toward the house. Milroy was in the doorway, and they stood talking for a moment.

Cairns tried to steady his shaken nerves, but as soon as he had pulled the trigger he knew that he had failed. At sound of the shot Rod bolted into the cabin. Cairns turned to run.

Milroy and Randall looked at each other.

'Must be Bill Cairns,' Milroy said. 'But why? What has he got against you?'

'Don't you know why?' Rod asked, with steady, accusing eyes.

'How would I know?' Milroy asked. 'I haven't seen anybody to talk to except you since I was locked up.'

'When did Cairns get here?'

'Last night. I somehow mistrusted him and wouldn't let him sleep in here.'

'He didn't tell you that he had killed my father?'

The amazed look on the desperado's face gave him a verdict of acquittal from Rod. 'He told me he had not seen Jeff for days, that he was on the dodge account of wounding Applegate.'

'I had Father kick him out. He has been lying around drunk ever since. Yesterday he killed Father at the south boundary cabin when he took a load of food there for you.'

Milroy came clean. 'I sent a note to Jeff by

Dick Spears. Asked him to get me food and send it either here or to the line cabin.' In the bleached narrowed eyes of the bad man was a hard glitter. 'Who told Bill Cairns your father might be at the line cabin?'

'I think Cairns was riding the chuck line,' Rod answered. 'He knew there was always some food there and figured he could bum a few meals.' The young man brushed aside explanation. He had a job to do. 'I've got to see he never gets away from here alive.'

'I'm with you,' Milroy said. He did not mention that by killing the boss of the Diamond Tail Cairns had robbed him of five hundred dollars he had expected to collect from Randall for destroying Bruce Sherrill. 'His horse is picketed near here. Bill has to have it for a getaway. He will sure make a break for it, and he dare not wait long.'

They decided that they would move their own horses to the spot where Cairns had left his mount and that Rod would wait to cut him off when the man appeared. Milroy was to swing around behind the fugitive and drive him forward from his cover. Cairns would reason that the two men had come out to hunt him and he would attempt to reach his horse. It was his one chance of escape.

'Your forty-five loaded?' Rod asked.

Milroy remembered the trick Rod had played

on him when he brought the pistol, but that was water under a bridge now. 'With Bill's bullets,' the desperado said grimly. 'Nice if I can give one of them back to him.'

Rod frowned. He did not like this set-up. There was a faint lingering doubt of Milroy in his mind. He might go out to find Cairns and throw in with him. But if he was on the level with Rod, a six-shooter was no weapon with which to go hunting a desperate man with a rifle. Yet the spot where the horses were picketed was the focal one. Randall did not intend to leave it.

'You'd stand a fat chance against a Winchester with a forty-five,' he suggested.

'He won't even see me if this works out right,' Milroy said. 'All I need to do is to fire a couple of shots from cover and push him back this way. You're the one entitled to rub him out, not me.'

Rod could not think of a better plan than the one they had made and he let it go as arranged. He waited in the brush forty or fifty feet away from the place where the nearest horse was picketed. As long as he had the three mounts in sight, Cairns was tied to the neighborhood.

Milroy crept up the creek, making the most of the willows and the wild plum trees that grew on the banks. Unless Cairns exposed himself at the entrance of the hill fold where he was hiding, he could not see the stream, and Quint's judgment was that the man he stalked would keep out of sight as long as he could. The gunman stayed with the stream till it left the valley and cut into the hills.

He left the brook, to take a fold that led to a clump of aspens above. These he skirted to a rise from which he could look down on another dip. On the opposite slope of this were more aspens. He watched them, patient as an Indian, and observed a shivering of the branches more sharp than that made by the breeze. Somebody was crawling through the young trees.

Presently his keen eyes focused on a moving object. The distance was about a hundred yards. He took aim with his forty-five and fired, with no expectation of scoring a hit. The foliage of the aspens was violently agitated. He fired two more shots. Cairns broke from cover, appeared for a moment silhouetted against the skyline, and disappeared over the brow. Milroy charged down the slope in pursuit and up the hill on the yonder side. From the top his glance swept the panorama below. He saw Cairns running toward the hollow where the horses were picketed.

Rod's voice came to him sharp and clear, from too great a distance for the words to reach him. Cairns fired. There came an answering shot from Rod. The hunted man dropped into a gully and raced for the house, evidently with the idea of holding it against attack. He reached the cabin.

What occurred then was a total surprise to Milroy. Cairns stopped, abruptly as if the loop of a rope had pulled him up. He flung up his rifle and fired. Quint knew there must be a fourth man in the Roost.

'Both of Them Are Better Dead'

XL

The sound of the pistol shots held Bruce frozen for a moment, so unexpectedly had they broken the deep silence. He stepped to the door and looked in the direction from which he thought they had come. In the pleasant sunshine the scene was peaceful as Eden before the serpent incident. A meadowlark on the branch of a willow lifted its head and flung out a full-throated burst of joy. Yet with the sixth sense that men who lived on the frontier sometimes acquired Bruce knew there was something sinister in those three tightly packed shots.

His rifle he laid against the door jamb. He did not want to be hampered with it if trouble came quickly at close quarters. He did not draw his revolver yet, but the thumb hitched in the sagging belt was scarcely four inches from the butt of the weapon projecting from the pocket of his chaps.

The landscape looked as deserted as when he had arrived. He walked as far as the corner of the hut, to sweep with his eyes the view from that side of the house. What the shooting was about he did not know, but for the present he meant not to venture farther from the cabin. Cairns might not be alone, and in case of attack he might need a fort of refuge.

Once more the stillness was shattered, this time by the whiplike reports of two rifles, much nearer than the pistol shots had been. He heard the slap of running feet coming toward the house.

Bill Cairns burst round the corner of the shack and stopped with shocked alarm at sight of him. The killer could not take time to aim. He jerked up his rifle and fired, almost from the hip. A fraction of a second later a revolver slug slammed into his belly. The big man gave a great gasp of pain. He half-lifted the Winchester for another shot, but a second bullet tore through his throat. The weapon clattered to the ground. The spread fingers of Cairns's hairy hands pressed in against his stomach. He lurched forward a step or two before the hinges of his knees gave way and let the heavy body slump to the ground.

Bruce watched him, not moving from where he stood. A trickle of smoke rose from the barrel of the revolver in his hand. During the past brief seconds there had been no time for fear. Every sense had been keyed to intense concentration. He had to kill or be killed. But as he looked at the sprawled body, a moment ago filled with malevolent life and now stilled forever, a kind of horror grew in him. By no desire of his own a crook of his finger had destroyed a human being. He had neither remorse nor regret, only a feeling of dismay that some quirk of fate had made his the hand to put an end to this evil force.

The pure sharp song of the meadowlark lifted again.

He became aware of somebody moving through the brush a hundred yards from the cabin. As the crouched figure crossed an open spot he recognized Rod Randall.

Bruce shouted his name, and Rod came forward. He looked at the prone body and then at Sherrill.

'So you got him,' he said.

'He didn't have a chance,' Bruce explained. 'When he showed up round the corner he wasn't expecting me. It startled him, and he fired too fast.'

Rod looked down again at the outstretched figure. 'Both your shots were bull's-eyes.' On his grim face a sardonic smile showed. 'Might have been me instead of him, the way I felt about you a month ago. It's a damned uncertain world. Then you were an infernal nuisance. Now you'll be the boy for this country's money. I'll say this, Sherrill. You're turning out quite a lad.'

'Because I was forced in self-defense to kill a murderer?' Bruce shook his head. 'Nothing to be proud of in that. I wish you had done it.'

'I wish so too. I had a crack at him and missed. You landed solid both times. How in Mexico did you happen to show up here?'

Bruce explained. Before he had finished Rod interrupted. 'Hell's bells! I had forgotten. You had better light a shuck out of here, Sherrill. Quint Milroy is just over the hill.'

'You're not kidding?' Bruce looked at him sharply.

'No. That's why I'm here. To bring him grub.'

'Yes.' Bruce spoke after a moment's thought. 'I'd better go.'

'Unless you would like to turn hunter.' There was in Rod's eyes a gleam of impish mirth. 'He has only a forty-five, and if you're careful you can pick him off with a rifle at no risk.'

Coldly, Bruce replied, 'I'm not a murderer.'

'He'd get you any way he could,' Rod mentioned.

'He would. You wouldn't.' Bruce spoke harshly.

Rod laughed. 'All right. I didn't expect you to take good advice. Better be hitting the trail sudden, fellow.'

'My horse is back on the rim,' Bruce said.

'If you hurry he won't know who was here until you've gone. Dust along.'

Bruce showed no signs of haste, perhaps because the desire to get away fast was so strong in him. It hurt his pride to run away from any man, even though he knew that a pistol duel with Milroy was as unfair as it would be for him to shoot down the other with his rifle. He counted himself a good shot, better than average, but he had never known anybody else who possessed the swift deadly accuracy with a revolver Milroy was reputed to have.

'Get going, you lunkhead,' Rod snapped. 'He'll be here soon.'

'Be seeing you,' Bruce said.

He retrieved his rifle and walked back to the fringe of bushes along the creek. By keeping close to the shrubbery he might reach the rim without being seen. There was one stretch of about forty yards where he would have to come into the open, but by that time he would be near enough to his horse to reach it in spite of Milroy if the man appeared in the pocket.

On the rim a wind was blowing. It picked up the dust of disintegrated sandstone and swept it across the bluff in a small cloud. Bruce looked across at the three twisted pines. A warning stirred in him sharply. Back of the trunk of one was something that had not been there thirty minutes ago. He stopped, the rifle half-raised.

The blast of a forty-five sounded, and the hat was lifted from his head. His heart began to pound. There was a tightness in his chest. He felt the icy crawling of fear along his spine. Quint Milroy was here before him.

From that first bullet the distance and the wind had saved Bruce. Before he could move, a second slug struck the rifle barrel and glanced off in ricochet. A cold anger brushed away all fear and scruples. Milroy was an assassin trying to ambush him, a desperado entitled to no more consideration than an Apache in covered-wagon days. He raised his rifle, took deliberate aim at the crouched figure, and fired.

That he had hit his foe Bruce knew, but the chances were that the wound was not a fatal one. He drew back a dozen yards to be out of range and made a half-circuit of the pines, watching the center of the circle every foot of the way.

Milroy broke from cover, reached the horse, pulled the slipknot, and swung to the saddle. He fired, body bent low, just before he jumped the cowpony to a gallop. He headed straight for Sherrill, evidently aware that if he tried to escape he would be a mark too plain for a good rifleman to miss. As he charged, his revolver barked again.

The man was less than twenty yards from Bruce when the rifle bullet tore through him. His body slumped. The frightened horse swung away at a sharp angle and the rider pitched out of the saddle at the feet of Bruce. The fall jerked the weapon from the slack fingers of its owner. The glaze of death was already in the eyes of Milroy. He gave a strangled cough, and his frame shrank in collapse. The killer had gone out to the sound of roaring guns, as so many of his victims had done.

Bruce followed his horse down into the pocket and found that Rod had caught the animal.

'You killed Milroy?' Randall asked.

'Yes.' Bruce had fought down the wave of sickness that swept him after the battle. 'I saw him back of one of the pines. He had to try a long shot, and the wind was blowing. He knocked my hat off. I wounded him with a rifle shot and circled round to get him from behind. He made a break for it on my horse—came right at me, his gun blazing. I couldn't miss.'

'Both of them are better dead,' Rod said bluntly.

'Maybe,' Bruce agreed bitterly. 'But who am I to play at God and decide that?'

Rod grinned. 'For a tough hard rannyhan you're too soft, fellow. They both asked for what they got. What else would you figure on doing when a pair of wolves start for you?'

Bruce had no answer for that, but he knew that what he had done made him heartsick and wretched.

The Quartercircle D C
Finds a Mistress

XLI

Rod rode over to the Bar B B with Bruce. The story of what had occurred at Renaud's cabin had preceded them. For the first time the voice of Cliff Applegate was warm when he spoke to his neighbor of the Quartercircle D C.

'What in Mexico you trying to do, son?' he asked. 'Clean up all the riffraff so the sheriff won't have anything to do but sit on his behind?'

'I hope to God I'm through forever,' Bruce said fervently. 'They came at me smoking, and nothing but gilt-edged luck brought me through.'

Linda had just come into the room. 'Or Providence,' she amended. 'Maybe God thought it was time for them to die.'

Their eyes met. They had things to say to each other that could not be said before an audience.

'Who wants to ride down and get the mail with me?' she asked a few minutes later.

Rod jumped up, mischief in his eyes. 'You're speaking to me, Lindy?'

'I want to talk with you about yore plans for the

Diamond Tail, Rod,' Cliff interposed. 'Is Mary expecting to stay there with the children after the funeral?'

'Sure. It's their home. I reckon I'll run the ranch.' Rod waved a hand at Linda. 'If you ask him pretty please maybe you can get Bill Hickok here to ride down with you.'

'I'll do the asking,' Bruce said. 'Miss Linda, will you—?'

'Yes,' she interrupted.

Rod looked up at the ceiling innocently and began to hum 'Here comes the bride—'

'Oh you!' Linda scolded, her cheeks a deep pink.

After they were on their way to the mail box, Bruce mentioned that it was nice of Rod to propose for him.

'I thought you had already proposed,' Linda said happily.

'So I did, but it didn't turn out a very good job. If you remember, I was in the doghouse before I left.'

'Maybe we had better start all over again.'

'I think so.' The road had dipped into a hollow through which a small stream ran past a clump of cottonwoods. He pulled up his horse, dismounted, and lifted her from the saddle. 'How do you think this place will do?' he asked.

'Any place that suits my lord will do,' she murmured.

'Hmp! That sounds to me. I'll probably be the most hen-pecked husband in the county.'

If he thought so it did not seem to worry him much. After much warfare and many troubled days, they had come together at last, and out of this nettle danger they had plucked something much dearer than safety.

Center Point Large Print
600 Brooks Road / PO Box 1
Thorndike, ME 04986-0001 USA

(207) 568-3717

US & Canada:
1 800 929-9108
www.centerpointlargeprint.com